THE MERCHANT MURDERERS

Also by Michael Jecks

The Jack Blackjack mysteries

REBELLION'S MESSAGE *
A MURDER TOO SOON *
A MISSED MURDER *
THE DEAD DON'T WAIT *
DEATH COMES HOT *
THE MOORLAND MURDERERS *

The Templar mysteries

NO LAW IN THE LAND
THE BISHOP MUST DIE
THE OATH
KING'S GOLD
CITY OF FIENDS
TEMPLAR'S ACRE

Vintener trilogy

FIELDS OF GLORY
BLOOD ON THE SAND
BLOOD OF THE INNOCENTS

* *available from Severn House*

Visit www.michaeljecks.co.uk for a full list of titles

THE MERCHANT MURDERERS

Michael Jecks

First world edition published in Great Britain and the USA in 2022
by Severn House, an imprint of Canongate Books Ltd,
14 High Street, Edinburgh EH1 1TE.

Trade paperback edition first published in Great Britain and the USA in 2023
by Severn House, an imprint of Canongate Books Ltd.

severnhouse.com

British Library Cataloguing-in-Publication Data
A CIP catalogue record for this title is available from the British Library.

ISBN-13: 978-0-7278-5092-8 (cased)
ISBN-13: 978-1-4483-0772-2 (trade paper)
ISBN-13: 978-1-4483-0773-9 (e-book)

All Severn House titles are printed on acid-free paper.

Typeset by Palimpsest Book Production Ltd.,
Falkirk, Stirlingshire, Scotland.
Printed and bound in Great Britain by
TJ Books, Padstow, Cornwall.

Clive and Keith
Thanks for the support, boys

PROLOGUE

When the fellow hit me on the cheek the second time, my skull struck the side of the rolling, creaking bucket, and I felt the bile rise to choke me. Not that he would have cared, of course. He just grinned.

Spray rose over the ship's side as the waves buffeted it, and my head lolled. In truth, I felt so sick and unhappy that death would have been a welcome relief. Life was misery and hardship. It would be no loss, were I to die. The shipman turned at a bellow and suddenly moved away. As he did, a huge bird of the sea came and took its rest on the rail above me.

I was jealous. This creature could fly away whenever it wanted, safe from the tribulations of men like me. I had a warming sense of comradeship with the bird. It was, I felt, a symbol – of freedom, of safety, of life away from this present hell. A proof that my life could improve. I attempted a vague motion towards it, hoping to stroke its head or body, but it gave a loud squawk, tore an inch-long gash in my hand, defecated on my arm and flew off with a sardonic cry that sounded like laughter.

It struck me that the bird had summed up my life perfectly. My life was shit.

But what was I doing on that ship?

That, my friends, is a good question.

ONE
I Arrive at Exeter

6 August 1556

A dead body is not particularly exciting.

It has always struck me as odd that people would be keen to view one. After all, it's not as though the figure is likely to rise and entertain everyone by dancing a galliard on the spot. Yet still the public will gather and stare, whether they knew the dead man or not. It's a spectacle, I suppose. Everyone likes distractions, and the fascination of a dead body is not the fact that it was once *someone*, but that it was someone *else*.

Not that the people here in this heaven-forsaken hole were capable of much in the way of rational thought. It was, after all, the absolute boundary of human advancement, and for my part, I was convinced that all concepts of civilization had swept up to the eastern walls of this city and there been held at bay forever. Nothing had penetrated the city. All I could say in its favour was that it did not smell as foul as other places. On the way here, I had passed through the nearest real town, Crediton. That place simply *reeked* of sheep.

Not that the poor fellow on the ground would have cared. Not now.

He was sprawled out, the back of his head stove in, the blood clotted on the ground beside his head. When I moved round to get a closer look, it was enough to make me blench. Someone had sent a herd of cattle to trample his features, or so it seemed. His nose was mashed, his temple crushed, and a bloody slice had been torn from his cheek. One arm reached out before him as though pleading. The other was under his body, his legs crossed at the ankles like the knights in my church who had been on pilgrimage. He was definitely dead.

I watched rather glumly as a pair of wealthy-looking men

appeared, one short and fat, the other taller and slender as a willow. The latter stared at the corpse with a face twisted into a sneer. The fatter man looked wary and rather nervous. With them was a priest, who peered down at the dead body like a judge viewing a guilty felon. Behind them, the bailiff stood in an approximation of attention. His sagging belly and dewlap made him more a figure of ridicule than a terrifying officer of the law.

And then there was an interruption. A slim, rather gaunt woman in a threadbare shift and cotte, dark hair straying from beneath her coif, shoved the merchants from her path and stood staring down at the body. With a scream, she flung herself on to the corpse, and rolled there in the filth, shrieking and pawing at the dead man like a cat testing its claws. It was overly dramatic, I felt, but she was entitled to her display. I had little doubt that she was the man's widow.

It was enough for the trio. The priest made a perfunctory sign of the cross, and then all three made their way along the passage, a henchman or two with them pushing other onlookers from their path.

When the trio had left, the bailiff returned to picking his nose and investigating the results with interest, like a gourmet discovering a fresh dainty, before sticking it in his mouth. A woman pulled a face at the sight and averted her gaze. I did likewise.

Such manners would not have been tolerated in polite London society. However, I was many leagues from London – and heavens, didn't I feel every single mile of them! Besides, the average watchman in London would be just as uncouth. I had seen enough of them in my time as an employed servant to the household of Lady Elizabeth Tudor.

Looking away was all very well, but it brought my eyes to the figure of the dead man again. I have never liked the sight of death, and this one was a peculiarly ghastly sight.

He was a scrawny fellow of some thirty summers, in clothes that had once been fashionable but which now looked faded, scruffy and filthy. Mind, that could have been the result of his lying in this alley, from the muck and trash that filled it. If it had been placed in one of the farmyards just outside the city's walls, I would not have been able to tell the difference. Excrement of all forms, mud and the detritus of the city lay all about, and the body appeared to have soaked up many of the less pleasant forms of dampness.

I was in Devon, in the city of Exeter. As you may have guessed, I did not like it. I was only there to make my way home by the speediest route. After some weeks festering in the hell hole that was Okehampton, very close by the ancient waste of Dartmoor – and as far from civilization and the attractions that make life bearable as was the moon – I had at last escaped. But how to return to my house and real life?

My visit had not been planned. In the summer, I had been advised that my safety might depend on my rapid disappearance, and I had taken the hint most willingly and swiftly. As a fellow whose patron was, by a slightly circuitous route, the Lady Elizabeth, and whose occupation was supposedly that of assassin – although I have never intentionally killed any man, unless it was during the short-lived Wyatt Rebellion, when I was a soldier for the good Queen Mary. Even then, it was more by chance than deliberate. However that may be, nonetheless I was now a servant in the pay of Lady Elizabeth.

Her sister, Queen Mary, had always harboured suspicions against her. During the Wyatt Rebellion, which led to the execution of poor Lady Jane Grey, and for months afterwards, Lady Elizabeth had been incarcerated at Woodstock. Recently, a pair of blockheads, Ashton and Dudley, had decided to rob the Exchequer to pay for an army to depose Mary and replace her with a more accommodating ruler. The only person with a near claim to the throne was Mary's half-sister Elizabeth, so as soon as the plot was uncovered, the poor lady was arrested and transported to the Tower. Soon, by the grace of God, she was released and returned to her former position, but a scant month later, a bull-headed schoolmaster contended for village idiot of the year by claiming that he was the Earl of Devonshire, that he had been bulling the Lady Elizabeth, and that they were the rightful King and Queen of the realm. He immediately demanded that all men should rally to his side to remove the Queen.

This news came to me while I was at an inn outside the city. On hearing it, I was instantly sobered. Not only would Lady

Elizabeth be likely returned to her second home in the Tower, but many of her household would probably be arrested and persuaded, by various means within earshot of Lady Elizabeth's chambers, to divulge all they knew of her iniquity and treachery.

Most of all, it was plain to me that my safety and security would be best served by making myself scarce. I fled with all speed.

At first, I planned to ride for the Kentish ports, thence to take a ship to France or elsewhere. But soon I came to realize what the Queen's men would likely think of that. I might outride them as far as the coast, but then, if there was no ship, I would be forced to wait for their arrival, mournfully gazing over the expanse of water until some hoary old buffoon appeared to arrest me. That was a most unappealing prospect.

Thus, to Devon. Taking that longer route would mean confounding them. No doubt, emissaries would be sent to arrest me in Kent, perhaps others to harbours to the south and east as well, but with good fortune, no one would expect me to ride two hundred miles to a port quite so far away as Devon. Making my way to a ship that far from London must baffle them.

Of course, I was soon to find that no matter where a man is, a stranger will always be the victim of accusations, no matter how unfair and irrational.

Thus now, on the sixth of August, here I was in the collection of barns and shacks that they were pleased to name a 'city'. It would not have sufficed to hold an army of scavengers in London. The houses were shabby, many thatched still, most of them built from timber that had been felled a hundred years or more ago, and the general appearance of the populace left much to be desired.

A breeze from the west wafted the odours of urine and rotting flesh past my nostrils. There, on the island just south and west of the city, lay a befouled wasteland where tanners worked. Of all trades, surely that of tannery is one of the most disgusting. The men work with dog turds, piss and all manner of similarly disgusting substances. No man of taste or a sense of smell could participate in such a hideous task as making leather, surely.

At least I knew that I was on my way out of this city. Soon, with luck, I would be back in London, in my warm house, a pot of spiced ale or wine in my hand, and all memories of this horrible journey dispelled.

All I needed to do was hire a horse to take me east.

The bailiff, having exhausted the possibilities of both nostrils, was now sitting on his rump near the dead man's head. He looked thoroughly bored, as well he might. After all, there was no telling how long it would take for the coroner to appear. Some coroners took their duties seriously and would quickly visit every suddenly dead body. Theirs was not a simple occupation. Many, especially in a county like Devon, lived a peripatetic existence, with long hours spent nursing their piles on a hard saddle. And when they arrived, they would be shunned by all right-thinking folks, since their existence involved imposing fines.

They must amerce the first finder, to make sure that the poor devil actually appeared at court; they must amerce the locals living nearest for the same reason, so that any witnesses would give evidence when the justices appeared. They must consider the value of the weapon used to commit the homicide so that they could charge the deodand, and record every aspect of the killing so that the justices would be able to read what had happened, just in case a jury reluctant to agree to the more expensive taxable details might suffer a sudden memory modification when the case came to court in the future.

To be a coroner in a wild land like Devon required a man of intelligence and bravery, or a knave and a fool.

The bailiff looked up at me mournfully.

I had a certain fellow feeling for the poor man. He looked so miserable, sitting there. 'Do you know how long before the coroner will arrive?' I asked.

For anyone who has not spent time in Devon, the language is nigh on impossible to understand. The bailiff was a particularly strong example of a man who spoke the dialect to perfection; that is, he was almost incomprehensible. I translate for you:

'No, 'e were off to Morchard Bishop yester e'en. None know

when un's likely to return.' He glanced down at the body with grumpy bitterness. 'And I 'ave to stay here till he do.'

You see? A fellow like me, who was used to English being spoken normally, found it hard even after spending some weeks with people who spoke in this manner. 'Who was this fellow, do you know?'

''Im? Aye, he were Roger Lane, poor bugger. The women will regret 'im goin'. Leaves a wife and a child, too. Don't know how they'll bear 'is loss.'

'I think I saw one of them.'

'That were 'is wife. She'll have to shift for hersel' now.'

'Not a wealthy man, then? He didn't leave her much?'

'Look at un's clothes.'

I didn't need to. As I think I mentioned, his clothing might have been valuable once, but now it was old and a mess, not helped by the mangled skull. It really did look as if he had been struck by a steel mace or heavy lump of rock. The back of his head was a blackened scab with occasional pale chips showing. I didn't want to look too closely, but they reminded me of chips of bone from the butcher's. I swallowed uneasily. 'Does the first finder have any notion who might have done this?'

The bailiff's mouth pulled into a sneer. 'There were many wanted to see un dead. He was a troublemaker, for many.'

'How so?'

''E were a priest with the new religion, and randy as a goat. Many a man thought as 'e'd been made to wear the cuckold's horns by un, and would've spoke to un, but you don't beat a priest. But when the Queen took the throne, all changed, eh? 'E were told, *If you want to be vicar, you'm give up your women.* Well, others knew what he were like, and didn't want him priesting in church again. So he lost his church, and since then 'e's not been safe. Plenty of cuckolds wanted to do this to un. Larnin' who did for un, that'll be a bugger.'

'Which was his church?'

'St Petrock's. He were 'appy there, so I heard. Not since.'

'He found life hard without his position as a priest?'

The man sneered. ''E made it hard for 'imself, what with women and whoring. 'E did well at first. 'Ad training, didn't he? Could read and write. 'E were popular, first, working for merchants and suchlike, who trusted a man who'd been a priest – specially them as 'ad no wife to worry about, but then all soured. I reckon 'e were drove mad wi' women, that's what I think. Couldn't keep 'is cods in 'is piece. Many members of the Cathedral and City's Freedom will be happy to see un dead, I 'ave no doubt. The dean was.'

I made my way out of the alley. At the road, I saw the dean and his two companions, heads down in deep discussion. As I approached them, they all nodded to each other, and then the priest turned left and made his way along the road. The other two, I saw, wandered along behind him, heads leaning towards each other as they continued to speak, their henchmen at their heels, for all the world like two minor lords on a perambulation of their estates. They stopped outside the Guildhall, an imposing building in the High Street.

One, who must have been a fabulously successful merchant from the gold chain about his neck and the rich garments he wore, had a gross belly that overburdened his short frame. His paunch was so huge it looked as though he was constantly at threat of toppling over. He had to lean backwards as he walked just to balance the weight of it.

His companion was similarly wealthy, although he did not display it by the breadth of his paunch. He preferred to wear it in a vulgarly ostentatious display, sporting jewels and expensive stones in profusion on his fingers and about his neck, all entrapped in gold. On a man so tall and cadaverous, it looked as though the weight must crush him.

'My apologies, masters,' I said, sweeping off my hat and bowing low. 'I wondered whether you could advise me on the best stables to hire a horse?'

'Do you think I look like a groom?' the fatter of the two said. From closer to, he had the pale, soft skin that proved he never worked out of doors, with blue eyes of a watery nature, as though he was on the verge of tears.

His companion peered at me. He had arched eyebrows over half-lidded eyes that viewed the world, and especially me, with contempt. His long, thin fingers were like a scrivener's, and he tapped them on his dagger's sheath as he looked me up and down with every indication of revulsion.

The two bodyguards suddenly noticed me. One was the kind of fellow who would find it taxing to count with his fingers. The other was more intelligent. He could at least count to ten – if first reminded where his fingers were.

'I meant no insult, sirs. I am a gentleman from London,' I explained, 'a stranger to this city, and just thought—'

'Leave us. Begone!' the other said, dismissing me with a flick of his hand, like a man giving a beggar short shrift. The fat man laughed. It was not a kindly sound.

I was about to protest when the first henchman appeared before me and gave me a shove with both hands, almost throwing me to the ground. 'Leave Master Wolfe alone, you piece of shit!'

His companion, clearly feeling that he was being left out of things, curled his lips at me. 'Aye! And Master Shapley, too!'

I staggered back under their onslaught, and you can be sure that my expression told the churls exactly what I thought of them. The two merchants barely glanced at me and continued on their way.

Only a short distance further on, the tall man was met by a willowy woman with the sort of sultry looks that would make the Pope howl. She had olive skin, and a fine, slender face with large eyes that were angled slightly, giving her an exotic appearance. Her hair was concealed in her coif and under a delicate hat that gave her a regal poise. While the short man entered the Guildhall, the other man took the lady by the hand. It was enough to make me feel a stab of jealousy to see how she submitted to him. They must be married, I thought.

Their guards blocked my path, sniggering unpleasantly.

There have been many times when I have been insulted. Obviously, for a proud man like me, it is insufferable to be treated in such a manner, and as soon as the two had disappeared from view, I gave them the finger. A couple of women walking past were shocked at my gesture, and the younger of the two, a pretty little thing with tight ringlets of dark hair protruding from her coif, gaped at me, plainly surprised to see such coarseness from a man of my obvious rank and position.

I smiled back at her as she passed, and she coloured delightfully, while her maidservant – or perhaps mother? – clucked angrily and propelled her charge on more swiftly, but not before I had seen her throw me a second glance over her shoulder. She seemed to lift an eyebrow and then smiled – an entrancing sight – just as she was hidden by the crowds.

I was left with my own company and a need for a horse. Well, horses would often be found nearer the gates to a city, whether at an inn or a stable, so I made my way back the way I had come that morning from Crediton. Surely there was a stable there.

The journey from Dartmoor had taken a day. I was weary after the events of the previous few weeks, but I was desperate to escape from Okehampton at any cost after my experiences there.

Originally, I had planned to take the road west and south, skirting, so I was told, the great waste of Dartmoor. That would have brought me to the coast, where I could have taken a ship to France. But now I had no need to leave for France, and besides, that route involved passing close to tin miners and other thieves and outlaws, and that itself was not appealing. Instead, I chose to take the more direct route of the road to London, which took me past Exeter. At Crediton, I had managed to hire a mount as far as Exeter, with a small, snot-nosed brat who trotted along at my side, and who took the brute back once I had dismounted at the West Gate to the city. He looked as relieved to be going as I felt at his departure. The peasants of Devon really are incomprehensible. Their language is a series of grunts and wheezes that no Englishman of quality could understand. And they smell of the animals they live with. That little urchin smelled mostly of old goats and piss. I tried to have him trot downwind of me, but the wind kept changing direction.

I reached the city from the west. After I had clattered down from Newton St Cyres, then up a small hill and down to the bridge at Cowley, I could hear the noise of the city: bellows, bangs, rattles and clatters. It was a relief to hear the sounds of civilization. I bent my way southwards, following the river, past tatty buildings at the outskirts, until the great wall rose before me like an island of calm in the grim misery of all the countryside about it. Red walls emerged like cliffs from the river, and I could see the roofs of hundreds of houses, with the two towers of the cathedral standing as if guarding the population, a mother hen sheltering and protecting her chicks. Before the gate was the bridge, an impressive construction with many arches that must have taken years to build. There were a number of ruins before the bridge itself, and as I approached it, I was struck by the desolation. On the western side of the river, there was a small church and the remains of a few houses, and everything near the wall was half demolished. I gazed about me at the clutter of stone, and I was glad when, soon after, I was over the bridge and inside the walls.

At least Exeter itself was more congenial than Okehampton or Crediton, both of which were noisome towns with the ever-present risk of footpads knocking a fellow on the pate. Exeter, I was relieved to see, had a gallows with a rotting corpse in chains dangling from a gibbet near the river. At least here, it was plain, the rule of law held sway.

The rest of that day was spent seeking a mount. I was desperate to get back to London and escape these vile areas full of peasants, all of whom smelled of wet dogs. I recalled the trollops at the Cardinal's Hat, the saucy wench who lived opposite my house, and a myriad of other faces whom I missed. It was enough to make a man weep, looking about me now: shabby buildings in dirty streets. Loitering near a stable, where I had again been refused a beast, I felt as lonely as a fox in a pack of hounds. It seemed to me that everyone in that horrible city despised me as a foreigner and stranger.

Not that my view was entirely fair, I know. There were not only the unintelligible voices with their 'zurrs' and 'ziderz', and the thick, harsh tones of the Cornishmen, but also a fair intermingling of Frenchmen, some Italians, and others. This was not a place where I was alone in seeming exotic. More than once during my wanderings about the market, I had seen blank confusion on the faces of more than a few store holders when confronted by a customer who was less than fluent in the local dialect. However, that could have meant the 'foreigner' was from a town fifteen miles from the city walls. Really, the people in this area have a fabulously overbearing sense of their own importance in the world.

As soon as people heard my accent, they closed their mouths like bullocks chewing the cud, glaring at me as I explained what I sought. No one was prepared to aid me. It was as though they all assumed I was some sort of thief – or worse – from the farthest border of the kingdom, and that as soon as I clapped spurs to their beast, I would be off and over the horizon with my ill-gotten gains. Would no one trust a traveller? Even the inn at Crediton had been more helpful.

At last, having passed near Exe Island, where my nostrils informed me the tanners plied their trade – the noisome fumes were very easily recognized – and had walked along Little Southernhay and Southernhay roads, I found myself at the square bulk of the East Gate.

My bag was growing to be a great weight, and I was miserable. The only saving grace of this city, to my eye, was the fact that it at least appeared to be less wet than Dartmoor. There, the wind and rain were constant irritants. Just now, I was glad to be within the city. There must be some form of entertainment within the walls, and with a little good fortune, if I found a suitable bed for the night, there was also the chance of some mattress-thumping. In the morning, a friendlier man might be willing to let me make use of a horse. Perhaps ten or fifteen miles, as far as the next large town. That was all I needed, after all.

I accepted defeat and was about to return to the city when I saw a welcoming church. St Sidwell's. A cleric stood sweeping the dirt, and I wondered whether he might know of a horse dealer.

'Good day, sir. I hope the weather finds you well?'

The cheerful-looking priest looked up from his labours. He had been bending to sweep the mud and dust from his threshold, but when I accosted him, he stopped, his round, friendly face beaded with perspiration. 'I am indeed glad to see you, my son,' he said, adding in a confidential manner, leaning on his besom, 'for it gives me an opportunity to cease in my labours.

Although I know my work is pleasing in the sight of God, I confess it is more pleasant to rest and speak to others. Good sir, can I offer you a little refreshment?'

He held up a costrel, and I gladly took a gulp or two of apple-flavoured drink while he stretched his back, his hands on his hams. I had tried some of the foul brew that they made in Okehampton, the sort of drink that would dissolve your teeth in a single mouthful, but this was altogether different, a kind of watered apple wine, with a fragrance and lightness that was delicious, especially in the warmth of the late morning. It certainly was refreshing, and the priest – whose name, I learned, was Walter – was pleased to hear my effusive thanks. I was merely glad of an educated man who could speak plain English.

'I am seeking a horse,' I said at last, when discussion of brewing apple juice had petered out.

'Where to do you wish to ride? Cornwall?' he asked. There was that Devonian expression: *Where to?* He must have taken on some of the stranger linguistic forms of his parishioners.

I shook my head emphatically. 'I have just come from that direction, Father. No, I would not return that way if ordered on pain of death. I am a civilized man, as you can see. My path lies in the opposite direction: east, to London.'

'There are some few horse dealers about the city, and some who will rent you a day's ride on one. But none down here, I think. Perhaps in Heavitree over there.'

He was pointing towards the east.

I was downcast to hear that. He slapped my shoulder. 'Come, fellow, I am sure you will soon find a mount. Volk here are helpful when they can be.'

All about, there were broken buildings, with several in the process of being rebuilt, and I watched a couple of carpenters lifting a great frame for a new house. 'What happened here?' I asked. 'There are so many ruined buildings – what caused this?'

'That was the rebellion.'

'Which rebellion? Wyatt's?' I shivered. It had been terrifying. Wyatt had gathered together supporters in Kent who, like him, didn't want to see Mary on the throne. They preferred to return poor Lady Jane Grey to the seat. She had been Queen for nine days, and many felt she was a better proposition than Mary. Wyatt had believed that there would be risings up and down the country, and that Londoners would flock to join him. The poor fool was mistaken and captured out at Temple Bar with the remains of his army. The executions went on for an age.

'Who? No!' My companion threw me a baffled glance. 'This was the great rebellion over the prayer book.'

My expression displayed my ignorance.

'It was seven years ago now. The people of Cornwall wanted to keep the old ways, and when the new prayer book came, the folk wanted no part of it. They burned copies and revolted. Many castles and fine houses were burned. They marched up here, joined by the men of Sampford Courtenay and Crediton, and posed a real threat. Here, at Exeter, they laid siege. The gates were barred, and everyone helped build solid ramparts of stone and soil behind them so they couldn't be broken. It was fortunate that the city had provisions. The rebels sat outside for a week or more, firing their guns at the city from places like St David's Hill. A shot from there killed a man in North Street as he stood in his doorway. They pulled up pipes and conduits to melt for shot – and to deny water to the city.'

'Did they take the city?'

The man shook his head solemnly. 'Nay, they did their best, but my Lord Russell came from London with an army, and the rebels fled. They ran all the way to Sampford Courtenay, where they made their stand. And Russell won the day.'

There was a note of appreciation in his voice that seemed to show support for the protestant Church of England defenders of the city. It was brave, if so. Queen Mary would have been for the rebels fighting to have their old prayer books returned to them.

'This was before I was installed here – I was studying at Oxford – yet I have heard that the city was reluctant to open the gates to the rebels. It must have been terrible, with all the foul consequences of war. Cannon, mining of the walls, weapons loosing projectiles over the walls . . .'

'So the rebels destroyed these houses?' I said, hurrying him along.

'Oh, no. That was the city. The people removed any buildings near the walls that could give succour to the rebels; they were torn down before the rebels arrived. Furious, the rebels wanted to fling fire into the city and set it ablaze, but the poor vicar over at St Thomas's persuaded them not to. Not that it helped him. When the city was relieved, he was captured and hanged in chains on his own church tower. They only took him down a couple of years ago. It was a melancholy sight,' he added thoughtfully, his cheery face suddenly glum.

'If he saved the city, why hang him?' I asked reasonably.

'There are always reasons for men to kill others,' he said mournfully. 'He had helped prosecute a spy. The King's men sent a fellow to watch the rebels and see where they were placing their weapons. Their spy was caught, and it was the vicar's prosecution that led to the man being hanged. But to hang a vicar – that was evil. Still, now we have a Catholic bishop once more, and we have returned to the good, Christian ways and services, so all is gradually returning to normal.'

I nodded as if in full agreement, although I admit I had doubts. 'At least, all is much more peaceful now,' I said without thinking.

'Hah! You think so? If I were to tell you some of the things . . . why, I should turn your hair white!'

'What do you mean?'

He gave me a shy smile. 'Here, even merchants squabble among themselves. They blame each other for their misfortunes, and sometimes quarrels begin.'

'It is the same in London.'

'Perhaps. Here there are constant disputes about the price of ships and their cargoes, they complain about the behaviour of each other, and claim that each is trying to hurt the other financially. And some of that is true! At the same time, there are many who deplore the fact that the true Church has returned. They agitate. There are attacks on Catholics, and I fear more attacks on those who have not yet come to realize the true path to God.'

I nodded. 'Yes, so I have seen already. There was a man murdered today. The man looking after his body said he was once a priest but lost his position because he wouldn't desert his wife and children. He lies in an alley while they wait for the coroner.'

'Who?' I was suddenly aware of his sharp attention.

'I don't know. A scrawny-looking fellow; someone who had been wealthy once, but now fallen on harder times, I would think.'

'A man about my height? Mousy hair, thirty years?'

'Yes, I should say so. The man said he was the priest at St Petrock's.'

But I was talking to the air. My new friend had hurried into the church. He soon reappeared, a cap on his head, hurrying up the road towards the city.

Following him at a more sedate pace, I entered under the gate and continued up the High Street. It was less shabby from this side, I admit. On the right was the gatehouse to Rougemont Castle, an imposing building in reddish stone like the city's walls. On the left was a large house that was plainly converted from a religious institution and was now a house for one of the richest men in the city, from the look of it. Further on, the merchants' houses took over, and Exeter had a great profusion of them. Windows had their boards set down on trestle legs, with their wares piled high to tempt passers-by.

Naturally, the women were most interested in the shops selling fabrics, trinkets and gewgaws, while men were more keen on the metal workers, smiths or the bowyer and fletcher who owned businesses side by side. Dogs barked or scuttled about expecting to be kicked. Riders trotted past, casually ignoring all pedestrians, apart from the women that took their fancy. These they subjected to a vigorous series of comments on their carriage and appearance which were, frankly, offensive. If they had been relations or friends of mine, I would have been outraged. As it was, I shook my head at the way that these barbarians behaved.

Only a short way further on, I saw two women, and I realized they were the two I had seen earlier. The pretty little woman with the smile and the hair peeping in dark ringlets from her coif, and the more elderly, matronly companion. I caught the younger woman's eye, and she coloured delightfully to be noticed. She must have been not more than nineteen years, a slim little figure with a bulging bosom that would entrance any fellow with blood in his veins.

As I continued onwards, two men on horseback trotted past me. Seeing the two women, one of the riders called out, dropped from his mount and darted to the side of the younger woman, trying to take her hand in his.

He was a moderately good-looking fellow, I suppose, for a city such as Exeter. He was dressed brashly in the way these yokels sometimes will, thinking they look as refined as a London gentleman, which, of course, they can never pull off. He had a red cap, which was the fashion last year in London, and he wore a short riding cloak which was almost well cut, if I am polite. However, his square features had little of the elegance and casual good breeding of a man like me. From his appearance, he was, I suppose, an ordinary, lower-class man – by which I mean an arrogant, boastful, foolish sort. No doubt rather narcissistic. In any case, it seemed that his attentions were not appreciated by the chaperone, and I thought it possible that I might have an opportunity to get to know the dark-haired beauty. If I could do so at the same time as taking him down a peg or two, so much the better. Thus, I strode to the ladies and haughtily demanded that he leave the young woman alone.

'Whom be you?' he demanded. 'I am speaking with this lady. Mind your business, churl.'

I have been insulted by men before, but few would want to try it twice. Besides, although he could not see it, I had my wheel-lock pistol concealed under my jack. It gave me a sense of comfort, I have to say. 'The lady does not wish to suffer your brutish attentions,' I said.

'My . . . you should watch your language, fellow!'

'I doubt you would understand if I were less direct,' I said. 'This lady does not wish for your impertinence. Leave her and be on your way.'

'There's no need,' the young woman said anxiously.

'There is every need,' the matron snapped. 'Come, Alice. Leave these two.'

'But, Margaret, may I not just speak to this man?' she said, indicating me. 'He is trying to help us.'

'And he can, by detaining this ruffian!' the matron said, glaring at the man and bundling her charge away.

Which left me in the interesting position of standing before the man who, now I took a closer look at him, was moderately well built, and bore a sword whose hilts, I noticed, were well worn, as if the sword had been drawn regularly and used in practice. My own, I should say, was much more polished and clean. I had only rarely used it.

'Um,' I said.

It was suddenly borne in upon me that I stood before a man with a well-used weapon, and also his companion, who was behind me. Here I was, in a strange city, with no friends, and two brutes who looked competent to skin me alive. It was not a pleasant reflection.

Over the course of a life that has regularly involved interesting adventures, I have learned that the best means of escaping danger is generally the most obvious one: run very quickly from the source. Over many years, I have proved to my complete satisfaction that running away, while it may lead to some ill-informed jibes, does at least prevent my coat from being slashed and my body punctured, let alone the risk of my face suffering unpleasant bruising.

There are many who would consider that their reputation for courage in the face of danger is more important than the imminent threat of pain or worse. I have never subscribed to that view. To me, the crucial consideration is not demonstrating my bravery – which is, of course, of a high standard – but preventing my own suffering. It may well be that my prowess with blade and gun means that I am saving someone else from suffering, too – my opponents, for example. But my strong conviction was that today was not such a day.

To mention the obvious – that my best action would be to flee – is surely unnecessary. The fact that it was less than realistic was more relevant to me. After all, while my opponent before me stood ready and waiting, I had no idea what his friend was doing behind my back – why had I chosen to step forward in such a foolhardy manner? He was still, no doubt, on horseback, and that meant that any attempt to run would surely lead to my being speared in the back by my pursuer.

In short, I was left in a quandary: whether to draw my sword or to treat these fellows to a cup or two of wine or ale.

I glanced at his sword once more. It was enough to decide me.

Smiling profusely, I bowed low. 'Good day, sir. I hope I find you well?'

'You insulted me!'

'I fear, after you called me a "churl", my naturally proud nature rose in bitter denial. But come, if you are offended, allow me to buy you a flask or two of wine. There is no reason for gentlemen to fall out over a trifle. What is a word? You did insult me, but I would rather make a friend of a bold, courageous gentleman than come to blows. What purpose would a fight serve? Nothing. But forming a new friendship, that is worth much.'

He was glaring at me with the look of a man who suspects that he is the target of a humorous pleasantry, but after some moments, during which my heart thundered like a galloping horse, he suddenly gave a half-grin and nodded. 'Wine, William, what do 'ee think?'

I should have been warned by their enthusiastic acceptance of my largesse. The two men, who were named William Carew and Richard Ralegh, were both of the class that expected many things to land in their laps without effort. They were in their early twenties, rumbustious, bold and, in Richard's case, as eager for mischief as any man in his early manhood.

Richard was the louder, more brash of the two. He had robust good looks and the sort of jawline you could crack nuts on. His eyes were shrewd, but a little sly. He was obviously of the opinion that he would get the better of any man in a fight, whether it be of arms or wits. That was pleasing, for I have often noticed that those most convinced of their own capabilities are often those who are most easily gulled of their money.

The other, William Carew, was a very different character. William, when I turned, was still athwart his mount, leaning on the beast's withers with his arms crossed, shaking his head.

When he turned to me, I saw his eyes flick all around me, from my hat to my bags, to my feet and back. He wore a contemplative expression, like a wolf studying a deer and wondering whether the chase would be worth the meal. I thought him the more dangerous of the two and considered him closely.

He was not dressed with obvious care like Richard. His dark hair was cut more for efficiency than fashion – short at the sides and back – and he wore a woollen cap. A beard followed the line of his jaw and emphasized the squareness of his chin. A scar on his cheek tugged at the eyebrow above, too. That wound must almost have blinded him. The blade had raked over his face and just missed his eye. When he sat upright in his saddle again, I could see that he had the figure of an athlete, with broad shoulders tapering to a slim waist, which was where his riding sword hung. Both hilts and scabbard had also been well used, I saw.

However, it was his eyes that caught my attention. They were alert and missed nothing. I mentioned that he noticed my bags, and the two that took his interest were the small ones – my powder bag and the bag of lead balls for the pistol. He nodded, as though to himself, and then, 'Come, Richard, we don't have time for frivolity. We should get to your father's.'

'I would prefer to sit in a tavern for an hour first,' Richard said, and thus we were soon ensconced in a small chamber, served with a flagon of wine, and taking our ease on a settle and a bench.

'Why did ye interfere between the lady and me?' Richard said, when we were comfortable.

'She seemed unwilling to be propositioned in the street like a common drab,' I said. 'Although I cannot fault your choice and taste.'

'She's a pretty little thing, isn't she?' he said, becoming quite animated. 'Alice Shapley is her name.'

'You know her?' I said, surprised. I had thought this was merely a chance encounter.

'Not so well as he'd like,' William observed caustically.

Richard flushed. 'Don't talk like that. I'd do nothing to offend her. She is a sweet, tender little thing. I . . . well, I adore her.'

'Her chaperone didn't take to you,' I said.
'Her parents and mine have a dispute,' he nodded glumly.
'He has been told not to speak to her,' William said.
'Ah,' I said.
'But I want to marry her,' Richard said, slumping in his seat.
'What is the dispute?' I asked.

That was when it all came out. Apparently, Richard's father, Godfrey, was a master merchant who was in competition with Alice's father. The two merchants had flourishing businesses, but that led to competition. When a ship owned by Shapley was attacked at sea, he suspected Ralegh was responsible. That gave rise to arguments, and there was even an attack on Ralegh's father in the street. But a little later, Ralegh learned that one of his vessels had been attacked and captured, and blamed Shapley for his losses. Now neither man would speak to the other.

'Their losses must have been very high,' I said.

'They were. But my loss is greater than both of theirs together,' Richard said. He did indeed look as mournful as an Italian banker discovering he had lost a silver crown and found a penny. 'I love Alice.'

'And your father would have enjoyed the thought of the two houses being joined by marriage,' William said, I thought a little cynically. 'But not now. He brands Master Shapley as a thief and pirate.'

'Were both ships lost?' I asked.

'Yes. With all their cargoes,' William said. 'It was a hard loss for both families.'

'Not if they stole each other's cargoes,' I said. 'Although I suppose they can't just reuse each other's ships.'

'Hardly. They would both be easy to recognize,' Richard said.

You'll notice he did not deny that the families may have been involved in plundering each other's vessels.

'We are due at your father's house,' William said firmly.

'I know. But when I saw her . . . I just wanted an opportunity to speak with her one more time.'

His expression was glum. I sought to distract him with a

reminder that others had their own troubles to bear. 'Meanwhile, gentlemen, I have been searching for a mount to carry me eastwards, but there seem to be no beasts for hire. Do you know where I might procure one?'

'There has been a celebration here – the raising of the siege in the rebellion – and all the stables are full of the mounts of visiting people, here for the parade and feasting. There are some inns that may have old brutes for hire. You could ask here, for example,' William said.

'I have already searched high and low for something that could carry me to the next town,' I said. I was quite knocked back by my lack of success. 'If you can think of any, I would be glad of your advice.'

William frowned a little, staring into his cup. 'There is one, old Hawkey. He might have one, but beware! He is a devious courser. If he has something that would do, you'll pay extra for a beast from him.'

'If it would get me home, I would pay much for it,' I said with feeling.

When I arrived in Devon, I had been riding a vicious brute that could not decide whether to bite me or kick me. When I was offered money for him, I could not agree fast enough. There was also a scrawny, spavined thing I had won at dice, but that, I was sure, would never make the journey to London. I thought it better to sell both and hire others at intervals. A courser is only a seller of already used mounts; a dealer would have spent time training his mounts, which would be reliable, but more costly.

I took directions from the young gentlemen, and was soon following them from the door, and turning up towards the North Gate, where I was assured that 'Hawkey' Kempton the Courser had his business.

I had only made a short distance along the High Street when I was stopped by a procession. Priests in vestments, censers swinging and the fumes of exotic spices led the way, causing more than a few people to cough and choke, while others behind carried the religious folderol and marched along, trying to look enthusiastic. The bishop had a face that would have suited a stuffed toad, as if there was an unpleasant smell under his nose, but then again it might have been the natural reaction of a refined man when surrounded by such rabble.

A couple of rows behind him, I saw the same priest whom I had first seen in the alley with his two friends over the dead body. The priests made their slow way past, impressive in their haughty disregard of the men and women lining the road, and then came the city dignitaries. In their midst were the other two from the alley. They strode like dukes behind their king, and I was forced to wait, irritably tapping my foot as they proceeded down the road towards the cathedral. And as I waited, I suddenly realized that I was the victim of a crime.

A slight tug at my belt. Almost imperceptible, but – to a seasoned gentleman like me – enough. Someone had cut the laces of my purse and snatched it before the last thong had been fully snipped. I turned in time to see a foul tatterdemalion of some eight or nine summers stare at me. His moon-face was appalled, and mine was no doubt reason enough to look terrified, for he held my purse in his hand.

If you have followed my adventures, you will know that I had almost lost my purse while staying in Okehampton. I was not willing, having had to rediscover it once already, to see it stolen by a thieving peasant from Exeter's underworld. When he sprinted away, I was after him like a greyhound after the hare.

He was fleet, I'll give him that. For such a short, slender figure, he could have put many a pony to shame, the way he jinked and jigged, making his way along the High Street, right along an alley, then left and left again until I was lost. Being foreign and not having been here for any time, I was completely befuddled, darting along narrow ways where the jettied buildings smothered all light and left the packed earth of the paths in a perpetual gloom.

Before long, I was blowing and puffing like a vat of water in a laundry house, but I was gaining on the little scrote. It's one thing to try to outrun a fit and healthy youngster when he's been fed and generally well looked after, and quite a different thing when he's a little rascal who's been half starved for most of his life. I, on the other hand, was nourished and fit, and had the enormous advantage of incentive. I had a long way to go and *needed* that money.

It was in a dark alley that the boy ran out of oats. He stopped, panting, leaning against a wall and staring at me with wide eyes. I stood sternly, heaving for breath, and grabbed the urchin by the shoulder of his thin waistcoat. The little creature suddenly sobbed, 'Don't kill I, master, please! I were just so hungry . . .'

That was when I realized my captive was no boy at all. It was a girl.

God's nails, but I missed London.

I suppose, to a child brought up in the midden that was this outpost at the wilder ends of the kingdom, being taken by a man like me, with the advantages of wealth, culture and elegance, must have been terrifying. The fact that the wretch had my purse in her fist didn't make her comfortable in my presence, obviously.

A wild choler rose in me, and I lifted my hand to smack her, but she flinched like a puppy. A tear made a track in the filth on her face, and I gritted my teeth, but could not let my hand fall. It would be like striking a hungry memory of myself.

I know: spare the rod and spoil the child and all that; but the simple fact was, I had been as hungry as her when I was young; when my mother left us and my father spent more and more time in taverns draining barrels of ale with every spare penny he earned. I was left hungry while he spent his time drinking.

'Give me my purse,' I snapped.

She held it out at arm's length, averting her face in expectation of a slap. I snatched it from her. 'You're coming with me,' I said.

'No, no, please, master, don't . . .' she began, and her wailing accompanied us to the end of the road, where I spied a tavern and dragged her to the door. 'When did you last have a meal?'

'What – here?'

'A real meal.'

'I never . . .'

I pulled her inside. She was instantly struck dumb and tried to conceal herself behind me. A thick fog of sweat, sour ale and smoke assailed my nostrils, and I inhaled happily. The chimney must have been blocked, for clouds billowed from the hearth, and the overall reek reminded me of home in London. There were full benches at the walls, but the room grew silent as we entered; suspicious eyes narrowed observing us. Spotting a pair of seats at the far side, I pulled the suddenly silent child behind me. The host appeared, glowering, but took my order for a quart of ale and wine for the child. With food ordered, soon we were alone. Conversations started up again, gradually.

'Where are your parents?' It seemed a natural first question.

'Mother's ill.'

'Your father?'

'He's . . . gone.'

I nodded. It was a common enough story. 'Where do you live?'

Her eyes grew hooded. 'Why?'

Our food arrived, a thick and meaty stew with a mess of wilted salad leaves, strongly scented with garlic and onions, and a hunk of bread. I waved at her. 'Eat!'

She gazed at it, then at me, then back at the trencher as if in disbelief. I took a long draft of the ale, which at first tasted of goat's piss but then settled into a more tolerable flavour. 'Go on, eat,' I said, dunking my bread into the gravy.

You may say, *Why, Jack? Why feed someone else's daughter? She was only a thief and beggar, after all. She was almost certainly due a visit to the gallows as soon as she was old enough.* And I wouldn't disagree. But there was something about her fragile appearance and desperation that called to me. Perhaps it was a sense that she was, in some way, a reflection of me. I saw in her poverty a reminder of my own childhood before I escaped my father. So it was a form of sympathy. Yes, she was a thief, but perhaps, with a little kindness, the little chit could find a route to gentility, as I had. I had been a cut-purse myself, not so terribly long ago, after all. Now look at me: a man with a trade, a profession – admittedly not one which I could confess to, but it was at least a rewarding occupation. It showed that hard work and commitment could win rewards.

I ate my own dish of food with enthusiasm. It was at least

adequate. For her, it was almost too much. She scoffed hers like a hungry mastiff falling on a long-anticipated burglar. I thought she must be sick, the way she gobbled it up, constantly throwing sidelong glances at me as if expecting to have it snatched away. For my part, I ignored her – and kept a firm hand on my purse.

When we were finished, she looked at me with increased suspicion. The food had sharpened her wits. 'What do you want?'

'Nothing. I saw you were hungry. I have known hunger, too.'

'You going to take me to the bailiff for that?' she said, nodding towards my purse.

'No.'

'So you want *that*, then.'

I swear it took some moments for her words to sink in, and when they did, I recoiled. 'No, I swear! You can only be some . . . What do you take me for – a pederast? *God's hounds*, but I'd rather . . . no, child. I do not want "that". I just wanted to feed you. Nothing more.'

She absorbed that, considering me as one might an exotic flower sprouting in a midden. 'What now?'

'You go to your mother, and I will go about my business. Your mother should be worried about you.'

'Suppose.'

'And your father has gone away, you said?'

'Yes.'

'Your mother must depend on you.'

'Yes.'

And that was that. Soon thereafter, she rose, giving me a curious look, and was gone. I took a cup of wine, avoiding the glances of the other men in the room, and then took my leave, searching for a shop selling laces for my purse. Soon I had it affixed to my belt once more, and I felt less undressed.

Damned child. Still, I felt I had at least achieved one good thing that day.

The man recommended by Ralegh and Carew had a small-holding and pasture outside the North Gate. He was not one to whom I would enthusiastically entrust my money. He was a sallow-skinned, thin man of about forty, with barely a tooth in his head, a cast in one eye, and a manner of speaking that was both suspicious and sly. Before speaking, he managed to give the impression that no matter what your position, he would not believe you, but there was a cold, steely glint in his eye when he spoke of money.

'Nay, master, I couldn't let you have a beast for London. I don't have many beasts. Few enough even to rent. The roads are dangerous. You could lose your life, but I'd lose my mount.'

It was as clear as the nose on his face that he would not settle for a reasonable sum. Strongly desirous of a beast as I was, I had no wish to pay him an exorbitant sum for one. Uppermost in my mind was his trustworthiness. Buying a second-hand beast from a man such as he was risky.

Mulling over this as I walked, I became aware of a soft sound behind me. A light-footed step, but when I turned, there was nobody there.

When I had been stuck on the moors recently, stories of ghosts, ghouls, sanguisuga that drank the blood of men, had frozen my own. The thought of an invisible pursuer chilled me to the bone, and I confess that my pace quickened considerably, until, by the time I reached the city's gate and passed under its welcoming arch, I was pelting along like a racehorse.

It was a relief to be back in the city, but my relief was short-lived. There was a loud step, and I realized a man was following behind me. I was hard put to it not to peer over my shoulder. It wasn't Kempton, and it wasn't the light step from outside the gate.

It was gathering dusk now, and you know that feeling of trepidation as the light fails, and you find that someone is behind you? I had that feeling now. The sweat formed icy trails where it ran down my spine.

I was inside the city. This was a place where I should be secure. After all, even in a poor, wretched huddle of houses like Exeter, a man knows he is safer than outside where felons held sway. Within the walls, a man had the reassurance that people would hear a cry for help. Inside the city, footpads, cutpurses, drawlatches – and still more rapacious thieves such as bankers – are more prominent. Nowhere is entirely safe, but almost anyone would feel safer in a city than walking the woods and dark lanes outside, where felons might lie concealed behind every bush and tree.

So it was easy enough for this parcel of brutes to waylay me.

In my mindless wanderings, I had entered a strange network of alleys and clogged lanes in which some of the poorer peasants and denizens of the lowest classes lived. I mean to say, I have been poor in my time, such as when I first moved to London from my family home in Kent, but these were the worst dregs of this rather awful city. Rough, ill-bred denizens of the lawless areas of the city, clad in tatters and rags, some with a leather jerkin, most with little more than scraps and a blanket to act as a cloak. It was the sort of place you'd often find dead bodies lying in your path, and no one would be likely to worry the coroner. He had enough to deal with looking after the better-off corpses.

What can a city do? In London, the wealthy and better classes, among whom, naturally, I would place myself, tend to avoid the worst dives where such folk might gather. Oddly, of course, it means that those places where I had spent my youth were now excluded from me, whereas my usual haunts now were those very areas that would have excluded me.

But to return to that evening.

My wanderings had been perfectly aimless, and I took no note of my general direction until men in front and behind made themselves known to me. I had little choice: to stand still and try to negotiate my escape, wait for them to attack, or flee. This was not a moment for indecision. I studied the huge man before me, glanced over my shoulder at the thief behind me, and came to a decision.

I chose flight. It has, after all, saved my life on many occasions. There was an alley on my right, and I suddenly threw myself into it, hurtling along like a cat fleeing a dog.

Have you ever seen a reckless hound happily chase after a cat, only to discover that a trapped cat can metamorphose into something terrifying and deadly? I once saw a neighbour's fearsome mastiff discover this. He saw a cat and exploded into action.

Jowls flapping, slobber flying, every muscle rippling like waves on a violent sea, he set off in hot pursuit. And then something miraculous happened. The cat, cornered between two walls, had no escape. In an instant, their roles were reversed. Instead of a petrified feline, the dog found himself facing an evil black shape, with fur that stood out like a hedgehog's quills, emitting a coarse, spitting snarl of pure hatred.

Clearly, the mastiff's slow-witted mind was quick to adapt. This was not a fight he would easily win. The cat was no longer a victim. It had become the devil's avenger.

Nonchalantly, instead of continuing after the cat, the mastiff gradually slowed to a trot, then a gentle amble, and paused here and there to sniff at some choice plants as though the idea of chasing this cat had never entered his mind.

I was to experience a similar event, by which I mean that as I pelted down the alley away from the imminent danger of two footpads, I became aware of a greater danger. A large shadow seemed to fall over me.

It was rather like running down a roadway without looking, and striking a massive oak at full pelt. If one is not involved in watching the scenery, such an appearance can be a surprise, and thus it was that evening.

The massive object in this case was a man of some thirty years, and from his appearance, every year had been spent in combat with bears or wrestling with tigers. His face had no surface that had not been damaged. His nose was bent at a curious angle to the rest of his face, his eyebrow on one side had been disfigured by a sword or dagger, and there was a half-inch gap. When his mouth opened, there was a lack of ivory, as if he had been punched with a metal tube, removing the two upper and lower incisors, but leaving his other teeth intact. His ears were large and without definition, as if someone had grabbed them and blown into them until they had swollen like inflated pigs' bladders.

But it was his eyes that grabbed my attention. He had small, glowering eyes that I knew would be sure to come to me in dreams on those nights when I might have consumed a little too much strong red wine or cheese.

'Good evening,' I said, and if my voice trembled slightly, what of it? This was a man from a nightmare.

''Ave un paid your toll?'

'I . . . *toll*?'

'This'n's our lane. Us don't let just any'un in yere, do us?'

At first, I thought he was talking to me, but then I heard the two voices behind me agreeing with this fellow. It was enough to make my knees become wobbly. 'I'll just go back the way I came, then,' I said hurriedly.

'Mayhap. After thee'st abin an' gone vor to pay your toll,' the grim creature said.

That took me a while. I stared up with perplexity as my mind unravelled his peasant speech: *Maybe. After you have been and gone for to pay your toll*, I realized. 'But I'm not entering your lane.'

'Ye already 'ave. You must pay,' he said, leaning down conspiratorially. 'Arter all, us wou'n' want folk to think us'd bin an' allowed a traveller to pass through our lane without helping t'wards the upkeep.'

I smiled up at him. It might be readily appreciated that I was not feeling particularly sunny at this stage. There was a strangely unpleasant dampness seeping into both boots, and I was sure that it was not mere rainwater.

'Thee going to puke?' he demanded, and there came the sound of sniggering from behind me. 'Because if'n ye are, us'll charge for fouling the roadway.'

I glanced about me. It was hard to see a single square foot that was not already perfectly covered with its own layer of filth.

He held out his hand, and I backed away from his grimy flesh.

'I have no money with me,' I said hurriedly.

'Tis a pity, in't it, boys?' he said. He withdrew his hand, slipping it into the neck of his shirt. When he pulled his hand free, he was gripping a short-bladed dagger with a wicked, oily sheen to it. He smiled. 'Us best take som'else from thee instead.'

I stepped backwards into a wall. At least, it felt like a wall. When I glanced around and up, I realized that this was less a wall and more a block of stone shaped into the resemblance of a man. Perhaps he was a troll. The features above me subtly moved until the gargoyle-like face had shifted into a vague semblance of a smile. At least he had teeth.

Behind him was the third man. This man was fey, touched by a fairy and sent mad. He giggled, widened his eyes and all but danced with excitement at the thought of my being injured. Like a willing dog, he constantly looked up at the other two as if he was seeking their approval. He certainly was not winning mine.

'Gentlemen, let me suggest,' I began, but as I spoke, the two behind me took hold of my arms, the one with grim resolution, the other with a slight caper and high-pitched chuckle. It was the sort of sound I might have given myself, with the small difference that mine would have been driven by terror. That blade, you see, was still before me, and now it was moving as though to attack my cods.

I gibbered and then gave a shriek as the knife touched my codpiece. 'No, no! God's teeth, man, please, I beg . . .'

The evil man grinned and set his knife against my belly. 'Be you so sartin sure thee have no pelf?' he said.

I swear, I could have fainted away right then. All I could think was that if they took my purse, I would have no means of returning to London, and I was convinced that they were intending to do just that.

He had seen my purse, and now his grin broadened. He reached forward, the knife severed my new laces, and he had my money. He opened it and peered inside. His friends craned their necks to join him, and they gave a sort of collective sigh, as if the view of my money was enough to send them into a trance. It was plain enough that my purse held considerably more coins than any of the three – perhaps all three collectively – had seen in their lives.

It was my moment, and I took it. As the two gripping my arms leaned forward to gaze into my purse, their attention was diverted. I lifted my arms suddenly, snatching both free, then brought them down again over the top of my purse, wrenching it from the man's grasp with a speed and ferocity born of desperation. With it in my hands, I bent low and did what I am good at.

I ran.

* * *

That race will stay with me no matter how long I live. I have considerable experience of running from danger, but few cases have been so fraught as this. I knew that to falter would be to die. They had seen the value in my purse, and they would do all in their power to win it back. Since I was equally determined that they would not succeed, we were all four engaged in a battle to the death. That was plain.

The way ahead was filthy, with trash and garbage of all sorts lying in the lane. An occasional drunken figure could be seen slumped against walls, and I must hurtle over them, carefully preventing myself from hitting their heads with my feet as I went. Not because I was anxious that I might hurt them; no, it was more that if I were to do so, I'd certainly fall into the muck and my pursuers could take hold of me. And that must mean emasculation and probably death. I had good reason to be swift.

It was a horrible chase. I was constantly aware of the feet behind me, their panting, the snarls and grunts that spoke of their efforts, but I was not going to turn and look. I was far too desperate to risk looking over my shoulder.

I clung to my purse like a man clutching a rope in a drowning sea. The purse was my salvation; it was my guarantee of returning home. If it were stolen, I would be forced to remain here in this horrible city until I could acquire more coin. So I held to it like a dying man holding a rosary. I would not let go for any reason.

And then I had a brilliant idea. My wheel-lock pistol was still nestling at the back of my trousers.

No sooner did I have the thought than I put it into action. In an instant, I had reached round to the back of my belt. I grabbed the pistol's handle, set the dog to the wheel, turned a little so I could point it behind me, and pulled the trigger. I heard the familiar whine of the flint striking the wheel, saw the flash and smoke of the first ignition and heard the boom. I saw the thick, greasy smoke, the long flames reaching out to the three men, and knew satisfaction. Startled, all three tried to evade the bullet. The capering fool was slowest, looking at his companions as though they were gone mad, but No Teeth dived for the ground while his companion the Troll sprang behind a broken barrel.

My achievement gave me a delicious, warm glow in my belly.

I had bested them. Now I could run on, safe in the knowledge that they would never be able to make up the distance between us. I think it is fair to say that I was smug. There is no better feeling than evading danger at the hands of ruffians. Yes, I was smug. Who wouldn't be?

Once I heard a man say that pride comes before a fall. I don't recall who the sage was – it was probably one evening in a tavern or a fellow in the Cardinal's Hat – but I was now to learn that the same is true of smugness. In fact, almost as soon as I was aware of the recoil of the gun's explosion in my hand, I was also aware that something was amiss.

I don't know whether you have ever had a similar experience. A moment when everything seems to be going well after a period of disaster, only to suddenly be thrown off course and be reminded that no matter how rosy life can look, there is always the possibility that Chance and Fate had only been pulling up their shirt-sleeves, cracking their knuckles and preparing to make life sticky. A moment similar to one in which the bride and groom are preparing for their first kiss, when a fellow at the back of the church sticks his hand up and says, 'May I have a word, Vicar?'

You see, as I fired and felt the gun kick at my hand, I was aware that my aim appeared to be rather off. Instead of the gun pointing at the trio of chuckle-headed head-bangers, the gun was pointing at a darkening sky. Perhaps it was the recoil, I recall thinking, but then I grew aware that my legs were not functioning as I would have expected. Although I was continuing forward, for some reason I had the impression that my feet were not striking the ground. Contact with the soil and night soil of the lane had been lost. But that was soon to be rectified.

Something hit me forcibly on the forehead. It was the ground.

When I was able to open my eyes again, I found myself staring up at the stars. Most, I think, were genuine, but there were three or four red and blue ones that appeared to be dancing and occasionally diving down to belabour me about the head. I suspected these were no more than vicious nymphs enjoying themselves at my expense.

I tried to rise, but there was a weight resting upon my breast. I had an instant's horror, thinking I was held and this was the *peine forte et dure* for something I had said or done, but a moment's reflection told me that such torture took time to set up. The executioner must collect the requisite weights before squashing his victim, and he would only conduct his experiments on human survival in the safety of a torture chamber, not here in the open air. Peering through the fog of attacking stars, I discerned a boot, and attached to it a leg. My eyes travelled upwards until they were granted the sight of my friend with the knife but no teeth. He smiled his black hole of a smile, reached down and took hold of my purse. I squeaked and clutched it to my breast.

'Oh, ye wan' me to cut un away, then,' he said, lunging for it.

'No! No!'

'Ye squeal like a merchant!'

'Sounds like that puppy Lane!' said the Troll.

'At least this un has money.'

Of course, I had no idea what they were speaking about. Or whom. It didn't matter. I had other things on my mind than analyzing their speech.

Just then there was a sudden noise. A shriek of some sort, and the three stiffened. I gave a gurgling laugh. They would soon regret their attack, I thought. This must be the watch, here to see that poor travellers like me should be safe from their depredations. They would be captured, arrested and forced to decorate a local gallows for their impetuous assault. I looked up to see my attacker scowling at someone other than me. Having his attention elsewhere was good, I felt.

The boot was gone. I rolled over and tried to stand, but my broken head was throbbing so, I could barely move without vomiting. I remained there, head hanging. I imagine I looked like a cur that's been starved for a week and kicked routinely. You know the sort – the kind of beast that has so little energy it can barely lift its head. The sort of dog every unpleasant churl or child will mock because it's easy to beat a brute which is already suffering.

No Teeth must have thought that too, because suddenly his

boot was all too evident as it connected with my flank. My arms and legs left the ground – it felt so, anyway – and I curled up, clutching at my belly and moaning. A hand reached down, took hold of my purse and snatched it away from my grasp. All I could do was moan and whimper despairingly. I had little strength and could not keep my grip. My purse, my fortune, my return home were stolen from me.

Before I could recover, the three were gone, and there was a shout. In an instant, two men had overtaken me and were hurtling off in pursuit of my attackers. I stared after them, wishing to urge them on, but lacking the energy to do so. My belly hurt so much that I wanted to vomit, but had no ability – my stomach muscles were one enormous bruise.

I would have joined the chase, both because I was reluctant to remain in the alley all alone and because I would have really enjoyed kicking the thieves – once they had been knocked down, of course – but just then the thought uppermost in my mind was whether I would ever stand again.

My head was a throbbing mass of pain. There were shooting pains at the side of my body, and I was convinced I was going to be sick. I had a feeling that, were I to stand, my head might well fall from my shoulders, and although that was not usually a thought to comfort me, it did occur to me that at least then I'd have no more pain. My flank felt as though that villain had broken every bone in my ribcage, and I would have liked to have seen him have similar grief inflicted upon him.

It was plain enough what had happened. When I turned to fire my pistol, the distraction had prevented me from keeping close attention on the route ahead. I had stumbled and gone flying, striking my head on something. Casting a bitter eye over the ground nearby, I saw a large, broken cartwheel. If I had hit that, it was no wonder I was stunned.

A foul old fellow with a leather pottle at his side was probably the explanation. His outstretched legs were almost certainly the cause of my fall. I gave him a grim look. If there was any justice in this city, he would have combusted on the spot, such was the virulence in my glance. As it was, he merely snored, squirmed and continued his drunken dreaming. A cat or a rat scurried over some trash in the alley behind me. When I peered down it, I could almost have imagined there was a small figure there, but when I blinked, it was gone. With my head feeling as it did, I wasn't surprised to see things that clearly weren't there. Besides, I had more pressing concerns.

By slow degrees, I was able at last to bring myself upright. I stood unhappily, swaying slightly. A brief investigation brought my pistol to hand, and I retrieved it, installing it once more in the place of concealment under my jacket, placing my hand against the nearer wall while I waited.

And then, naturally, it struck me. The two men who had taken off after my thieves had no doubt caught the scoundrels. Perhaps even killed them. And yet there was no sign of them. They were no doubt even now enjoying their unexpected windfall at the nearest tavern.

There are times when I am appalled by the degeneracy of my fellow man. These two had appeared like good Samaritans, eager to rescue a visitor to their city in his moment of distress. But as soon as they had discovered my wealth, they had succumbed to their baser instincts. They had taken my purse and were even now ordering sack by the bucket, no doubt. Could any man be so mean? Well, obviously, yes. I had known enough in my time in London, for example, but even though I knew that people who lived in such vile and degenerate areas among peasants would naturally be more base than the lowliest carter in London, somehow I had not anticipated that the two whom I had considered my rescuers would suddenly prove as venal as those who had robbed me. It was a sad, reflective Jack who stood there.

The drunk snored. I kicked him in the cods, but it gave me little satisfaction. He muttered reproachfully and rolled over. I was all alone, adrift in this city with little possibility of even a bed for the night, now that my little all was stolen from me. Yes, I was filled with melancholy.

Which is why it was a surprise shortly afterwards to be accosted by my two friends of the afternoon. Richard Ralegh and William Carew.

* * *

As they led me from that noisome alley and out into the High Street once more, they were full of the adventures of the evening. They had been walking to a tavern when they heard a shrill voice calling on the hue and cry. Shortly afterwards, there came the report of my gun, and they saw my abortive flight into the wagon's wheel, then the appearance of the felon who stole my purse.

'Who called you?' I wondered.

'A child or a woman. They must have seen the three attack you,' Richard said with a shrug.

'That felon had the feet of Mercury,' William Carew said thoughtfully. 'He could have outrun a hare!'

'He sped along like a galloping horse,' Richard Ralegh agreed with respect. 'Who would think that a man so large and unprepossessing might achieve such a turn of speed?'

This was all very interesting no doubt, but, 'What of my purse?'

Richard looked at me with a dumbstruck expression, like a spaniel suddenly aware that while chasing a rabbit, he had forgotten his ball.

It was William who spoke with simple compassion. 'We did all we could, but the man was too fast for us. He made good his escape with your purse.'

At that, I admit, I let out a groan of despair. I had lost my money again. The likelihood of retrieving my purse in a city like this was slight in the extreme. What could I do? I was adrift in a foreign city, without friends or patrons, and without money, there was little chance that I would ever make my way home again.

What could I do? Walk? Beg for food from local farmers or other peasants? No gentleman would allow me under his lintel as a beggar.

'What will become of me?' I said, and it may well be that my voice came more as a wail than my usual bluff and confident tone. I succumbed to despair, thinking of my comfortable house, the taverns and bordellos, the women . . . 'How can I survive? How can I return to London? What am I to do?'

The two were silent a moment, perhaps stunned by my evident grief.

William Carew grunted and shook his head. 'Richard, you will have to help the fellow. He did stand us a good drink, after all.'

'I don't think my father would appreciate my bringing home a fellow just now,' Richard said slowly and reluctantly.

'Your father may need a reminder of his responsibilities. It is a Christian duty to help those in distress.'

'He would say he does enough by leaving food at his gate for the poor.'

'But he would be wrong.'

'Please, either of you, if you could help me, I would be very grateful,' I said.

The two exchanged a look. It appeared to me that William was keen that Richard should take on responsibility for me, but not to help me himself. Later, I learned that he had no property of his own in Exeter, and he was himself to shake down with Richard.

In a short while, we were retracing their steps out of the little alleyways and along a large wall. This, I learned, was St Nicholas's Priory, which Richard's father had acquired after good King Henry's reappraisal of the Catholic Church's position in the country. I heard that his father had made a small fortune by purchasing the old buildings, first by selling off the stones from some of the buildings to help restore the bridge over the Exe, then by building new, cheaper homes which he rented out for very high fees. Those who could not afford to buy a house were glad to be able to rent one in the city, and if they soon found themselves running out of money and into debt, well, there were many more to take their places.

Of course, I was too young to know all about the confiscations of Church lands and the demolition of so many monasteries up and down the country. All I knew was that there were many men in positions of some authority who had taken over large buildings and made use of them, for a small consideration in the King's purse. If Richard's father made a small fortune, the King must have made a huge one in those days. Taking excess silver and gold, destroying many buildings and selling off the lead and stone and timbers, and then taking money from men who wanted to keep their abbeys as great houses – I wish I had thought of a scam like that.

Richard's home was a long, low building not far from the alleys.

'We were just going to find a watering hole where we might sit and talk things over,' William said.

Richard nodded glumly. 'We spoke earlier of Alice, that angel who treads so softly, her hair like—'

'Yes, he remembers,' William said quickly. I soon came to realize that if Richard was not halted quickly when he started to speak of Alice Shapley, there was always the risk that he would grow maudlin and continue in a similar manner for an hour or more, singing the maiden's praise to the heavens and generally boring all about him to death.

'There's no need to snap,' Richard said.

'You were the same over Agnes Causley two months ago. Before her, it was Margaret Efford, and before her it . . .'

'They were not the same.'

'Yet you would still visit the whores?' William said.

My ears pricked. I was in the mood for a little horizontal wrestling after my injuries and excitement.

Richard pulled a face. 'I am no better nor worse than any other man,' he said, a trifle plaintively, I thought. 'When temptation is presented . . .'

'Your response rears immediately,' William said caustically.

'You mentioned Alice to your father?' I guessed, trying to get to the point.

'I merely brought her to my father's memory,' Richard said mournfully. He looked like a bloodhound who'd lost his sense of smell when presented with the scent of a cat.

'He was not best pleased,' William continued for him. 'The words "traitor" and "ingrate" were raised. As was his voice.'

'He doesn't understand real love,' Richard said. 'What can an uncouth old man like him know of love? I am motivated by a pure, fine adoration. He thinks only in terms of money, of financial matters. Love is for the young. He couldn't understand.'

'He told Richard to spend himself with one of the whores rather than tying himself to a young daughter of a viper like Isaak Shapley,' William confided.

It seemed excellent advice to me, if there were any wenches

available in this city, but I didn't mention it. I might have appeared unsympathetic. Not that Richard would have listened. He was engaged in kicking stones of various sizes across the road like a frustrated choirboy.

We turned in at a large gateway, which brought us into a small courtyard. Beyond was a welcoming stone building with a front door covered by a small portico, which had benches on either side. The windows gleamed with light. Richard looked at William and then at me, sighed like a seamstress who felt her tip was inadequate, and led the way to the door.

Soon I found myself in the presence of Richard's father.

It was the fat man I had seen that morning at the corpse.

In the opinion of Richard Ralegh's father, Godfrey, he had been content without a Jack Blackjack in his house. His language was abrupt to the point of rudeness and, with his deplorable accent, nigh on impossible to understand. I translate for those of happier upbringing.

'What the devil were you doing down there in the alleys? Gracious God, any man should know that it's the sort of place where a man might be in danger, even in a model city like ours! Do you London folk have no sense? And now, because of your stupidity, you wish to claim sanctuary from me?'

'Father, the man was attacked,' Richard said. 'It was not his choice or his fault. What, would you blame any victim who is robbed? After all, you yourself were robbed only recently.'

'That was entirely different! Shapley is a pirate and murderer. It was no fault of mine that he took my ship and goods.'

I hotly declared that it was not my fault that, while walking in his supposedly splendid city, I had fallen prey to representatives of a particularly unwholesome form of roadside pirate, at which he stepped forward, thrust a finger like a steel peg into my breast and pointed out that a stranger to any town would be a fool to step into the darker alleys and byways. 'Especially carrying a well-filled purse on your person!' he added nastily.

'I was not to know that this city would hold such dangers – and wretches who would attack a foreigner,' I said.

Godfrey's finger was still prodding at my chest as though he intended to learn whether he could actually stab it through to my heart. Now he leaned forward – his paunch was so vast, he could barely approach within a foot of another man – and I was fain to turn my head to avoid the foul fumes of sour wine and garlic.

'Do not dare to blame our city, you coxcomb! You come here, a walking temptation to any man with ballocks, with less brains than my morning's turd! You should be glad that your life was spared! Hah, you should be grateful that they took your purse alone to teach you a lesson. Many would take your cods as well!'

I winced at the memory of that knife at my ballocks, but then gathered myself. After all, this was only a merchant from Exeter. He was no match for a man of my standing. He took his finger away and stood glaring at me. Glancing at Richard and William, I shrugged myself more comfortably into my jack and rewarded them with a haughty smile. 'My friends, I am plainly unwelcome here. If you could direct me to an inn, or introduce me to a friend of the Queen or Lady Elizabeth, I would be grateful.'

The merchant threw me a suspicious look. '"Friend of the Queen"? What does that mean? Why do you ask that? Speak! What do you mean by those words?'

Now, in case you think that I was over-aristocratic in my demeanour, I should just say that at that time a man's livelihood could depend upon his religious choices. In this house, there was a singular lack of Roman fripperies, which was a surprise for a man of such obvious wealth. After all, during the reign of young King Edward, men of sense would proclaim their support for everything to do with the Church of England. King Henry would piss acid if he learned of men remaining Catholic. Since his own and his son Edward's death, Queen Mary had taken an equally strong but opposing view. Now a man must carry a rosary at all times to avoid suspicion. It mattered less for those with no money; peasants were safe enough. But those who did not profess their rediscovery of the Roman faith – well, life could grow intense very quickly.

A wealthy merchant would be well advised to return to the old faith, or else it could be suspected that he was still a believer in a Church that the Queen considered heretical. She would not shower contracts or rewards on such men. Rather, she might invite such folks to visit her accommodation at the Tower.

So, gazing about me and seeing nothing in the way of Roman religious items, I realized that I might have an opportunity here. Were I to find a loyal supporter of the Queen, a reward could soon be forthcoming for denouncing a merchant of local status. A reward that might even be adequate to allow me to reach London.

'If you will not help me, I shall be forced to use my own contacts,' I said coldly.

'With the Queen?'

'I serve the Queen's sister, Lady Elizabeth. Even now, I carry important news to her.' Such as it was. The news was that I had not fled over the water to Europe. Many people would be keen to learn that I was still in the kingdom, although most probably Lady Elizabeth would not be terribly interested.

But Ralegh was not to know. He stood contemplating me for some little while, before gruffly muttering that it would be ill-mannered for a man to force a visitor from his door. There was an evil glint in his eye as he spoke, and I was all too aware that if he suspected that I had invented this, my stay could become painful. Still, I had not lied. I was assassin to Lady Elizabeth, and if that did not make me a part of her household, I don't know what would.

I graciously accepted his offer of a bed for the night, with just enough hauteur to make my contempt clear without being so insulting I risked eviction.

TWO
Hunting Thieves

6 August

The chamber to which I was led was a pleasant enough room with a small but comfortable tester bed. I sat on it and reviewed the poor luck I had endured throughout that day. At least now I was in a comfortable room, and I could still denounce the merchant Ralegh and perhaps earn my passage to London; I had not been murdered by the three thieves in that alley.

The three were much on my mind. They had been happy to insult a man on the ground and kick him. With that thought, I rose and methodically went through the process of reloading my pistol. I scraped out the burned powder, poked at the vent, blew into it, wiped the pan and refilled the barrel with powder, wadding and ball, setting a little powder under the cover and winding the gun carefully. It settled my mind for a while, and while I did it, the name Lane returned to me. *Squeal*, indeed. They had said how I squealed like a merchant, and then something about Lane – that was right, that I squealed 'like that puppy Lane'. Lane was the name of the man who was dead, surely. It made me shiver. Surely these three were the men who had slaughtered that fellow today. Why? Because he carried money? That would have surprised me. Surely, if he had coin, he would have spent a little on his clothing.

It made me think how lucky I had been not to be killed. I should count my blessings. The trouble was, as I considered my position, I was forced to conclude that the scales were not balanced in my favour.

On the plus side, I was alive, had a safe room with a good bed, and I would not be charged for it since I was a guest. However, on the opposite side of the ledger, there was the loss of all my wealth. I had plenty of coin stored safely at my house in London, but that was as much use as moonshine to me right now. I would not be able to escape this city with money lying seventy leagues away. No, I must arrange, somehow, to return. Finding the three thieves and recovering my wealth would not be easy, and for certain a large amount would already have been lost, for they were the sort of fellows, I reckoned, who would have made their way to the nearest lowly alehouse as soon as they could, there to sprinkle their ill-gotten wares as liberally as they might, purchasing wenches, ale, sack and capons to their hearts' and bellies' content. And soon all my money would be lost forever.

It didn't bear thinking of.

I suddenly had an urgent desire for drink. And not a mere jug or so: I needed a flood, an inundation of ale. My flank was hurting, my head was joining in, and waves of misery all but overwhelmed me. Could I ever return to London? Send a message to my master? He would be unlikely to be keen to send me money. In his view, it would be up to me to make my own way, and he would be delighted, I have no doubt, to learn that I had been beaten by three town toughs. He would probably expect me to find them and kill them. As if that was likely!

And then I hesitated. After all, I was a guest in this house. The two ruffians who had tried to chase after my attackers were eager to see justice, and if the master of the house was keen to be rid of me, he might be willing to supply me with two or three of his servants armed with good oaken cudgels. That way, he might be rid of me completely.

Of course, if there was a fight, I would endeavour to be well away from the front line, perhaps somewhere to the rear, so that those more trained in combat could earn their spurs, but the main point was to ensure that I found my purse again before all its contents were spilled.

It was no surprise to me that Godfrey Ralegh was glad to see me leave. He would have been perfectly happy to see me leave his house carried on a door – or just dragged out through the back and dumped in an alley, I have no doubt. Still, he was happy enough to give me the aid of three brutes who, so Richard said, were willing and eager. Richard and William joined me too, and all of us bore staffs of stout wood, so the six of us made for a moderately intimidating army, I would think.

We marched into the darkness with the resolution of knights errant. We had our quest, the search for my grail, and we intended, I thought, to search every drinking den until we had found it. It soon became moderately clear that the others might have had different ambitions for the evening. Richard was set on testing the ale in each hostelry, as were two of his servants. William and the remaining fellow watched them with jaundiced eyes, but I confess that after watching them quaff a quart each, I decided to join them. After all, what harm could it do? The evening was chilly, and I was thirsty, so a pint or two of spiced ale was necessary to warm my bones.

The taverns we visited did not seem to have had any view of the men, but in the fourth, or perhaps the fifth, the host recognized the men from my description. 'That's Ned Hall, the man with no teeth,' he said. 'He got into a fight with a man, but his opponent had a staff with him and poked it into his gob. Served the mazed bugger right. Mind you,' he added reflectively, 'Ned didn't ought to have done that to him. He couldn't walk for weeks after that.'

'What?' I asked, rather foolishly.

'He shoved that stick where it didn't ought to go,' the man said knowingly. He gave me a meaningful look, and I suddenly had an urgent need to cross my legs.

'Have you seen him today?' William asked.

'He was here a while ago, but I told him to bugger off. I won't have him here, not since the last fight he started. Took a month to get the furniture replaced.'

I looked about me in the dim interior of the tavern. If anything in there was less than ten years old, I'd be surprised.

He continued sharply, glaring at me as though guessing I doubted his words, 'Him and the other two, they went off. I heard someone say the Black Pony, up along. There's one thing for certain.'

'What's that?'

'You won't have to look hard. Just listen for the sound of screaming and breaking tables. You'll soon find them.'

We left that tavern and went in search of the Black Pony. One of the servants knew of it, he admitted, looking shamefaced at the fact, from which I gathered that it was a place where more than ale and wine was available. We followed the road down to the steep road that led towards the West Gate, and turned left. Soon we found ourselves in a warm little chamber that was almost filled with labourers, apprentices and lower classes of servants, as well as a high proportion of friendly young wenches with excellent proportions of their own.

The place reeked. On the floor, the reeds must have been over a month old, and the smell of sour ale and sack filled the room. I walked in and could feel the moistness sucking at my boots as I went. From the smell, I could almost imagine the soles dissolving.

Richard and William were not foolish. They moved together, and I was aware mostly of many men behind me, especially the servants. I was glad to have them behind me, but I admit, the sight of the brawny gathering before me was not encouraging. Looking about, I felt that there were at least thirty men, and all appeared to have the strong arms and thick necks of masons. All gazed at us like crows spying an incipient battle: they looked hungry. I swallowed, and I was about to suggest that perhaps we should find another hostelry when the door at the far side of the room opened, and in walked my friend the Troll. He seemed to notice something was amiss as soon as he entered, and in a moment, he had caught my eye. I was wrong: his face could register emotions, if he was given time. Now it showed shock and disappointment, as though he had been expecting to be left alone for a while to enjoy the use of his money – *my* money!

I pointed, and we barged through the crush to him. Seeing us, he gave a roar, which I thought was merely a battle cry, but then he span about and chased from the room, with us in hot pursuit. There was a low, menacing growl, as though the landlord had brought in a pack of deerhounds, and then the crowd closed in.

This is the problem with fighting in an enclosed space: you

may have a six-foot length of oak or beech, you may have a sword or a lance, but when the ceiling is only six feet and two inches overhead, it is damnably difficult to wield such a long weapon. The gathering in that room was better qualified for such battles. They all wore short daggers or knives, and they were not afraid to use them. Some had two-foot-long cudgels, which served them to great effect. However, two of our servants held their lengths at half-staff, with half the staff between their fists, and used these to push at the crowd. One of them received a slash on his fist, which made him redden with anger, and suddenly he snapped the stick into one man's face, stabbed the opposite end into another's throat, sending him choking to the ground, and then rammed the centre into his opponent's nose. There was a great effusion of blood, and with all those three out of the fight, the rest seemed to lose interest in us. We hurried from the scene and after our quarry.

Behind the tavern was another alley. One wall was used by drinkers as the privy, and we pelted through the puddles – I tried not to think what I was splashing in – as we sprinted after the Troll. He was tiring, from the look of him, and as we gave chase, he threw a look over his shoulder as though in disbelief.

On we rushed, six men with fitness and youth on our side, chasing after a man built like a bear, but with the speed of a three-legged cat.

He just couldn't go any faster. The Troll was not built for speed but for steadiness over a long distance. Having us sprinting after him was testing his stamina, and as we hurtled down the hill, we were gaining on him. Through more puddles, almost slipping on ordure, on we went, crossing over one road, then another, staying in the alleys where, I suppose, he felt safer, until we fetched up against the city's wall. He slammed into it, both palms against the rough stone, and then pelted off towards the South Gate on the perimeter lane, but we were much closer now. I was puffing and blowing, and the pain in my bruised flank was growing, but I was not going to give up on this opportunity to catch one of the men who had robbed me. On and on we sped, all of us panting – apart from Richard, who appeared to have boundless energy and kept up a loud bellowing as he went, in a manner that I found quite deafening. No matter: I continued, gradually allowing Richard to overhaul me. After all, the Troll was still a big man, and I didn't want to run the risk of being the first to grab him in case he swung a fist at me. He could break my head with his hands, and I had no desire to put my skull's resilience to the test.

The end, when it came, was an anticlimax.

Richard's shouting had roused the porter at the South Gate, who came to his door with his staff to see who was raising the hue and cry. Seeing the Troll being chased, he came to a swift conclusion and swung his staff with vigour. It caught the unfortunate felon on the shin with a loud crack, and the man fell, yelling with pain, rolling over and over.

We caught up with him in a moment, and soon we had our captive held in the small cell at the gate.

It was a tiny cell, designed more for holding two or three men of normal size for misdemeanours while trying to enter the city. With the Troll and six of us, it was full to capacity and beyond.

The Troll stood scowling with his back to the wall. His shin was painful, or so I hoped. Behind him, I knew, was the road down to Southernhay and the fields beyond, and I had an impression that he was almost trying to be as close to freedom as he could manage while still being in custody, as if he could walk backwards a couple of paces and melt through six yards of stone wall to the open air.

'You remember me?' I asked nastily.

'Yes. Squeaker,' he said.

If he had been only a little smaller, I would have hit him.

'You were bold enough when your friend Ned held a knife to my throat.'

'He only held it to your cods.'

'That's not the point!'

'Nothing to lose there,' he smirked.

William touched my shoulder and pushed slightly. I was at that moment spluttering with outrage, but William was calm and precise. 'What is your name?'

'Hugh Miller.'

'You were there when this man Blackjack was robbed, weren't you?'

'No.' He smiled.

I kicked his bad shin. He howled and made a grab for me, but I had already retreated.

William treated me to a frown of disapproval. 'No more of that, Master Jack.' He turned back to the Troll, who was gripping his shin in his hands and glaring at me malevolently. 'You were with the other two. Ned Hall and one other. Who was he?'

'I don't know who you mean.'

'That's good. You can stay here until the justice can listen to your pleas. But we all know what you did, and that you threatened this man's life. So when the matter comes before the court, you will be alone and you will hang alone.'

'I won't hang!'

'What, you think Ned and his friend will come to save you? They are not the sort of men to put their necks into the noose, are they? But that is fine. You know what you did, so perhaps you think you deserve to be punished.'

'Don't know what you mean,' he said.

'Well,' I said, 'there is another aspect to all this, of course. When you had me at your mercy, you declared that I' – I edited my words as I spoke – 'was no better than Lane, whom you killed yesterday.'

'That's a lie!' he said, and if I was not so convinced of his guilt, even I might have been persuaded to believe him.

'Really? You didn't mention him squealing as he died?'

'No!'

'Was he carrying much money?'

'No. He had nothing at all. Why would someone rob a beggar? He might have been important once, but he hadn't had money for years.'

'Who was this?' William asked.

'Roger Lane. His body was found in an alley not far from the Guildhall,' I said. 'Your father knew him, Richard.'

'My father? A beggar? I doubt that!'

'He was the clerk who worked for Wolfe,' William said.

'Oh, him.' Richard looked shifty.

'He was there at the body,' I said. 'I saw him.'

'Yes, well, a man like him could be useful,' Richard said.

'Eh?'

'A clerk in another merchant's house might be able to offer . . . *advice*.'

'What of this, Miller?' William said. 'Is it true that you had a part in this Lane's death?'

'No!'

'Because Master Blackjack here heard you mention him.'

'That was different,' he said, looking daggers at me. 'It's true we . . . spoke to him earlier. But we just tickled him up a bit. We were paid to. But I swear we had nothing to do with his death!'

'Who paid you?' William demanded, but the man turned away and refused to answer. There was something in his manner that said his master was an important man. He wasn't cowed or anxious at the thought of being placed before the justices.

'You swear? We should accept the word of a felon and thief?' I said.

'I'll—' he said, lunging at me. I gave a startled cry, stepped back and ended up on my arse on the straws of the floor. Fortunately, one of the servants struck him on the head before Miller could reach me, and he fell over my legs, trapping me while he grumbled and moaned, semi-conscious. I managed to scrabble from beneath him and get to my feet once more, appreciative of the efficiency of Ralegh's servant. My flank was giving me pain again. I had a bruise from armpit to hip, and the breath was sobbing in my lungs.

The servants dragged the fellow to the wall again, and one took a bucket of water and tipped it over the recumbent figure. He coughed, spluttered, and gazed about him blearily, at first with baffled incomprehension and then with increasing rage as, I presume, the events of the recent past caught up with him again. He made as though to rise, but there were several weapons pointing at him, and he took the hint.

'I had no part in his death,' he muttered sulkily.

'That's a shame. Without witnesses, you'll hang for it all the same.'

'I won't hang,' he said sharply. 'Besides, we only beat him a little. Ned told us we'd been paid to hurt him, but nothing more. We weren't paid to kill him.'

'How do you explain his death, then?' William said.

'I don't. We left him bruised. That was all.'

'Why were you paid to beat him up?' Richard said.

'Ned said it was because he was rabble-rousing. Someone wanted to persuade him to shut up and stop making people angry.'

'Who did?'

'I don't know. You need to ask Ned.'

He was persuasive. It was obvious that even if he knew, he would say nothing about the man who had commissioned an attack on Lane, and was offended to be accused of killing the man. Apparently, being robbed as an innocent traveller was my own fault for wandering about the city. I should have known better, as Godfrey Ralegh had said, but the idea that he would break Lane's head and leave him to die in an alley was anathema to Miller.

We did, however, learn that Ned Hall and the other man were brothers. They had been with Miller earlier in the tavern, but after a few drinks, they left and went somewhere else. Miller didn't know where. After a little more discussion, he admitted that the two lived over a shop near South Gate itself. That made me wonder whether he had been running to reach their house for sanctuary. Having two companions would make him feel safer against the six of us.

'This man Lane,' William said, looking across at Richard. 'You knew him.'

Richard shrugged. 'I can't keep abreast of all the priests and canons in the city! As for those evicted from their livings . . .'

His words were left hanging. Obviously, no one could keep track of all those who had been deprived of their living. Many had been burned for heresy as well, but trying to recall all their names – well, it would take a man who was determined to keep records of all martyrs to bring everyone to mind.

'You said he gave advice. I think you mean he was a spy. He kept your father informed of Wolfe's business.' He didn't deny it. 'When your father was at the body, there was another man with him. Tall, slim, but clearly wealthy,' I said. 'And a priest. The dean of the cathedral, I think.'

'That sounds like Master John Wolfe the merchant,' William said. 'Lane worked for him. Why the dean was there as well, I don't know. He has clerks a-plenty.'

'I don't see why my father should have been there, unless he happened past and the dean and Wolfe were already there. He might have joined them to study the body,' Richard said.

It left me wondering why any of the men would bother. After all, Lane was already dead, so there was nothing in that little alley to interest the three.

'I have heard that the city was besieged over prayer books,' I said. 'Did that lead to much dispute afterwards?'

William Carew sucked in his breath and then cast a look at Richard. 'The city has been on tenterhooks since then. We don't talk much about such matters, but there was a lot of bad feeling. The city itself was mostly supportive of the rebels. No one knew much about the new religion, and the idea of all the services being held in English – well, that did not appeal to all. And then there was the costume the priests wore. A sober confection compared with the Catholic vestments. People here, both in the city and in the country all about, tend towards a conservative attitude. They dislike change. So when the rebels arrived, most thought the city would welcome them. Nobody thought of insurrection, I think. It was only a movement to persuade the King – that would be young Edward, God preserve his memory – that the people would prefer to reinstate the Catholic faith, renew the churches, monasteries and nunneries, and return to the old ways.'

'But it didn't work?'

'Of course not! The Freedom knew it must support the King and uphold the law,' Richard said. 'It is one thing to stand firm when a siege is offered by raggle-taggle peasants, and a different matter if the King were to send his artillery. The King could destroy the city. All the merchants were bound to be on the side of the King and the new faith.'

'Aye, and Lord Russell came with a firm determination to

punish those who sought to bring back the Catholic worship,' William said. 'He raised the siege, forced the rebels into retreat and destroyed them.'

I frowned. 'So when Queen Mary reimposed the Catholic faith, it must have been difficult?'

'There have been reprisals. Most have accepted the fact of the new demands,' William said carefully. 'The city was split, much like the rest of the country, but in the interests of peace, all were careful to support the new Queen's law. No one wishes to overturn the applecart here.'

He was quiet then, as I expected. Everyone in the country knew that the faith they held was the true one. The difficulty was that the two faiths were in opposition. The Catholics refused to agree when King Henry decided to cut the nation adrift from Rome; his son upheld his decision; now his daughter Mary was determined to return to the Roman faith. It left many confused. It was not as though a man should change his faith every time the throne changed.

I glanced at Richard. 'Lane must have been an irritant to someone for him to be murdered.'

'Any man can be an irritant to another, whether by design or by accident,' William said, casting a look at me that seemed full of meaning. I had no idea what it signified. Perhaps he wanted me to stop speaking of Lane.

'Did you know him?'

William chewed his lip. 'I have heard of him, yes. He must have been known to most merchants. Any who might require a clerk would be the target of his advances. But few would use him; he was tainted after losing his job with the Church. With the new regime in the cathedral, it would be dangerous to take him on.'

'Surely the cathedral would not persecute him?'

William grimaced. Perhaps he chewed too hard. 'You have to understand, this is a small city. People gossip, and rumours fly more speedily than an arrow within these walls.'

'What rumours?'

'That he had been blackmailing someone in authority.'

'Who?'

He shrugged. 'Perhaps the dean?'

* * *

I was intrigued by this. After all, if a merchant had been foolish enough to allow Lane to learn something worth money, perhaps I could learn it too, and make the money Lane had failed to earn? Of course, I was aware that there was a risk that I could end up like Lane, dead in an alleyway, but I was cleverer than him. I was a London lad when all was said and done, and that meant I could easily win over any number of yokels.

But there was a small, quiet voice in my head that told me not to try something that could be dangerous. I didn't want to end up like Lane, lying in an alley with a broken head. If it was the dean who had seen to Lane's punishment, the matter was not one in which I should become involved. He was no peasant. The dean would have received a good education in Oxford.

I could ask nothing more. We had arrived at Ned and his brother Adam's house. Richard put his hand to his sword, while one of his men lifted his staff and beat on the timbers. William was crouched at Richard's side, head low, staring at the door, his sword sheathed, but there was an alertness and readiness in his posture that spoke of swift retribution to any man who attempted to attack.

A thin, reedy voice from the other side of the door said, 'Who be that at this time of night? Our household is asleep. Begone and return in the morning.'

Richard leaned forward. 'Mistress, we are here to speak with Ned Hall, who lives here with his brother Adam. Let us in.'

'G'wan! I shessent! What! Open my door to thieves? This be a 'spectable house! They'm zleepin', as gude Christians men shude be. G'wan, git awa'!'

'If you don't open the door, we shall break it down,' Richard said. Then, in deference to her tongue, he sighed, and shouted, 'Come out therevrom thease minnit, awd Mistress!'

He looked at me with a smile of embarrassment.

At the same time, William nudged a servant, and they hurried up the road to an alley that led behind the houses and disappeared from view. It was clear there was a rear entrance to the house which Ned and his brother might employ to escape.

There was much grumbling, and finally a scraping sound indicated that a bolt was being wiggled in its slot. A sudden crash came when the stiff metal slipped free and ran back to hit its stop plate. Then a second began to make a similar rasping noise, the jiggling and metal-on-metal squealing, until an abrupt yelp could be heard. Suddenly, a bolt was slid back and the door opened to display William. Behind him stood his servant with an elderly woman. She had suspicious, deep-set eyes under a louring brow and looked like a thunder cloud on a hot summer's day. Her scrawny neck looked barely strong enough to support her head, and she cast sidelong glances at the servant. 'A-breakin' into my 'ouze like zo many drawlatches and burglars,' she muttered, and when her eyes caught mine, I swear I would have been glad to apologize, offer money and make my way out of that hovel with all haste. If there was ever a witch in Exeter, this was her. An evil, ravaged old hag if ever I saw one, and I've seen a few.

'She was sliding the bolts back and forth to delay you,' William said. 'But she wasn't going to open it. Luckily, she hadn't locked the back door.'

'I were trying to open the doower,' she said, hunched over like a miser protecting her money. Not that she had any, from the look of her hovel.

It was little more than a single room, with a ladder at the back which led up to a chamber set in the eaves. A fire in the grate sent up a pathetic and hopeful strand of smoke. A tiny flame, which was clearly feeling lonely, sputtered and choked. A bench and two three-legged stools and a table were standing against the wall, while wooden trenchers and some spoons rested on the table. All were in threes, I saw. If Ned and Adam lived here, clearly she was living with them.

'Where is Ned?' I said.

'Who?'

'The man lives here with his brother,' William said. His tone was sharp, and her eyes flew to his stern figure. She seemed to shrink into herself a little more. If she hunched her back any further, I thought, it would be likely to break.

'Whot's 'e a tellin' of? I lives 'ere alone,' she said.

I looked at William, and we both stared meaningfully at the table with its trio of eating implements.

Richard gazed at us. He had the look of a man who sees

clearly. In his mind, women don't tell lies, and if this woman said she lived alone, she must be telling the truth. I think he was about to suggest that we left the poor old dear alone, since she couldn't help us. I have rarely seen such an expression of gormless innocence on any man's face.

From looking at her, I was pretty sure that she must be the brothers' mother. Who else would live with her, other than her own flesh and blood, after all?

Just then we were interrupted. A servant had gone up the ladder and had dug around among whatever passed for valuable possessions in the old crone's family, and now he gave a cry.

The woman span to stare with fury as he began to descend the ladder. She snapped some curse or other, which was enough to make me blench in case it might rebound on me, but then she was hopping across the room like an angry raven, trying to snatch something from his hand. William caught her shoulder as she passed, and she was suddenly pinned to the spot. I saw her turn and look up into his face, and she suddenly seemed to slump, as if she was nothing more than a bladder full of water, and someone had stabbed her in the midriff.

'What is it?' William said.

'A purse,' the man said.

'Hey, that's mine!' I declared, glaring at the woman.

She cringed. 'I ban't zeen it avore. You brung it with 'ee to accuse me! I zee what you be up to! You'm lying, makin' out I done zummat, but I . . .'

'Your sons. Where are they?' I demanded.

'Eh?'

'The men who live here,' Richard said. He seemed quite shocked that the discovery had been made. Not that I was interested in that just now. I had grabbed the purse from the man at the ladder and was clutching it with a sense of disbelief, for it was empty. Someone had emptied it. There was nothing left, not even a clipped penny.

Have you ever had that kind of shock? I felt as though my heart had stopped beating. There was a whirling, as of smoke, about my eyes. My hands felt like lead, and the purse, which should have felt heavy, was instead as light as an empty felt bag. I opened it and peered inside, closed it and took a deep breath, and then slowly opened it again, as though the first glance was a horrible mistake, an ocular illusion, and that if I could only give the purse a little time, it would miraculously refill itself.

It didn't. It remained resolutely empty.

There are times when things happen so swiftly that it's difficult to take it all in. I had been hoping against hope that I would be reunited with my purse, and now that I was, I was forced to confront the unfortunate fact that the purse itself was perfectly pointless and pitiful without my pennies to fill its belly. Now *I* felt like a stabbed bladder. I was weak and distraught and light-headed, as though I was sensing the emotions through a fog, a kindly dulling of my wits that prevented my full appreciation of the scale of this new disaster.

'My . . . my money?' I said at last. The shock made me mumble. 'It's up there? It's there somewhere. It must be!'

The servant was on the ground now, and he shrugged. He appeared to believe that there was nothing else to be found.

'No, it must be there. It *must* be. Surely, it's concealed! The robbers have found a place to hide their pelf! It must be up there. Is it up there, Mistress? Could they have shoved my money into the thatch? Or have you hidden it here, down here, in the wall or a floor?' I began to search about me, gazing at the packed earth of the floor, at the walls, at the table, and thence to the ladder.

'Hold!' William said to me as I began to stumble towards it. 'Mistress, we don't want to see you held in gaol. Where are your sons, and where is this gentleman's money?'

'Whot money? Now, lookee zee, an' I don't know what money, I don't have money. The boys wouldn't do a thing like robbing this vule. Whot vor would they do that? He 'abn't the . . .'

'Mistress, if you don't help us, we will have to take you to the gaol. You can wait there until the stay loosens your tongue,' William said firmly. Richard looked quite appalled at his tone of voice, but William continued in a similar threatening tone, 'You live here. This gentleman was robbed in the city and his purse has been found here. You know that my word, the word of this gentleman and my friend, the son of a Guild member, will carry weight in court. Just tell us where to find your boys and we'll leave you alone.'

'God's teeth, I'll be dalled if I do!' she spat, huddling further into her clothes. I once saw a tortoise, and the way that he withdrew his legs and neck into his shell was remarkably similar to the way she retreated into herself now.

She said nothing more. Which left Richard, William and me looking rather foolish.

We could have dragged her to the gaol. We could have hauled her by the hair or grabbed her arms and legs – she wouldn't be heavy – and make her join Miller in the South Gate's prison. But we had no real authority. I suppose, as citizens of the city, Richard and William would be justified in holding her since she wouldn't talk about where Ned and Adam had gone, and they could demand that a Justice of the Queen's Peace speak to her. And yet I detected a reluctance on the part of both William and Richard to take that route. No matter how much I protested, they were resolute, and I found myself being removed from the hovel. All of us ended up in the street while she sneered at us.

William, Richard, the servants and I looked at each other with dismay, while the old hag laughed with a hideous cackle. 'Call yourself gentlemen? You can't even defend yourself against a poor old woman, can you? You dung-filled bladders, you whoreson's whelps, you—'

She continued in the same vein for some time, and I confess, I was impressed by her range of invective. She had a real talent for insults and could have taught some of the women in London a thing or two – even the fishwives and whores. However, a swift kick to her rear from one of the servants sent her howling for her door, rubbing her arse. With her sons safe and well, there was little point in her trying to detain us any longer. It was plain enough that we had no idea what to do.

The door slammed behind her, and we heard the bolts quite clearly, shooting home with great ease, as well-greased bolts will.

'Well!' William said.

'That was not entirely as I had expected,' Richard said.

A second slam could be heard in the still night air. We heard more bolts slide across.

'That'll be her back door. You won't get inside again in a hurry,' Richard said.

'We should have taken her,' I said reasonably. Not that I would have wanted to grab her by the arm or anything.

'Stop your sulking, London,' Richard said. 'It would not have done.'

'Why not?'

'Because the justice is Isaak Shapley,' William said. 'He has a lot of authority in the city – plenty enough to willingly see Richard's father irritated by having his son and two friends gaoled for molesting a poor old woman.'

I began to see their point. 'You mean . . .'

'He would happily install you in the gaol for no reason. It would not be a good idea to give him one.'

That was a compelling argument, I felt. We began to walk away; me more than a little disconsolate, William and Richard less so. They, of course, had not lost all their money; they considered our visit to the old woman had been useful. I couldn't see how, bearing in mind that although I had retrieved my purse, it was empty. I wanted my money back, and I didn't care how I managed that feat.

'I suppose we should leave things till morning,' William said.

He was right. After all, it was late. I had already risked much in the search for my purse. At least in Richard's father's house, I could get a good sleep and hope to wake to better news, but when I looked at Richard, his face was still grim. 'We cannot allow the fellow to disappear and spend all your money, can we?' he said.

'What else can we do?'

'There are some taverns and other welcoming houses where he might be hiding,' Richard said.

'Oh, no,' William said.

I saw no reason to dispute Richard's logic. It was a fair thought. After all, thieves and robbers are not the most intelligent of men. Many, having almost been caught, would be likely to throw caution – and the money from a stolen purse – to the winds in search of happiness and forgetfulness. It was likely that Ned was even now settling into another tavern, a quart of strong ale before him, and preparing to carouse the rest of the night away.

'Where would he go?' I asked. After all, it was my money he was spending, probably profligately.

'No, Richard,' William said again. We had walked little more than twenty yards, and now, before Richard could respond to him, a man appeared in a doorway.

He was a local, I could see. His trousers were ragged, his beard unkempt, his feet bare in the dirt of the road. Clearly, the neighbour to the old crone.

'Did her tell you where to they gone?' he said.

His square face was not built for happy conversation. It looked more like the sort of face you'd see on a bull, moments before he lowered his head and charged.

Richard and William separated slightly, and William smiled. 'You mean Ned and Adam's mother?'

The man hawked and spat into the street. 'Her? Her bain't their mother. Her's an old hag who saw an easy way to keep house. She rents it to Ned, and he pays her when he can. Not that he can terrible often. Not until now, anyhap.'

'Why so, friend?' William pressed.

'They seem to have money just now. Started a fortnight hence. Now they can afford food and drink and the rent.'

'Do you know where they might be?' Richard asked.

'You'm try Moll Thatcher's place. If there's money in his purse, he'll be there like a schoolboy after his first fumble.'

'No, Richard,' William said again.

'Moll Thatcher's place?' I questioned, glancing at William. To my concern, he did not look content. 'What is it, William?'

'It is not a good place. Not a good place at all,' he said.

There were plenty of seedy places where a man could go to spend money even in Exeter, apparently. Many were not the sort of place a fellow with style and distinction would usually care to be seen to visit, but tonight I was prepared to throw caution to the wind if it meant I could get my hands on my money.

London, that queen of cities, has several brothels which I

would personally avoid. These stews cater for the meanest types, and a gentleman like me prefers not to mingle with the costermongers and shipmen in such areas. Besides, the women who frequent such houses tend to be on their way down. Their looks have been ravaged by hard living, too many nights lying awake, and generally by encroaching old age. It was a place like this that I expected Richard to take me, but no! It was soon clear that Ned appreciated a better class of hostess than would be offered down at the quay or up near the castle. For his fornication, he had selected a brothel that was more in keeping with the wealth he had stolen from me, the . . . But I must not grow vituperative.

William frowned and shook his head. 'No, I will not enter such premises. Neither should you, Richard.'

'We're only going to see whether Ned and his brother are in there, not to pursue our own natural pleasures,' he said reasonably.

I confess I was rather hoping for some horizontal engagements as well. If I could find my purse, I would deserve a little relaxation. And would be able to afford it.

It was plain that William did not think the same. 'I am going back to your father's house to sleep,' he said to Richard.

'Why, don't you like women?' I asked with genuine surprise.

'Very much. But I don't think that going and swiving a maid for money is the right behaviour.'

'He is considering a post in the Church,' Richard chuckled. 'He thinks visiting a whore might harm his immortal soul.'

'I know it will, just as it will yours, too,' William said. He lifted a hand and pointed to the sky. 'Up there, the angels watch over you, but if you will persist in such rowdy and incontinent behaviour, it will be noted. When you reach the gates of—'

'Yes, I know. I'll be left standing in purgatory for an age or more. But just now, it can't hurt anyone for me to visit a friendly house with Master Blackjack to see whether these two felons are inside. And I don't think it would hurt your soul to join us in that search.'

'I will return to your house with the servants and my conscience clear,' William said. 'And you should come, too –

both of you. What would Alice say if she were to hear of your visit to a place of ill-repute, Richard?'

'I doubt she has the faintest idea of what men and women do in such places,' Richard said with a broad grin.

William rolled his eyes and was soon marching off at the head of the three servants. I watched him go with sadness not unmixed with relief. He was a good man to have alongside in a fight, but he was more than a little prudish. If he had joined us, and we learned Ned and Adam were not inside, he would have drained our enjoyment. His presence would have made the evening much less amusing. Better by far that he should return to his bed, while we enjoyed the exercises on offer at the place Richard proposed.

But that supposed that Adam and Ned were not in there. And right now, we had to believe that they were. Before I could think of grappling with a willing wench, I had to try to recover my money.

We walked up South Gate Street, right at Carfax, and thence along almost to the Guildhall before turning up into a maze of streets near the northern wall. Here there was a quiet-looking house, and Richard turned to me and placed a finger against his lips, saying, 'Don't mention Ned. If he's there, we'll see him, but if the hostess learns we're here to catch the man, she won't let us in. She won't want a fight in her house,' before knocking moderately quietly.

'This is an area where the neighbours get annoyed by rowdiness,' he explained. A moment later, a flap was opened in the door and a suspicious eye peered out at us. It glanced up and down the road, and then snapped shut. A slight metallic squirling announced well-oiled bolts being drawn, and soon we were invited inside by a woman of perhaps five-and-thirty years, wearing a dress and blouse that did nothing to conceal her figure. Her hair was glorious, red-gold and entirely unconstrained by a coif. It was permitted to hang down to her shoulders in a most lubricious manner. She had large blue eyes and a mouth designed for kissing. She was altogether delightful.

'Mistress,' Richard said approvingly. 'You are as lovely as the most perfect rose.'

She cocked an eyebrow at Richard. 'You are almost a stranger, Master Ralegh. I swear, it has been five weeks since we last entertained you. And you now come knocking at this late hour, expecting to be welcomed? I am not sure that I should allow you entrance.'

'This is a friend of mine,' he said, taking my arm and pulling me forward. 'He is from London and knows little of our ways down here, but he has had a most trying day. He was robbed, you know, and set upon. It's a miracle he's alive.'

'There is too much death outside our walls,' she said seriously. Then she smiled at me, and it was the fresh, contented smile of a young woman, setting her head just slightly to one side and giving me the advantage of her white teeth and long neck. I could have grabbed her bounties right then and there, but she was entirely professional, and before I could launch my assault, she took a step rearwards and indicated a door. Through there, I understood, were more hostesses.

But before I could walk inside, I was intrigued and must ask, 'You say "too much death". Do you refer to Roger Lane, the poor man found dead in the alley?'

She smiled again, this time at my purse rather than my face. She was entirely professional. 'Yes, poor Roger Lane. We'll miss him. But also the men of Richard's father's ship, and those of Shapley's, too. So many men have been lost recently.'

I had not thought of that. 'Both ship's crews are lost?'

Richard nodded mournfully. 'It is very sad and troublesome.'

The room was stylishly decorated, with comfortable chairs, warm tapestries on the wall, rugs and blankets on the floor, and enough large cushions to stuff a moderately sized elephant. I had the impression of softness and comfort in every direction, and that impression was only enhanced when I studied the women. Some were languorously draped over benches, their plump posteriors resting on soft pillows, while others were disposed over the laps of a number of men. A cluster of wenches was gathered about one fellow, while others were set to bringing drinks. As usual in a recreational room like this, I noticed that the women were all terribly thirsty. They would demand drinks of the most appallingly expensive kind to help boost the profits of the brothel, and then drink but a little of it, while their guest would sup up like a paviour at the end of a long summer day's work, get stupendously drunk and be still more easy to fleece. Pots and cups were set all about the room where the women had placed them. For such expensive drinks, it looked horribly wasteful to leave the drinks in such a fashion, but then again I was more than a little certain that the drinks for the girls would not only be expensive to buy but also be heavily watered.

It was, in short, a delightful room, and I allowed my hand to be taken by a happy harpy with curling black hair falling luxuriously about her shoulders, a delightfully curved eyebrow, and eyes that managed to look both lewd and innocent at the same time. She drew me to a couch with a stack of soft goose-down pillows, and I was just settling down, pulling her delicious figure on top of me, when I heard a sort of a gasp.

Yes, in a chamber of that sort a fellow expects to hear sounds of that nature, but this was not a satisfied, relaxed, relieved gasp, but a tense, shocked type. I was unwilling to be distracted and tried to concentrate on the dark-haired beauty lying atop me, but then I heard a muffled '*Jack!*'

I was in a quandary. There were two basic thoughts running through my mind at that moment. The first was the simple one, which was that I was otherwise engaged and would give my attention to the name-caller in a few minutes; the second was that I have heard people call my name in the past, and occasionally it was to my benefit to respond. It would be a good idea to harken to the warning, were there a risk that a bailiff was about to enter to tap me on the head, or a felon was trying to feel for my purse (as the sultry besom on top of me had, just now; she was to be disappointed if that was her main desire). There were several occasions when I would have regretted not heeding such a warning, and so now I somewhat irritably opened my eyes and glanced over to Richard.

He was staring beyond me to the bevy of beauties I mentioned a few moments ago, his face showing a kind of wondering surprise. Even as I caught sight of his expression, assuming, naturally, that some form of vile act was being perpetrated on one of the women or their guest, I was fascinated enough to move my own companion aside in order to gain a better vantage. I am always keen to learn.

What I saw was a man involved in pleasuring a maiden, or a woman pleasuring him. However, that was not all. It also afforded me the sight of a man who was, if you will excuse the pun, rigid with shock. He was at the moment standing with his hosen resting about his ankles, and a happy woman before him playing hide the hog's pudding. That was nothing new, and I was not taken with a flare of rage to see that. What I was furious about was the fact that the man was my assailant – Ned Hall. Even as his eyes met mine with a kind of shock, I heard a loud giggle and saw his brother a little way behind him.

'You bastard!' I yelled, leaping to my feet. My cuddly beauty fell from me with a squeal, and Richard put his hand to his dagger. Ned Hall slapped the bare buttocks before him, and that maid gave a sedate little scream before falling to her knees, and Ned turned to execute the fastest possible escape, completely failing to recall the hosen about his ankles. He made a move, flailed with his arms and fell in a heap on top of another maiden, who was sprawled in an entirely relaxed fashion, and who gave an earthy guffaw, saying, 'What, you want more, dearie?' while he attempted to clamber to his feet.

Meanwhile, Richard had sprung upon his back and now held his knife to the man's throat, while I had sprinted forward to retrieve the one thing that truly mattered – my money. It was lying in a sadly depleted manner at Ned Hall's feet, in a revolting soft leather purse that had seen far better days, and I grabbed it before any of the shrieking wenches could. They were obviously not as professional as the women in the Cardinal's Hat in London. There, a purse lying unattended would have been snatched up and handed to the madam in moments. In any case, they were sounding like a choir of banshees as they caught sight of bare steel, and the noise was quite alarming.

Anyway, I had managed to grasp his purse and feel its heft, with a sense of relief not untainted with rage that so much had been spent in so little time, and for that moment was incapable of any other thoughts.

Thus it was that Ned managed to snatch hold of Richard's wrist and push the knife away from his throat. Richard clung to his back as Ned rose to his feet, apparently heedless of the weight. He stood, his hands gripping Richard's wrists, his hosen still bundled about his ankles, while Richard went red in the face, struggling to pull the dagger back to the thief's bare skin, but without result. Ned was much more powerful, and the dagger was slowly forced away, Ned baring his horrible gaping maw with the strain.

I watched them struggle with mild disinterest. After all, if Richard wanted to take on a man quite as alarming as Ned Hall, I felt he was welcome to it. However, it quickly dawned on me that, were Ned to overcome Richard, my situation might become rather more questionable. After all, Ned had recognized me; in any case, he would be bound to demand that I return my money to him. He was a large man, as I have said, and I was not convinced that I could bound from cushion to pillow and out through the door without being caught. I began to edge back now as the thought came to me. And as I did so, Ned's eye met mine, and I knew I was lost.

With the determination of a man with nothing to lose, I pulled out my pistol. While Ned watched, I set the dog on the spinning steel wheel and held it at his head. 'Let go of him,' I said.

Now, the trouble is, of course, that when a command is given, sometimes it can be misinterpreted. I had thought that my words were perfectly plain. I was looking up at Ned's face, and it should have been perfectly understandable to the meanest intelligence that I was talking to him. But no, as I spoke, Richard clearly believed that I was instructing him to set his captive free. He let himself slide from Ned's back, with all the enthusiasm of a child sliding from a tree he'd just climbed, and suddenly Ned was unencumbered.

I goggled and retreated. As he moved towards me, it was rather like watching a bear approach. There was the same slow, awesome strength and power, and he kept on rising with a kind of ponderous majesty. My eyes were fixed on his, and my head tilted up and back. I think I tried to speak, but only a vague bleating escaped from my lips. The main thing I recall thinking was that I really did need a mastiff to restrain this brute.

Even as this was going on, I saw his befuddled brother make

his way, giggling, to Richard. He pulled out a knife of his own and was about to strike when Richard noticed him. He span, and this time he put the dagger into his left hand and drew his sword. That was a disincentive for more action. Adam Hall gave a sort of half-hearted gurgle, like a cross between his lunatic chuckling and a belch, and fell back. I saw him turn and flee. There was another door at the back of the room, and he disappeared through it.

Meanwhile, my attention returned to Ned. He reached down and took his purse from my hand. Then he took the pistol from my reluctant but insensitive hand. The dog was resting on the wheel, and he smiled then, a really nasty smile with that black hole where his teeth should have been. He reached forward and rested the barrel of my gun on my brow, and his smile broadened. Then there was a loud cracking sound, and the gun fell away to point at the ground. His smile did not waver, but his eyes acquired a mild bemusement, and then rolled up into his head.

He slowly slid sideways to reveal Richard behind him with the shattered remains of a large jug.

It took a little while to explain to the madam what had happened in her prized chamber. She was most put out at the loss of an entire jug of sack, as she put it. Personally, from the odour, I would say it was less than one-tenth part sack, the rest being water – although there could have been some cat's urine added. It certainly reeked of something.

Once I had calmed down a little from the shock of almost having my own pistol used to destroy me, I helped Richard. He had grabbed one of the less screamy harlots and persuaded her to fetch him some hempen cord. Now he and I sat on Ned's figure and tied his wrists together behind his back. Richard kept a long leash on the string, so we could walk our prisoner to the gaol with ease. It would be hard, we thought, for Ned to make a successful attempt at escape. Meanwhile, the hostess of the house stood and bickered constantly at us until I paid her a few pennies for her silence, while Richard kicked and prodded at the recumbent felon to tease him into life once more. In the end, our attempts having failed, the madam irritably called over some servants to assist us. They dragged the body from the room and out into the road, where they dumped him unceremoniously on the cobbles.

He was a dead weight. As soon as the servants had disappeared back inside, he opened his eyes and glared at us.

'Come along, Ned. You need to come with us,' Richard said.

'I'm not helping you. You want me to move, you'll have to carry me,' he said. There were a few other choice comments on our parentage and general style of life as well, but I closed my ears to those.

'You robbed me, threatened to kill me, took my money and spent it, and now you want sympathy?' I said.

'You didn't need it. I was desperate. You wouldn't understand,' he said.

The fool clearly thought I had been born with a golden plate and gilded cutlery to eat from. I didn't disabuse him.

He was heavy. It would be impossible to drag or carry him all the way to the gaol. He sat with his back to the house's wall, and Richard and I exchanged a look. Perhaps a wheelbarrow or small cart would allow us to move him? But he would be a reluctant and recalcitrant burden; that was clear.

'I understand hunger and thirst, and not having a roof to sleep under,' I said, 'but I was never persuaded to murder one man and then try to rob another in the same evening.'

He looked up at me with eyes rather bleary from ale. I imagined that he must have spent much of the evening and night so far drinking steadily on my account. It's what I would have done in his place. He tried to sneer. 'If I'd wanted, I could have killed you in that alley. I should have. I wouldn't be sitting here if I had.'

'You didn't dare with two men bearing down on you, though, did you?' I said with the poison sharpening my voice. 'When you murdered Roger Lane, you were very brave, with three men to murder the one!'

'Him? Who says I had anything to do with killing him?'

'You did – you said he squealed, remember?'

'We beat him. We were paid to, but not to kill him. We didn't kill him.'

* * *

Out of interest, I tried to elicit more information from him. 'What had Roger Lane done to you?'

'Nothing. No one paid us to *kill* him; just to give him a going over.'

I shrugged and gazed up the street. 'You'll hang, of course. And the man who told you to commit the crime will not suffer as you will, but if you don't want to talk, you don't have to. I could cut off a couple of fingers, but it's hardly worth my while.'

He was quiet then, and with him silent, conversation lapsed for a little. Then he appeared to make up his mind. 'Look, I don't see why me and the others should suffer for something we never did. I'll tell you all I know, but only if you'll let me go.'

'Let you go?' I blurted. 'You robbed me, you were going to stab me, you . . .'

'If you put me in the gaol, you'll come to regret it,' he said knowingly.

'Really?' I said. 'How much of my money have you spent, eh?' And with that thought, and the feeling of lightness at my belt where my depleted fortune dangled once again, I felt a sudden fresh rage flood me. He was sitting with his legs apart, and it looked all too inviting. I was about to kick him – hard – when I reflected that he might soon be free of his bonds and of a mind to let me know what he thought about men who hurt him while he was bound. Then I reminded myself that his release was in my hands, and I didn't have to worry about letting him go if I didn't want to. I'd prefer to see him hang for robbing me than for killing someone I never knew. However, I was also aware that a man kicked in the cods would find it difficult to walk to the gaol.

Instead, I kicked him in the belly, and he glowered up at me.

'Well?' Richard said.

'Tell this dog's turd that if he kicks me again, I will break his head open and eat his brains!' he snarled.

'How will we regret putting you in the gaol?' I demanded. 'You have strong friends, I suppose, who'll come and kill us in our beds? Or you'll have a witch like your landlady cast a spell on us?'

'More like the first,' he said. 'It's about Lane, right? Me and the others were told to scare him off, to warn him against any more of his rabble-rousing. He was always on at the cathedral and the canons, and they'd had enough, I suppose.'

'How so?'

'Jealousy. Lane wanted to be a priest again, but the dean and Church wouldn't have him back because he refused to leave his wife. Or his wenches. And there were several of them.'

'Where did you hear this?' Richard said.

'It's what the dean told me. Lane spread lies about the dean. That's why the dean wanted Lane warned off.' Ned shrugged. 'So the dean paid me to beat him up, but not to *kill* him. Why would we? There was nothing in it for us. We didn't kill him.'

I was frowning. 'What did he say that was so distressing to the dean?' There were always vague rumours about churchmen and their more ungodly activities – some about churchmen and nuns, others involving choirboys. There are stories I could tell you about the behaviour of the clerks at Westminster that would shake you rigid.

Richard took up the story. 'I have heard rumours: a man who denounced the canons and their profligate lifestyle; he said they were little better than thieves, the way they carried on, with women, food and drink. They should be praying for our souls, not carousing all hours. Perhaps that was Lane?'

Ned agreed. 'After he was thrown from the Church, he took a job with Wolfe, keeping accounts, but the dean heard he was speaking out against the Roman Church.'

'That would be enough to persuade the dean to kill him?' I said.

'No, to beat him up. The dean paid me and promised to pray for my soul. Who should I believe? A pest who shouts in the street telling people that the cathedral is a boiling pot of avarice and lust, or the man the Queen supports who can promise me a fast route to heaven?'

It took us some while to get Ned to the gaol. He was a dead weight, and it was only after we had kicked and prodded him with our staffs that we managed to force him to his feet. We had not released his hands, and now I took the precaution of binding his wrists to a strong cord. I took hold of one end after making sure that Richard had a firm grip on the other. If there was any danger, I could drop mine and flee, and Ned would still be held by Richard.

'What? You said if I told you what I knew, you'd let me go!' he said as I worked the thin rope through the tight bonds on his wrists.

I smiled nastily. 'No – you said you'd tell us if we said we'd let you free. We didn't agree to release you, thief!'

'You let me talk as if you were going to! You let me think you'd set me loose!' There was a low, nasty edge to his voice now that I did not like. It was rather like hearing the first low growl of a guard dog, and I instinctively drew away. For his part, Ned planted his feet and gave every indication of stubborn refusal to continue.

'If you wanted to think that,' I said reasonably, but with definite resolution, 'you deluded yourself. We didn't say it. And now we are almost at the gaol, so we can leave you to the gentle ministrations of the gaoler.'

'You aren't taking me there,' he said, twisting and peering around to see where we had reached. Only a matter of paces away was the great bulk of the South Gate, a cheerful light stabbing at the shutters over the windows.

'I rather think we are,' I said with certainty. 'And now, if you want to be treated better than the average felon, I would be a little more quiet and a lot less obstreperous.'

He looked at me then, and I have to confess, I did not like his look. It seemed malevolent. I recalled him talking about breaking my head open and eating my brains, and from the look on his face, he was ready to begin his meal. It was not a pleasant look, and I was not keen to remain with him.

'Not that it matters,' I said, keen to get away from the man but enjoying his discomfort. 'After all, you said you worked for the dean – no doubt he will come himself to liberate you. I dare say he's on his way already.'

Richard gave a loud guffaw, and Ned turned and stared at him with such a horrible intensity that I thought he was consigning Richard's face to memory, so no matter what – perhaps even death itself – he would be able to find Richard and me. The thought of his ghost appearing to me every night was enough to make my bowels desire a privy.

'You will regret this,' he said in a low, malevolent hiss.

Somehow, I felt quite sure that we would.

In the face of his obduracy, I thought it would be better to have the gaoler come and assist us. Richard helped me wrap the cord about Ned's ankles and tie them well, and then I trotted to the gaoler's door and banged on it until he appeared.

The old fool looked as though he had been canoodling with a barrel of strong ale. His eyes were bleared, his expression peevish in the extreme, as if I had just woken him from a delightful dream of strumpets and sack. 'What do you want?'

'We have another one for you,' I said, but he wasn't listening. He was peering over my shoulder.

There was a sudden commotion. I turned to see Richard slump to the ground, while Ned's brother danced a little jig of celebration and Ned bawled at the idiot – whether to cut him free or to stab me, I don't know. His hoarse bellow had the desired effect, and Adam jerked to a halt in mid-spin and drew his knife. I squeaked in terror – after all, I knew that Adam had the brain of a flea and would have no compunction in cutting my throat if he thought it would please his brother – but even as I darted behind the gaoler, who grabbed a heavy staff and raised it in both hands, Adam ignored us and instead attacked his brother's bonds. His must have been a horribly sharp knife, because the cords fell away in an instant, and Ned was released again.

I gave a little moan. Seeing the gaoler, Ned pulled his mouth into a leer of disdain and spat at the ground. He remained there, watching me, and then Richard groaned and murmured something. Ned peered down at him, then kicked Richard viciously. The poor fellow's head was spun like a football, and he toppled on to his back.

Ned glared at me like a bull seeing a stranger cross his field, before biting his thumb at me contemptuously. I tried to remain as inconspicuous as possible, and soon the two brothers were hurtling away up the road towards Carfax.

The gaoler glanced over his shoulder at me. I gave him a

reassuring smile. He appeared to take a dim view of my taking the precaution of stepping behind him, just in case Ned and Adam decided to launch an attack against me. Obviously, I am no coward, but I had to ensure that I was in a position to easily defend myself, and for that I would be best served by slipping into the gaol and sliding the bar over the door.

There was a shout from farther up, and I heard a clatter of metal, and then a bellow, and then silence. A short time afterwards, a lone figure appeared. He seemed to be staring along the road warily, as though he was looking for any signs of danger. Seeing only me and the gaoler, he seemed to gather his courage and beckoned behind him. Two more men appeared, each apparently as unwilling as him to venture far from their place of concealment, but then they made their way down towards us. From their tatty appearance and general caution, I was sure that they must either be felons or representatives of the city watch.

As they approached, they encountered Richard, and two picked him up and brought him to us, dropping him unceremoniously at our feet. He groaned again, louder this time.

'What are you doing up at this time of night, Tom?' one of them said to the gaoler.

The older man grunted. 'Trying to get back to my cot. These two fools appeared with a captive, but some other fellow knocked this one down and would have attacked me, I dare say, if I didn't have my old staff and ballock knife with me. If he'd tried anything on, I'd have gelded the bastard!'

'Aye, you're the sort of man who would terrify the fiercest thief with your old weapon,' the leader of the three said diplomatically, if unconvincingly. He nudged Richard and looked at me enquiringly. 'I don't know you, master. What happened here?'

'As the gaoler said, I was robbed today by a man called Ned Hall and two accomplices. His brother Adam Hall, and their confederate Hugh Miller. We caught Miller earlier, and he told us where the Hall brothers lived. We went there to try to catch them, and finally did get Ned Hall, but his brother just came and knocked my friend down and rescued his brother. They went up there,' I added, pointing up the road helpfully.

'We'll see if we can find them,' the leader of the watchmen said. His companions looked unhappy to hear this. One, the youngest, who towered over the other two by six inches or more, peered up the road as if expecting to see a rampaging herd of felons charging towards him.

It has often been said that those who join the watch are the least suitable. Such men should be hardy, bold, courageous fellows who are keen to get involved in a scrap. Those whom I have met have tended to be trepidatious, pusillanimous types who would prefer to wait in a dark doorway until any possible danger was long past. Only when any fighting was done would they emerge from the security of their places of concealment to remonstrate with those responsible for breaking the Queen's peace. I once saw two members of the watch in London observing a brawl between two gangs just off Cornhill. Once most of the combatants were left bleeding and bruised, the two happily wandered in and plied their clubs with cheerful abandon, knocking out the few who remained conscious and then arranging for the bodies to be removed to the gaol. Their motto seems to be something along the lines of *When in doubt, sit it out*.

These three looked much like any other watchmen I've seen. If there had been a fight, I have little doubt that they would have been on the other side of the city in moments.

Accordingly, I stiffened my back and spoke to them in a firm manner, as a London gentleman should.

'Help us to bring my friend inside. We cannot leave him out in the dirt of the street. Then you had best hurry up there to see if you can find the Hall brothers. Come along, be quick!'

And that, I thought, would be the end of my adventures for the evening. I had recovered my purse, I had seen to it that Richard was brought into the gaoler's room and set on a pile of blankets on a low bench where he could remain in moderate comfort, and now I bethought myself of my own comfort. I had a very pleasant bed in Richard's father's home, where I could return now. It was plainly my duty to get a message to Richard's family to the effect that he was now safely ensconced in the gaoler's chamber, and if they would like him returned, a wheelbarrow and a pair of burly servants would probably be in order.

However, after the excitement of the evening so far, I was unsure about returning straightaway to my cot. For one thing, I was unwilling to explain how it was that I had gone with Richard to a brothel. Not all parents would be happy to hear that their son had been injured after capturing a felon in a whorehouse. Besides, I was feeling thrilled and ready for some alternative entertainment, rather than a slow meander through the streets to Richard's father. The thought of the brothel immediately sprang into my mind. It had looked a pleasant venue for feminine companionship, and if the prices were as high as I believed, it was unlikely that Ned would return to it, unless he managed to find another poor devil to fleece on his way. And although that was possible, I did not think it probable. After all, he would know that the watch would be searching for him. Only a fool would wander the city waiting to be captured.

The more I considered it, the more I was taken with the idea of the buxom beauties inside Mistress Moll Thatcher's house. The smiling dark-haired hussy was much in my mind. Her chemise was fine, soft, thin material, and when she had sunk on top of me, her figure had felt as warm and soft as a puppy's. She had a specific fragrance about her too, which I couldn't place just now, but I was struck with the desire to inhale it once more.

Of course, there was an issue with any thoughts of marching to her door: it was at the northern wall, and that meant I would have to make my way to the opposite side of the city. At least I had the watch here, so I could perhaps persuade them to take me safely. I wouldn't want to make my way in the dark all alone.

It was soon agreed. One of the watchmen would go to Richard's father's house and bring news of their son before anyone grew too alarmed at his absence; meanwhile, the other two would join me and walk me to the brothel in safety. The watchman did not look happy at being delegated to visit Godfrey's house.

Before long, the leader of the watch and his youngest, lanky recruit were walking with me up South Street. They should have hurried off to see if they could catch Ned and Adam, of course, but I was now glad of their less-than-enthusiastic response to the idea of chasing after Richard's assailants. I think a quick look at his face was enough to convince them that they could easily find an easier occupation than trying to capture Richard's attacker, and I could not blame them for that. It was the same thought that ran through my own mind.

The hour was very late, and we walked without speaking much. The third man was already ahead of us. He claimed to know the house where Richard lived, and I was content that the remaining two were adequate for my own safety. I was mistaken.

There was a passage on the right that led to the cathedral, and as we passed, I could hear the bells ringing. The canons would be rising for matins, I realized. There was the sound of feet moving along passageways and men yawning. It was enough to make me smile. After all, I was a young blade with a night's enjoyment ahead of me. I had much to smile about, compared with canons and priests who must rise now and spend the rest of the night in prayer, kneeling on cold flagstones, muttering incomprehensible Latin and remaining there until dawn broke. No doubt they did good with their endless prayers, but for me, I was content to go and wrestle a maid in a warm, comfy chamber.

Or I would have been, because this was where my evening took a decided turn for the worse.

The first I knew of it was as we approached the tall, red sandstone church at the top of South Street.

There came a sudden slapping of feet from behind us, and I span with concern. After all, running feet in the middle of the night rarely heralds good news.

Behind me stood a pair of men. These looked like watchmen too, but they had some distinguishing features that made them stand out from the two at my side. These were well armed, well dressed, well fed and well capable of taking on any group of three or even five thrown at them. They had stopped a few paces from us, neither of them panting, but just eyeing us with glittering dark eyes that reminded me of old stories of men from the sea who would land and slaughter all, leaving with a ship full of stolen treasure and letting the bodies of the dead litter the fields. They were brutal, vengeful men with the build of wrestlers. And so were these two terrifying brutes.

'You are the one from London?' one said. He was the broader of the two and had eyebrows that met over his nose. The nose itself had been broken more than once and formed a zig-zag as it wandered down his face. His eyes held all the suspicion and brutality of the world in them. This was not the sort of man I would willingly offer to spend the evening with over a convivial quart or two of ale. This was the sort of man I would avoid meeting in the street. He was the sort of man I would turn and walk away from even if it meant I must walk miles in the wrong direction.

He lowered his head questioningly. I opened my mouth but could say nothing. I emitted a faint snivelling sound, but little more. After clearing my throat, I managed to get my voice under control. 'Who are you, and what do you want?'

'You're under arrest for assaulting a member of the dean's familia,' the man said.

'The dean's household? I don't know anyone from his household.'

'He says you do, and the dean wants to speak to you. Now.'

'It's the middle of the night!'

'You'll have nothing better to do, then.'

I tried to slip behind my two watchmen, but as soon as I tried to move, they also retreated. I turned to remonstrate with them and remind them that it was their duty to protect the innocent – people like me – but before I could speak, the youngster gave what I can only call a piteous braying noise and was suddenly away. If there had been a galloping horse there, I would have gambled on the boy winning. He put on a seriously impressive turn of speed, and in moments had disappeared round the corner of Carfax.

That meant there was me and the leader of the watch. We stared at each other, and then a thought struck us both at the same time.

I am a connoisseur of escape. If pitted against the average male, I will be able to outrun him. It is not that I am particularly fast, but more the degree of concentration I put into my task. When I am thinking about running, it is to the exclusion of all else. I do not give a thought to those behind me, only to the direction I am running. I do not look over my shoulder, for that would simply mean scaring myself; no, far better to fix the mind on speed and stamina. Speed I have, in abundance. Many was the time I managed to bolt just because I had a sudden burst of energy that allowed me to make myself disappear. Pursuers might be equally fleet of foot, but it was my ability to spring from a stationary and seemingly unprepared posture to full speed in the blink of an eye that made them fail. They would still be staring at me as I disappeared over the horizon.

Others, of course, were almost as quick off their mark, but in those cases, I had another advantage, because most men, when they run, will have either speed on their side or endurance. I was fortunate to have been trained from an early age, and my stamina was second to none. I could set off quickly, and maintain that speed over a long distance. Those who were capable of sprinting after me would rarely, if ever, be able to equal my distance.

Thus it was that when I saw the watchman's eyes narrow, I knew it was time for both of us to be elsewhere. My foot lifted, my body leaned, and I was off and away.

In my mind, I suppose, I was thinking that I must overhaul the watchman. After all, if you are being chased by a lion, it is infinitely better to be the one in front. Let the lion take the hindmost. It is, of course, much the same when trying to evade bailiffs. So my first objective was to pass the watchman and then let my feet do the serious work of getting me away from there.

On occasion, I have known moments of bemusement. Not panic, because that implies fear, but mere befuddlement. This was one such experience. My feet had performed a perfect about-turn and stamp to launch me into the distance, my arms had pumped, my body was leaning at the optimum angle to flee – and yet I had not moved. Twenty yards away, already, the watchman was turning into the High Street, and yet I was fixed, seemingly, to the ground. My feet moved, the soles of my boots scraping on the filth and cobbles of the roadway, but I was not making any headway. I turned to see that the brute of a bailiff had me by my belt. In his other hand, he was holding my pistol, and when I met his eye, he shook his head as if in disappointment.

I was perfectly in tune with his feelings there. Disappointment was a good way to describe my feelings on realizing I was going nowhere. And then he released me. The hand gripping my belt was suddenly gone, and, unbalanced, when I tried to pelt away, my feet were not in the correct position, and instead of charging off into the middle distance, I fell flat on my face.

'Like I said. The dean will see you now,' the man said.

He sounded quite smug.

The bastard.

I was pushed along the roadway, up to the red sandstone church, and then shoved unceremoniously right, into the cathedral close. A strong, oaken door blocked our path, and I turned and gave a sickly smile to the nearer of the two guards. He returned my smile with a grin of his own, while his colleague struck the door twice with the pommel of my gun. A shutter opened, an eye peered at us, and then the bolts were drawn and the gate opened.

My friend had his hand on my belt again and used this to direct me onwards, pointing with my pistol, the stinkard varlet.

The cathedral was a splendid affair, rising on our right, and the painted figures of saints decorating the image screen of the west front of the building stood out clearly in the cool night air. I would have to visit the place in daylight to see them more clearly, but even in the dark, I could almost feel their eyes on me as I was frogmarched across the graves, past the charnel chapel on our left, then over to the row of canon's houses. As we went, I could hear the voices of the choir inside, chanting and murmuring as the Catholics like to. All incomprehensible, of course. I never learned any Latin other than the Paternoster and a few bits of the Ave Maria, but what the words mean, I do not know. It made a lot more sense when I was younger and Henry and his son Edward had the lot translated into English.

Not that I was in the mood to consider such things just now, as I was pushed up to a studded and reinforced oak door. It was a pleasant-looking old building, with windows on either side of the door. The door itself was arched, like the entrance to a stable.

'Who are you?' I said, and I confess that my voice was a little tremulous.

'My name is Davy Appowell, sergeant to the dean of the chapter.'

Having said his piece, Appowell battered the door with my gun and stood a pace back while we waited. After a minute or two, we could hear the bolts slide back, and an elderly bottler stood in the doorway. Holding a large candle high to give him a better view of me, he eyed me rather like a man confronted by a pig in his parlour – with revulsion, but with the clear impression that this could be an opportunity. Not that I had the faintest idea what opportunity I might represent. Nothing as attractive as a roasted pig, I was sure.

A shove in the small of my back thrust me over the threshold, and I was forced to follow the man along a short screened passage, and thence into a small hall on the right. And there I met the dean.

It was the same man I had seen with William Ralegh and a third man at the body of Roger Lane when I first arrived in this God-forgotten city.

There were three tall candle stands about the room, all near the dean. They lit him with a warm, effulgent, mellow glow that made him gleam like an angel in the dark room. The room was panelled, and heavy tapestries tended to give the space a feeling of warmth that was helped by the fire sparking and crackling on the hearth. It gave him a kindly appearance that was pleasing, after the less-than-friendly approach of the two guards who had captured me in the street.

'Jack Blackjack, dean,' Davy Appowell said.

Dean Pycraft was a man of middling height, but slender as a willow. His shoulders would not have borne the weight of a yoke, and he had the look of a man who could be tumbled over and over by any strong wind. His face was almost unlined, as though he had never suffered any hardship that could make him strain or struggle. The only creases I could see in his face were crow's feet at the corners of his eyes. It could have been the light in that chamber, but his skin had a healthful warmth, and he looked kindly and understanding. He was the picture of the generous uncle who brought a present when he visited and always left a penny or two when he left. Not that I had one, but that was the sort of uncle I would have wanted.

'Ah, the gentleman from London,' he said, and his lips pulled back in the sort of smile you would normally see on a ferret just before you felt his teeth on your thumb. 'I am glad you could join me.'

'I did not seem to have much choice.'

'No. You didn't,' he agreed. Any impression of avuncular goodwill was dissipated by the certainty in his voice. He was one of those prelates who would turn up to a burning or hanging, not to offer prayers, but to watch with interest. 'I have need of a conversation with you. I believe you had an altercation with a servant of mine earlier.'

'I did?'

'Edward Hall and his brother are useful associates of mine.'

This was one of those moments when I felt a distinctly chilly rush of cold air up my spine. 'Oh,' I said.

'Edward is a rough diamond. But he is useful. I would not wish to see him imprisoned or accused of something moderately trivial.'

'Trivial?' I blurted. I couldn't help myself. 'He robbed me and would have stabbed me, and had already killed another man.'

'You have proof of this?' he said mildly.

'He spoke to me of how Lane squealed when he and his accomplices attacked the poor fellow in the alley.'

'Yes, but do you have proof? Evidence that can be corroborated?'

This struck me as distinctly unfair. After all, when I have been accused of crimes, there has been remarkably little evidence to convict me. Usually, a fellow needs only to be in the wrong place to be accused, and whether he is found guilty or not depends on the mood of the jury and how bad their hangovers are that day, or whether they know the real guilty party, and if so, how much they value his worth in the community. A good ploughman or thatcher is less likely to be found guilty than a stranger to the area.

'I see you have none,' he said after a few moments' consideration of me. 'You should know that Lane was not a popular man. He was a heretic who refused to accept God's own religion. Many would deplore his actions and seek to punish him. There is nothing to suggest that Edward and his brother had anything to do with his death, so I would be glad to hear that you have dropped your accusations against them and Hugh Miller.'

'But they robbed me and took my purse! They spent a fortune in the taverns and brothels in the city!' I protested.

'I can understand that would be frustrating,' the dean said, and then he did something that astonished me. He motioned to his bottler, who crossed to me and glared at me for a moment before passing me a small pouch. It was heavy and made a delightful tinkling sound when I weighed it in my hand. I could feel the silver inside. It sounded very friendly, as though the coins wanted to come and get to know me better, ideally across a drink or two in a bar.

I felt myself beginning to like this dean.

'I am sure you will forgive Edward for the unfortunate accident when he knocked you over. It was a misunderstanding,' the dean continued. His teeth sparkled in the candlelight. They were almost entrancing. I found myself gazing at them like a mouse staring into the eyes of a viper, incapable of arguing or moving away.

'He attacked Lane!' I said, but with little conviction.

'You would not wish to find yourself in a dispute with the Church, of course.' He added, 'The Roman faith is vital to the protection of souls. Those souls which deserve it, of course. Not the heathen religion that Henry, the devil, imposed on the poor innocents of the kingdom. Such men have no soul.'

There we were in full agreement. I had no desire to tempt fate – or the Church. Apart from anything else, it was dangerous just then to question the Queen's complete conviction that the Roman faith was the right one. Anything tending to imply that the Church was at fault was frowned upon, and there were many who had learned that to incur either the Church's or the Queen's displeasure was likely to result in a warm reception – generally on a pyre. But there was something else in his manner – this was a powerful prelate, and yet there was a note almost of pleading in his tone. I couldn't say he was begging, but there was a definite appeal about his request. Almost as though he knew I didn't have to, and he had no right to ask it, but if I would, I would be doing him a favour.

'No, no, of course not,' I said hurriedly, weighing his purse in my hand.

'I am glad. You see, there have been unfortunate cases of people, like Master Lane, who have been attacked and even killed. Many, I am sure, because of misunderstandings, but when a man goes out of his way to offend, those taking offence might well be seriously upset. Even to the point of chastising those responsible.'

I nodded furiously. I didn't want him to think I was in any way offensive.

'Some years ago, another dean had some little difficulties with a man. He was the precentor of the cathedral, a rather harsh, bullying fellow called Walter de Lechlade. He was a boorish man. The bishop thought it would be a good idea to have this Walter installed because he disliked his dean. Dean John was a perfectly good man, but because of some small, slight differences of opinion about how the cathedral should organize its affairs, the bishop decided to make his life difficult.' The Dean sighed and shook his head, then sipped from a goblet at his side before continuing. 'The precentor took over the dean's stall in the choir. He bullied the dean and his servants, and was rude and offensive. So it was not surprising that steps were taken.'

'What steps?'

'Dean John, my predecessor – curious that he had the same name, isn't it? – was upset by the insults raining upon his head, and others could see it. They decided to take action.'

'What sort of action?' I asked, but I had a suspicion already.

'Oh, twenty of his supporters came to the cathedral, at about this time of the night, I think, at matins. And here they waited for the end of the service, when the precentor and the rest of the choir left the church, and then they ran at the precentor and stabbed and bludgeoned him to death,' the dean said, with another of his fresh, open-faced smiles. 'So, you see, it can be a bit of a mistake to assail those of the Church or their friends here in Exeter. People can become inflamed.'

'What happened to the murderers?' I ignored the reference to flames.

'Them? Well, many men were accused. But fellows such as the vicar of Heavitree and the vicar of Ottery St Mary were not going to be punished too severely. They had their congregations to protect. And the dean at the time was a local man. He was even called John of Exeter, so it would be difficult to punish him. You see, Master Blackjack, those in power like to remain in power. And those who would take it away will often get more than their fingers burned. I hope I make myself clear.'

It was not a question. I nodded dully.

'Good. In that case, the affair is concluded. And now you may leave.'

I turned. The two guards who had escorted me stood back, and I went to the screened passage, but as I approached, the bottler joining me with his candle, I suddenly saw that there was another man in the room with us. An ugly brute who, when he smiled, displayed a black maw with no front teeth.

'I think you know my servant, Edward,' the dean called. 'He has witnessed our discussion, in case you decided to change your mind. And now he will escort you to your inn.'

'I don't need . . .' I began.

'Please be quick. It is very early in the morning, and Edward needs his beauty sleep, after all.'

It must be said that I was not at ease in the company of Ned Hall. I strode along the cathedral's green, and my impression of him was that he was always almost out of sight. No matter how I walked, how fast or slow, he was always just behind me. It made me deeply uncomfortable, and I began to walk more hurriedly as a result, but even as I did so, he began talking.

'Now you know the lie of the land, don't you? Thought you could bully me into submitting to you? Me and Adam are safe, and tomorrow we'll have Hugh out of the gaol, and then you'd best watch yourself. He don't like fools who upset him, and putting him into a gaol isn't going to leave him happy. Oh, no. You'll be back here in short order, I reckon.'

We were passing the charnel chapel now.

'See that? That's where the bones dug up here in the graveyard get put. That chapel stands on top of thousands of dead men and women. All the dead of Exeter come here to the cathedral graveyard. They get put in the soil to rot, and when the worms and ants are done, their bones are collected up and put in the chapel. One day, you'll be in there. Keep irritating Hugh and me, and we'll see to it. Unless we find somewhere else for you. Perhaps a nice crossroads where we can take off your head and leave you on ground where God'll never find you, eh? Take your resurrection from you.'

I was shivering now. 'Why did he hate Lane so much?'

'Perhaps he was asking too many questions. Anyway, he was a heretic. Wanted his women and to be a priest as well. Dean John wouldn't tolerate that.'

'Hardly reason to have him murdered,' I said.

Ned suddenly sprinted in front of me. 'We didn't murder him. We left him bruised, that's all, so you can stop all that!' His head jutted truculently. 'You forget the dean wanted him beaten!'

'If you stop trying to rob me, I'll stop suspecting you and him!'

'He only wanted Lane taught a lesson. Lane was annoying him. And in the same way, other people who annoy him might regret it!'

'I . . . I . . .' I swallowed hard, but he just sneered and chuckled deep in his throat. He held out my pistol to me.

'You're a pathetic, feeble little man, aren't you? Go to! Take your toy and go away! Out of here: *go*!'

The porter was standing at the gate and, hearing his words, yanked the heavy timbers of the wicket gate wide. Beyond it was the vast expanse of Exeter city, and I almost ran through the gateway, so full of enthusiasm was I. I hurtled up the road to Carfax and then over towards Godfrey Ralegh's house, passing on the way the alley where Lane had lain, if you'll excuse the pun. Glancing in, I saw a body. I was going to continue on my way when I realized that it was not Lane.

It was another man.

There is a simple rule that I have discovered to my benefit over years of living in London, and this is that it is better, when you see a body, not to approach it. If you are listed as the first finder of a corpse, the coroner will demand money, the magistrate will demand money, and your journey home will be hugely delayed. No, when you see a body, leave well alone and go home quickly and quietly.

I did not do so. In my befuddled frame of mind after the last hours, I noticed the body, and my attention was drawn to the fact that the man was lying in a different posture. His arms were spread out on either side, his legs were apart, and if that wasn't enough of a clue, his head was towards the road. Lane had been lying with his head facing into the alley. Besides, his clothing was different. It was more like the items that the bailiff guarding Lane had been wearing. This man had a huge belly, too. There was a groaning noise from somewhere. At first, I thought it was me, but then I realized it was the snoring of a man knocked down and left with his nose in the mud – or so I hoped – of the gutter.

Yes, the sensible thing always is to run from a dead body. But I couldn't leave this poor fellow lying in the filth. I gingerly entered the alley, keeping a careful look about me as I went. I didn't want to be surprised by someone else suddenly appearing and knocking me on the pate. I've had that too often already in my life.

When I crouched at the man's side, he was still moaning and snoring. I wasn't too sure which was the loudest, but both, I felt sure, were symptoms of a man who had been struck hard on the head and forced to go to sleep. I pulled his shoulder to try to roll him over, but he was an appalling weight. In the end, I went before him, hauled one arm forward and then tried to roll him over on that side.

Yes, it was the bailiff. The poor man looked awful. In truth, I could say that he looked equally as bad as Lane when he had been here only a few hours before. His brow was bloody where he had hit the ground, I think, and the back of his skull had a bloody mess where something hard and heavy had struck him a glancing blow, tearing the skin so that the blood could run clear to his face where he lay face down on the ground. Now his eyes opened, the lids fluttering, and a look of incomprehension and distress slowly washed into his face.

'Why'd you do that?' he stammered.

'I just found you!' I protested.

He stared at me with wide eyes, and then his gaze slid away to the patch of ground where he lay. Suddenly, he noticed something was missing. 'What have you done with Lane?'

'He wasn't here when I arrived,' I said. I was smarting somewhat from his allegation that I might have knocked him down and stolen the body he was supposed to be guarding.

'Oh, *ballocks*!' he said.

THREE

A Maid, a Wife and a Ship

7 August

I woke to a hammering on a door and opened my eyes blearily.

The sun was high. She was as bright as only she could be. I could feel the heat like a lance of flame that seared through my eyelids. I grabbed my hat and pulled it over my face to give a modicum of protection.

As I pulled the brim down, I realized that my bed was extraordinarily uncomfortable. I recalled sitting on the mattress last evening in Ralegh's house, and it had not felt so lumpy and unforgiving then, but now, as the mists of sleep slowly faded in the sun's light, I realized that the sun should not be so bright in my bedchamber. And the bed was no bed; it was a stone bench, and when I tilted my hat cautiously, I could see that I was not in my bedchamber. Indeed, I was not in the house. Glancing up and around, I realized I was in the stone porch of Master Godfrey's house. I remembered now the hunt for Ned Hall and his brother, my own capture by the cathedral's guards, the discussion with the dean, the walk back to the Ralegh hall – and a long, long wait at the door.

Of course, all houses locked their doors against felons and thieves, but when they had a respected guest, like me, they should usually leave a servant waiting up so that the last fellow can be permitted to gain access. In my case, they had merely left me to sleep as best I could out here in the open. I was cold, uncomfortable, battered and beaten, and, all in all, I felt like an apprentice after a three-day drinking session. The cries of street sellers were like chalk dragged slowly along the slate of my nerves; a dog came and cocked his leg at my bed, eyeing me incuriously, and I saw figures moving about in the roadway.

One small figure seemed in a great hurry, rushing away as though the hounds of hell were at its feet.

'Awake, eh?'

The voice came from somewhere behind me, at the front door of the house. It was William, looking lugubrious and stern.

'You played us a merry dance last night, master. As soon as we heard Richard was injured, Godfrey sent us to fetch him and you, and we soon had him back home. But you . . . *you* were nowhere to be found. We hunted all the worst dives in the city, even the brothels, looking for you.'

I rubbed my head. It ached, but more from lack of sleep than any surfeit of wine or ale. My neck cracked. 'I was detained.'

'Really? By whom, I wonder? Who was she?' William asked in what seemed to me to be an unpleasantly cynical manner. The straight-laced fellow of the previous evening had not improved.

'Nothing of that sort,' I said grimly. I recounted my tale of being captured and forced to join in an interview with the dean. 'And I would have been back much sooner if it weren't for that. Why was no one left to open the door for me?'

'You go traipsing about the city in the middle watch of the night and ask that? A man was set to wait for you, but it was soon plain enough that you were staying out for the night. We all assumed with a woman.'

I sat up and put a hand to my head. It was as heavy and thick as a cannon ball of solid stone. Trying to think was painful. 'No woman, only the dean, and I came straight back here . . .' I jerked up and winced as an arrow of pain was loosed in my neck. Being stabbed would have been less painful. 'I have to speak to Master Godfrey.'

'Well?' Godfrey Ralegh demanded.

He sat at his table like a small, rotund emperor, a pile of appealing-looking coins before him, his clerk at his side. William was standing with me. We were both silent for a moment: I was longingly considering the money set in teetering towers, William trying to think of the best way to introduce his subject.

Godfrey Ralegh stood slowly and paced around the table, while I retreated slightly, recalling the pain from his stubby finger jabbing my breast. He shouldered William from his path and stood staring up at me. 'Well?' he repeated. 'What cock and bull story do you have now, eh?'

'The man who was killed, the fellow Lane, has disappeared,' I said.

'What?' He studied me with narrowed eyes, standing perfectly still, like a toad spying an approaching fly.

'I was coming back here when I glimpsed the alley where Lane was. The man guarding him had been knocked down, but Lane was gone. I raised a hue and cry, and soon locals came and helped. The poor bailiff was in a terrible state. That's why I was some little while later than I should have been. I'm surprised you didn't hear all the noise from the house here. No doubt you were all warm and comfortable in your beds,' I added nastily.

'As should you have been, instead of roistering at brothels,' Godfrey spat at me.

'I should have thought hunting felons in your city would win your support,' I said suavely, wiping his spittle from my jerkin. 'The Queen places high importance on clearing up crime. Interesting that things are so different here in the – ah – county areas.'

'I . . .' and then he snapped his mouth shut. Clearly, a little of our conversation the evening before had returned to him. His eyes bugged, and he swallowed harshly, like a man with a severe sore throat. 'I . . . may have sounded rude. I am sorry. I had no idea that this fellow Lane's body was gone, and it was a shock. But who would do such a thing?' His eyes clouded with suspicion as he peered up at me. 'First kill him, then steal the body of this fellow?'

It was interesting to hear him lie like that, as though he barely knew Lane. Perhaps it was easy enough to pull the wool over the eyes of other rural merchants, but it would not serve with a man of London. It takes more than a little dissimulation to confuse men of my sort. I had seen him at Lane's body with the dean, and his son had told me Lane was spying for him in Wolfe's business.

'Yes,' I said musingly. 'It is curious. Who could have wanted to see him dead? A business acquaintance, perhaps? Another merchant? Someone who despised his attacks on the Church? Someone who thought he was not making enough noise about the Roman Church, someone who disagreed and disapproved of the Queen's religious beliefs and preferred to see a return to the new religion of King Henry, perhaps?' and I gave him one of my 'honest Jack' stares. I've been told it feels as if I am peering straight into a man's heart. Certainly, Godfrey recoiled. It must have been his guilty heart.

'I am sure no one would think to question the Queen's beliefs or her actions, God bless the lady,' he said, breathing somewhat stertorously. He tottered away and rounded his table once more, slumping so heavily that one teetering tower of coins toppled over and clattered about all over the table and rolled to the floor.

It was a near-run thing. I have never seen a man succumb to apoplexy, but that was the day during which I almost did. Godfrey sat back as if recovering, but no, it was just in order to take in a deep enough breath so that when he bellowed, he could threaten to take down the walls of the hall itself.

'*Don't just stand there, you base, pricklouse knaves! Pick it up!*'

I left his chamber and made my way to the buttery, where I soon had a couple of slabs of pork and a hunk of bread on a trencher. With a jug of gravy to join them, I spent a happy while sitting at a window and eating. I was still there when William walked in with a pale and frail-looking Richard.

'How is your head?' I asked solicitously.

'Painful. No thanks to you.'

His tone was offended, but I was prepared to be likewise sharp. 'And what did I do? I went to get help, expecting you to be able to defend yourself against one half-wit, but you were so lackadaisical in your duties that you let the fool jump on you and break your head. I never thought you would be such easy prey to a man like him. In London, a fellow would always keep a close eye in all directions in case of a sudden attack. I was astonished to see how easily he knocked you down! And then I was captured by two henchmen from the dean's household and dragged back to see him.'

I told them both all about the dean's conversation. It was pleasing to see how both responded.

William scowled. 'He means to have that thief and scoundrel free to commit more depredations in the city? I'll be hanged before I allow that!'

'Ned Hall released without a stain on his character? And he wants Hugh Miller released as well? The effrontery! I want the man brought before the justice!' Richard declared.

'This is no lawless border territory like the Scottish march where thieves can run riot,' William said. 'How dare the dean suggest it!'

'He was persuasive,' I said. I tried not to think about the walk past the charnel chapel. 'He said such things have happened before, that a precentor was murdered in the close itself, and that it was local vicars who committed the act.'

Richard shrugged. 'That was true enough. But the vicars and Dean John and their accomplices were captured and punished. The city was, too, since the porter opened the South Gate for the murderers to rush into the city. He was hanged, and so was the mayor. If the city allowed the gates open after curfew, the city was complicit in the murder, and the representative of the city should suffer the penalty. The dean could not escape justice, and neither should Ned Hall.'

'Could he be the man who stole away the body of Lane, do you think?' I mused. 'He and his merry band accused me of making a little noise when they assaulted me, and said that Lane made more noise, but that would be curious . . .'

I was thinking hard now. In my years, I have had a considerable experience of bodies, and there was something that now struck me, as it were, with the force of a cudgel on the back of my skull.

'Why curious?' William asked.

'They said he made much noise, and yet when he was found, he had a great dint in the back of his head. That would surely have killed him. But after he had been struck with that blow, he would make no more sound. It must have killed him in an instant. So he could not have made the noise that they accused him of. Perhaps they didn't kill him. Instead, they were responsible for the blood on his face, when, for certain, he would have complained and protested.'

'Perhaps, but we cannot know that,' Richard said.

'You may not, but I am as sure as I can be that Lane was beaten up, and later knocked down with a blow that killed him.'

William shrugged. 'What does it matter? They beat him, and then clobbered him over the head with a weapon and killed him.'

'Why would they remove the body?' I wondered.

'Why, to take away the evidence of a culprit,' William stated. 'With no body, there is no murder. How could the jury comment on the corpse without the corpse to be viewed? How can we accuse Ned Hall of murder when there is no body?'

'Why was your father there, with Wolfe and the dean?' I wondered, glancing at Richard. 'Did they think they knew who was responsible?'

My belly full, I was called to the door by the bottler. I walked out to be confronted by a nervous-looking city watchman. He asked me to join him in visiting the South Gate because he had been told I was to drop all charges against the inmate, my friend Hugh Miller, or, as I still preferred to think of him, the Troll.

'You are mistaken,' William said. He had joined me and stood at my side. A slightly wobbly Richard leaned on the door's jamb. 'The man Miller robbed my friend here, and we think he was also involved in an attack on Roger Lane earlier. Miller is to be held until the justices can question him.'

The watchman had one of those vacant expressions that grew haunted as William spoke. He was a man with a hard, low-paid job, and he had no desire to question or give disrespect to a man in Godfrey Ralegh's house. He had begun with an anxious look on his face, but that now deteriorated into panic. 'But–but the dean's man told me I had to find you to come and order the fellow released. I can't say no to the dean!'

His expression put me in mind of a fly when it realizes that the pleasant landing it had anticipated was rather sticky, and that there was a large spider approaching. It glazed over when he looked at the three of us and saw neither sympathy nor agreement. I grew concerned that he might shatter into a thousand terminal, terrified pieces if none of us gave him any help. Besides, while William and Richard were determined that Ned and his companions should be held in gaol, I had formed a close, amicable relationship with the money in the dean's purse, and a strong opinion of the quality of his henchmen.

'I will come and speak to the gaoler with you,' I said.

'You will let them get away with robbing you?' Richard said.

I said nothing. I was thinking about the dean's shiny white teeth, the story of the precentor's murder and Ned outside the charnel chapel.

I was soon walking along the road with my watchman at my side, and it was as we passed over Carfax, almost stumbling over a meandering pig, and then being narrowly missed by a loud and insulting youth on a horse, which was being ridden at a ridiculous speed in such an enclosed lane, that I saw her again: the pretty little thing on whom Richard was so keen.

At this third sight, I could quite understand his infatuation. She was very pretty, in a coy, innocent way, and I could believe Richard's comment about her not having the faintest idea what diversions a brothel might offer to a man with blood in his veins. She had that look of supreme innocence that many would mistake for an angelic nature, but which I knew was often a mask to cover incredible stupidity.

She was walking towards me, and this time she did not have her mother with her, but instead a gingery-bearded man. He strode at her side, a burly fellow who looked all brawn and little brain, with a square face in which the eyes looked watery against the sun-burned flesh. His chin was solid and square, and his clothing was that of a working man: a strong, scarred leather jerkin, thick hosen and a belt a seaman would be proud of. He had a ballock knife in his belt, a purse that looked as though it had seen better days some thirty years ago, and he strode with the rolling gait of a man more used to the sea than the land.

He surveyed the people near him with a kind of fury, as though he was just waiting for the first insult to be hurled at him so that he could vent his rage. As things stood, he was already at a simmer, but a boiling fury was threatened.

I bowed, 'I am glad to see you are well, maid. I was concerned that the rude behaviour of those knaves in the road might have discomforted you.'

She also, I now saw, had pretty dimples. Her eyes were a clear, sweet blue, and her mouth was full and ripe. Yes, I could quite understand Richard's devotion to her. Any man would be glad to bed her. About her, there was a scent of citrus and warm summer meadow flowers that was quite intoxicating, too.

I was about to continue when my vision was blurred. A palm hit my chest and pushed me backwards. In place of her delicious features, I had a gingery beard with furious indigo eyes appear. His speech was so broad I was hard-pressed to understand a word, so I will translate.

He began, 'Keep your words to yourself, you whoreson drunkard! Don't speak to my daughter like some damned respectable suitor!'

'Father, I—'

'Shut up, child, and you, *you*, keep away unless you want me to cut your ballocks off and feed them to my pigs as dainties!'

'Father, he—'

'I said "shut up", Alice. You don't know these horn-makers as I do – he'd take a woman and make her husband wear the cuckold's horns if he had the chance! You don't know men as I do. This is the sort of fellow who'd take your virginity and then steal your purse, him with his fancy ways and smooth accent—'

'Father, he saved me yesterday. This was the man.' Her tone had a distinctly hard edge to it, a sort of tone of remonstration, if you know what I mean.

His eyes goggled and he visibly shrivelled. 'What? What d'you mean, saved you? This bowl-eyed bastard-maker?'

'It was he who saved me from the attentions of Richard Ralegh.'

The steam that had been coming from his ears, which was only matched by the flames emanating from his mouth, was suddenly quashed. He was like a dragon which, preparing to blast St George, was suddenly struck in the mouth by a bucket of cold water. The man looked at her and then at me. 'Master? That was you?'

'It was indeed,' I said, with a little loftiness based on my London accent. It doesn't do any harm to remind a peasant that a fellow has come from better stock. Admittedly, my stock was no better than any here in Exeter, but since I was living in London, I had several advantages, and my accent was one of them. I used it to the full.

'Master, accept my apologies. You will understand that when I heard you pay attention to . . . I mean, a stranger in the street . . . someone I had never seen before . . .'

He rambled on. I didn't help him but instead raised one eyebrow. I saw a fellow do so recently when a costermonger was trying to apologize for splashing him with mud and worse when his cart was rumbling along. The raising of that one eyebrow was enough to turn the usually loud and foul-mouthed seller into a gibbering, incoherent hardhead. It had a similar impact today. I rather enjoyed his capitulation and abashment. After all, he had been quite correct about me in his assumptions. And I had only saved her from Richard with a view to testing my luck with her. Not that I would touch her now. After all, Richard was young and fit. He would take my theft of his beloved with serious annoyance, and I was certain that his annoyance could bubble up into a rage more terrifying than this father could muster.

'I pray you, please, do not mention it,' I said, with a hand held up to stop the flow of his . . . I nearly said 'eloquence', but it was more a rabid rattling of incomprehensible half-sentences. 'I was glad to be of service to your daughter. Being a traveller, only visiting your – um – delightful city briefly, I was happy to help her. I drove the ruffians away. That is enough.'

'Where are you to?' he asked at last, his face gradually losing the dark plum colouring and becoming only a mild puce.

'I come from London,' I said, with casual indifference.

A swift calculation came into his eyes. 'Oh?'

I recognized that look. He was wondering whether I was a professional man or perhaps a merchant. His gaze ran down my body, taking in the piping on my suit of clothes and hat, which was admittedly a bit down-at-heel since the incident when the feather burned away in Okehampton. But any man who has travelled all over the realm will look a little the worse for wear after rain, mud and all the other little accidents of travelling. And then I realized that he was looking at me from the perspective of a potential suitor for his daughter. The man was keen to marry her into money, no doubt. Which sensible father would not?

Now, I had no desire to marry, and although I would dearly love to have a tumble with the dark-haired beauty, as I mentioned a moment ago, the idea of doing so when Richard would be certain to take offence was not one that I favoured. It would be a quick way to endure a lot of pain.

'I am glad to have met you, sir,' I said, bowing gracefully, and was about to walk on when the hand reappeared and blocked my path.

'You must visit us. I will expect you at midday for lunch. We are easy to find. Just ask for the house of Isaak Shapley.'

My visit to the gaol was not pleasant. When I reached it, I was confronted with a gaoler who was at least three quarts of ale happier than he should have been. With my poor evening and the pain still of the stones that had stuck into my back, I eyed him with a degree of jealousy. Worse was to come: when I spoke to him about the Troll, the gaoler was happy – very happy – to inform me that the matter was resolved to everyone's satisfaction. I had taken so long to make my way to the gaol that the gaoler had been happy to accept the assurances of a bailiff of the cathedral that Hugh Miller was to be set free, and all charges against him were to be forgotten. The Troll was, after all, a servant to the dean, and so fell under the jurisdiction of the Church.

I stood staring for quite some time, while the young watchman at my side muttered and complained that he'd been sent to bring me and it was all for naught. Which was fine for him. I now had all three of the felons ready and prepared to waylay me, and they were all free and at liberty to do so.

This was not a situation I relished. If it were not for the night before, and had I not reflected on the various aches and pains

I was already suffering from, I would have rushed to the horse courser. The thought of clambering upon a horse and getting as far as I could on unknown roads and paths was not appealing. I needed at least one good night's sleep before I undertook that journey.

I set off back to Shapley's house, the watchman grumpy at my side, bemoaning his fate as he was forced to make his way up through the city once again. His constant complaining was as irritating as a mosquito's whine and just as impossible to block out.

The only thing I discovered that could make his moaning recede was the study of the women of the city. True, most were the usual slatternly types a man would expect in any large city, but there were a few like Alice Shapley – small, young and refined beyond their years or place of birth. More than one caught my attention, and many returned my interest, one or two giving me languishing looks. I strode a little more upright and military at that, content to know that I was a fine figure compared to the run-of-the-mill fellows here.

One woman almost made me stop dead. She was slim and willowy, with almond eyes and the sort of looks that would have made Helen of Troy jealous. I was sure that she was familiar, but you must take my word for it that I didn't recognize her at first. So much had happened to me in the last few hours that the woman's face, for all its undeniable beauty, was just one more distraction in the crowds.

But then there was something else that caught my attention. It was the look in her eye. She saw me, and her face instantly changed from disinterest to keen scrutiny.

I know that not many men will receive such a favourable reaction whenever a woman sees them, but I have grown accustomed to it. My rugged good looks, slim but athletic build and upright stance make me a popular target of feminine regard. This woman was just the latest of those who have, at one time or another, paid me close attention. I gave her my special slow smile and was about to bend my steps towards her when her face suddenly froze and she became as still as the statues on the cathedral's image screen.

That was the moment when I recognized her. Her husband

– for he could be nothing else by the proprietorial confidence with which he joined her – took her hand and led her through the crowds. It was Wolfe.

I pointed them out to my watchman, and he gave them a cursory glance. 'That's Master Wolfe and his wife Margaret.'

Wolfe was the third man at Lane's body – Shapley, the dean and Wolfe. You can imagine that it was a slow and thoughtful Jack who made his way up through the jostling crowds towards Carfax, where my guard left me.

I had passed halfway up the road when I saw her again: Wolfe's wife.

She was standing at the corner of a small passageway, and as I watched, she began to make her way towards the Guildhall, idly peering at the wares on display at each shop. Looking about me, I saw no sign of her husband and, remembering his rudeness to me, hit upon a suitable method to pay him back. She was a beautiful woman, and I had not mistaken the way she had studied me: this was a woman who could be tempted into a brief dalliance, I was sure. I determined to make the attempt.

It took little time to catch her. I was like a hawk spying a field mouse; I made my way towards her on silent feet, and then, when I was ready, I flew to her as fast as a bullet from my handgun.

'Mistress, you must be sent from heaven. Only an angel could have a face of such beauty.'

She cast an amused glance over me, her mouth rising at either side. I had been quite right. She had a startlingly beautiful face, with large, liquid eyes and a mouth designed to be kissed.

'Oh, and you are an expert on angels?'

'I have studied many,' I said, 'but never before met one.'

'Really? Then I should be honoured, I suppose.'

'Can I tempt you to a little wine and some food? There is a passable inn over there,' I said, pointing to an accommodating hostelry.

'As an angel, I am sure I should refuse temptation.'

'But you might be able to save a misguided spirit by debating with me. And perhaps engaging in a little light discussion of sin and what is actually sinful. Can something pleasing to a man and woman be sinful?'

'Ah, you are a philosopher!'

'I am many things,' I said modestly. 'I am only in Exeter for a little while. Soon I must return to London.'

Her eyes lit up at that. She was as keen as any strumpet. Most bawds' eyes would glitter at the sight of a man's purse if it bulged well enough, but this was a well-born woman, who was as enthusiastic at the thought of the shops and wonders of a city like London. And my charm, naturally, overwhelmed her. I have that impact on women.

'I have little time,' she said.

'Let us enquire at the inn. Perhaps they have a quiet chamber where we could discuss London and drink a quart of wine in private,' I leered.

'You should be careful. My husband wouldn't appreciate a stranger making a pass at me.'

'He shouldn't leave such a precious jewel all alone in the road, then,' I said.

She dimpled very prettily. 'You are full of compliments, I see.'

'Only for those who deserve them,' I said. 'Look, the inn awaits.'

'And if my husband returns and finds me gone?'

'Tell him you were called to a privy – and give him hell for not waiting a little.'

She laughed at that. 'You are incorrigible.'

'I try,' I said, and was about to lunge and lead her to the inn, fully anticipating a mattress walloping, when I caught sight of Wolfe approaching. 'Ah, Mistress Wolfe, I fear I am too late,' I said.

He had seen her, and I slid away swiftly, blowing her a kiss. 'Until later.'

'I hope so, stranger,' she said. She turned to her husband, but not before I saw the smile turn into an expression of imperious challenge. Wolfe, I saw, wore a frown as he approached, and when he reached her, he stared after me as if seeking my face among the crowds. I kept low, confident that I was invisible. He was, after all, considerably larger than me, and I had the example of Roger Lane in my mind.

It was easy to be inconspicuous among the men and women of the street, and I made my way to Carfax once more, reminding myself of the route to Ralegh's house. But at the crossroads, I caught sight of a sly face ahead of me – it was Ned. His grin emphasized the black maw without teeth, and I stopped dead at the sight of him. He made no move towards me but merely stood threateningly, a block to any thought of continuing to the Ralegh house. I stopped and hesitated. Where else should I go? Glancing behind me, I saw a shadowy figure darting into a doorway, and that was enough to decide me. If I was being followed, and Ned was ahead of me, I was not going to continue in that way, nor turn back. In such a crowd, a man could easily have his purse stolen or receive a knife blow, with no one any the wiser.

I turned right, keeping with the crowds, seeking some safety in a new parish, but I had only covered a short distance when I was accosted as I approached Carfax. As I hurried past, I heard a voice call me. When I turned, it was Walter, the priest from St Sidwell's. He hurried to me, smiling, although he had the look of a man who was close to despair. It showed as a sort of thinness, even on his round features.

'Master, I am glad to see you,' he said. 'My apologies for departing in such an unseemly manner when you spoke to me.'

I looked at him and I confess that I was surprised. After our last chat, I had not expected to see him again. But here he was, as large as life and twice as ugly.

'I had thought—' I began, but he interrupted me.

'Come with me, I pray you. I am on the way to see my brother's widow. I want to bring her a little comfort, such as I may.' He met my gaze. 'Please? I am sure I will need the support of another man. This will be trying. She is greatly downcast.'

'I don't think—' I tried, but he took my arm and led me up to the great crossroads, and thence left, towards smaller houses leading down the hill towards the river. The buildings here all clung precariously to the hillside, so it seemed to me, huddling together like an anxious crowd trying to avoid monsters.

He stopped at a narrow entrance, and we passed into an alley that was little more than a tunnel. Plaster and cob walls rose on either side and suddenly opened into a little square space. A wooden staircase rose on the right, and Walter climbed this, carefully avoiding a broken step, and entering a door. I followed.

It was a small, cold chamber. There was a fire on the hearth, and smoke drifted idly in the air, but it was too small to change the room's chill atmosphere. A narrow, poor-quality bed, whose ropes were frayed and rotten, looked too small for two people. The mattress itself was little more than a palliasse stuffed with straw and looked scratchy and lumpy. For the rest of the furniture, a stool and low box served as a makeshift table and chair. That was all. On top of the box were the family's possessions: a pair of roughly carved wooden spoons, three wooden bowls of various sizes and a knife.

'Walter!'

The woman flung herself at the priest as he entered, throwing her arms about him, her eyes tightly closed. She was instantly recognizable as the widow who threw herself on the corpse. She had that fraught, drawn look of a woman at the end of her tether. But she was also a good height, and the thin shift she wore could not conceal the lines of her figure. It made me wonder whether if fate had been kinder, she would have been more attractive. As it was, her features were drawn. Weeping had made her eyes red and raw-looking, and her demeanour was that of a woman who had lost all hope. The sight of her made me ponder how my mother had coped when she ran from my father. She would have been destitute, too.

'Who's this?' she said now. Her eyes were open, and there was no welcome in them. No, rather it was the suspicious look of a harpy on seeing her husband wandering home utterly befouled with ale. There was little of the light-hearted, gay mistress of a house greeting a friend in that gaze. I suppose I should not have been surprised.

'He is a friend, Maud,' Walter said, and there was a tone of reproach in his voice, as though he had noticed her lack of good manners.

'What does this "friend" want here?' she said. She had withdrawn from Walter and stood now with her back to the box.

He was not likely to admit he needed my presence to bolster his courage in seeing her. 'I met him just now, Maud. Come, won't you be friendly?'

'Friendly? I've been widowed, Walter. You know that. And you expect me to dance and sing for any stranger, perhaps cater for them? You can see how much food I have, can't you?'

Her hand was flung towards a shelf, which teetered at the wall with a sort of horrible threat of falling. On it was a bare crust of bread and a fair layer of dust. It was a meagre amount of food for one person, and she had a daughter to feed as well.

It had not occurred to me until that moment, I swear, but looking at her, I suddenly thought of the waif who had tried to rob me of my purse. Similar scrawny build, not dissimilar faces, if you allowed that the girl was considerably younger, and markedly dark eyes, too. With a flash of surprise, I realized that this woman was possibly her mother. It put a different complexion on the matter of my almost-gone purse. I was glad now that I had at least given the child a decent meal.

I put on my most pleasant, amiable smile, and said, 'Mistress, I am sorry to hear of your loss. It must be—'

'Yes, it is. I thank you for your kind words.' She almost seemed to relent a little. Then her eyes filled. 'How could he? The fool! He left us with *nothing*! All his money was spent on his whores, I suppose, and in the alehouses. And now he's dead, and we have nothing! I could wish he was alive again so I could beat him!'

'Come now, Maud, you mustn't blame him for being murdered,' Walter attempted.

'Why not?' she demanded with vicious intensity. 'He has left us both hungry and without hope! He knew what he was doing!'

'Surely he was walking home,' I said.

'Not then! When he used to talk about the Church, with the women hanging on his every word. I know what he was really doing.'

'Maud,' Walter remonstrated gently. 'He's hardly even cold.'

'It was the dean. Dean John may give that smarmy smile,

but he has the mind and soul of a snake. He hated Roger for his religion, and when Roger started working for Wolfe, that was the final straw, I think.'

'The dean doesn't like Wolfe?' I asked.

'Dean John trusts no one,' she snapped. 'The city held out against the rebels during the siege! How could he trust the people in this city?'

'Well,' I began, but she wasn't listening.

Walter threw me an anxious glance, and I took the hint and my leave. I had no wish to be involved in any more tearful exchanges, and the woman was distraught and irrational.

Out in the street once more, I turned back towards the middle of the city. I suddenly recollected Ned's features in the crowds. I had no desire to see him again and stood irresolute for a moment. Then I had a happy thought and asked a passer-by for some directions.

'I am glad to see you,' Shapley said.

We were in his great hall, which was, of course, mean and ill-decorated compared with a great hall in London, and yet it was not entirely devoid of little details. I particularly liked the cupboard in the corner which contained not only pewter but a wonderful pair of golden plates. High overhead, the roof was well built, and the smoke from the hearth occasionally wafted about the room like an evening river's mist. He had a young bottler, who was obviously terrified of making some social faux pas and hovered at my elbow with a sickly smile whenever I turned towards him, refilling my goblet at every opportunity. It was clear that he had been told to ensure my cup was never empty.

Shapley's eyes were less bulbous now. Instead of looking like a dog that had swallowed a stick sideways, he looked more like a hound spying his prey. He had clear intentions which involved me, and although I was reluctant, I was keen to remain off the streets and in a place of refuge if I may.

His accent was of the thickest. 'So, you'm vrum Lon'on?' – which meant 'So you're from London?' It was one of the easier questions to answer, but it was also easier for me to comprehend. I had, after all, already been living with Devonians for some time – but for your benefit, as before, I will translate his foul peasant language.

I was able to answer in the positive.

'You came from Cornwall, I heard?' was his next enquiry, which, naturally enough, was intended as a demand for a lengthy life history, hopefully including aspects of my income and saved fortune. He was not a man to beat about the bush.

'Just now I am returning from business to the west.'

That made him raise an eyebrow. 'There's business west of Exeter? Hah! I thought there's bugger all there but sheep and felons!'

'And tin miners,' I added ruefully. They had made my life precarious in the extreme.

'But what do you do? Are you a professional man? Do you employ others?'

'I am professional, yes,' I said, adding loftily, 'I perform certain functions for those in high position. And employ some fellows who actually conduct the business.'

Informing him that I was a paid assassin for Lady Elizabeth's household would not necessarily endear me to him – although it is hard to tell with merchants. They appreciate the concept of individual enterprise and are often keen to hire men with my qualifications to remove potential business obstacles.

'Those in high position, eh? You mean lawyers, I suppose?'

'No. I mean those of noble birth,' I said, and if my voice had been any more lofty, my skull would have cracked the roof trusses.

'Oh!' he said, and his eyes began to goggle again. 'Do you have any belongings with you? A journey such as yours will mean you must have a bag or two for your essentials, surely. You must not leave them to the mercies of an inn. We should have them fetched for you and brought here. I hope you will not object to remaining here as my guest, my friend. It will be more comfortable than a bedchamber in an inn, I am sure.'

'That is most kind of you, but my goods are safely preserved in the house of the Raleghs.'

'Those incontinent bastard-makers? I am shocked, sir, that you would consider staying with such as them. The father is a scoundrel and the son a wastrel! Your belongings are likely to be pillaged if they remain there!'

'I have heard nothing to indicate that they would be any danger to me or my belongings,' I said firmly. 'In all their dealings with me, they have been entirely kind and generous.'

Not quite true, but it was how a gentleman might be expected to speak.

'Then you have been most fortunate. They have been a sad cause of trouble for centuries. Hah! Henry, one of Godfrey's ancestors, was a cunning old devil. He caused a rift between Bishop Stapeldon and the Dominican friars.'

'How so?'

'I will tell you,' he said, settling into his seat.

'Henry Ralegh was a shrewd old fellow, and when he died, he wanted his past . . . misdemeanours to be forgotten. So he tried to ensure that his body was one of those nearest the altar. But the cathedral would not guarantee such a prestigious place to a mere Ralegh. It upset Henry so much that he went to the Dominicans and offered them a large sum if they would permit him to live with them as a corrodian and then, when he died, to be buried near their altar. Well, the friars were more than happy to accept the offer, so he retired to the friary, where he lived out his days in gentle prayer so his past might be forgiven. And then, he died.'

'Of course.'

'Aye, but that was the beginning of the trouble. The canons demanded that they might take the body, for only the cathedral has the right to the bodies of the dead. Hah! A funeral is a valuable service, with money for the choir, the wax for candles, the hearse . . . the canons were not willing to give up such a venture just because some wealthy man wanted to have a place at the Final Judgement before all others. No! So two canons and their familias marched to the friary. Their servants broke down doors, smashed the rood screens, beat up the friars and lay brothers who tried to prevent them, and left them despairing of their lives. And these thieves stole the body, the furnishings, the candles and all else of value, and carried the body to the cathedral.'

I could see that a remark was required. 'Um. Goodness,' I said.

'They held the funeral service, pocketed the goods they had purloined, then sent a messenger to the friary, saying, "You can come and collect Ralegh now and bury him wheresoever you wish."'

I yawned.

'But the friars replied that they had no use for the body. The cathedral had taken the body and all the goods, so they could bury him. The cathedral canons were not pleased with that. They had no easy place in which to inter the man. The friars were as stubborn as a winter's gale and refused to discuss the affair further, so the canons had their men pick up the body and carry it to the friars. But the friars saw the canons approaching and locked the gates. So the body was dumped and left to putrefy outside the friary gates. And there he remained.'

'Really?' I was interested despite myself. It is not often that a body is deposited outside a religious institution. 'So the friars had little choice, then?'

'They had all the choice they wanted. The body had been stolen along with the funerary goods, so they refused to accept it. The cathedral denied responsibility. They had the right, of custom long-standing, of all burials and the proceeds. The friary had promised to bury the man without permission. It was up to them to uphold their bargain. And being a Ralegh, I doubt the friars would want him. In any case, the friars refused even to consider such a proposal. The cathedral staff had stolen the body and goods, so the cathedral must find a place for him. That was their view.'

He sighed and beckoned the bottler, holding out his goblet while the lad poured. 'Careful, you whore's brat, don't get wine on my sleeve,' he snarled and then turned his smiling face to me. 'It took four days, and this was mid-summer, mind you. You know what a decomposing body is like after that time in the heat? Appalling! And the city had noticed. It took men of standing and stature, the members of the Freedom of the City, and even the sheriff, to remonstrate with the cathedral. They had taken all the proceeds, so it was only reasonable that they should also bury the body. Shamefaced, the cathedral sent their fellows round to collect Ralegh's remains and conduct him back to the cathedral. I believe they buried him somewhere around the font, poor fellow.'

'And that was that.'

'Yes. Oh, there were more arguments over the years. The cathedral has always been in competition. First with the friars. They never liked the appearance of friars in the city – after all, the friars would take alms from people, and that money would not make its way to the cathedral itself – but for the most part, the two lived in moderate harmony. Since the destruction of the friary, the cathedral has been more in competition with the city itself. But you can see that the Raleghs have always been an immoderate family. Whereas my own family is honourable and decent. We have never had such scandals associated with *our* family name. And now there is the latest.'

'Latest what?'

'That bastard robbed me of my ship!' he burst out, and I almost felt I should have to catch his eyeballs as they were forced to fly from their sockets. Fortunately, there was no need, but the man's face took on the colour of an overripe plum, and his eyes blazed with fury.

'Tell me about it,' I said. It was the only way I could see of making him calm down a little.

'It was some months ago. I had a great cargo on its way from France, wines mostly, and I was assured that the ship would come back swiftly. There was nothing to oppose it. But the days passed, and there was no sign of the ship; in the end, I was forced to send a second vessel to enquire after it. You can imagine my rage when I heard that the ship had disappeared! No one knew what had happened to her. All they could tell me was that the ship had left harbour when planned, and no one had seen her since. She was worth a fortune. And there were no squalls, no gales, no intemperate weather. She didn't founder in a storm.'

'And you suspect . . .?'

'I don't *suspect*!' he spat. 'I *know*! It was that jaded pizzle Ralegh! Who else has the ships to steal one of mine? Who else would dare to take my wine and other cargo? He has hated me ever since I managed to snatch a cargo of wines from a French ship, and he thought he could have it! Hah! I showed him then!'

'But you have nothing to show it actually was him?'

'I don't need to. I know what happened as well as I know the sun rises in the east!'

He was getting himself into a fine lather, and his voice was raised loud enough to blow tiles off the roof over our heads, so it was a relief to hear a light step approach. It was the beautiful young Alice. She went to her father's side and smiled at him soothingly, stroking his shoulder as if he were a favourite pet spaniel, and generally making like a cooing dove in his choleric ear. His face once more began to lose the purple colouring, and gradually turned beetroot red, then puce, and finally returned to a wind-beaten leather colour. He gave me a smile in which embarrassment was mingled with pride – in his daughter, I assume. Making a quick apology, he left me alone with his daughter.

Now, you will know that it takes only an instant for me to win the heart of any woman. Leave me alone in the company of a sweet-natured wench or an older mother of six, and I'll soon have them eating out of my hand. It is a curse of mine. With my good features, ready smile and open face that is so apparently honest and without deceit, any woman will be mine in moments. And yet I was forced to try to prevent Alice from falling in love with me. This is no easy task, as you can imagine. Fortunately, she did not swoon to be left alone with me – which has happened, I assure you – but merely to be certain, I rose and took a couple of steps away from her, until the bottler blocked my path and refilled my goblet again. It was good wine. I took a refreshing draught.

'Master Blackjack, you must be so amused at our quaint ways here in the west,' she said. She held up a hand politely to refuse the offer of wine from the servant. He topped up mine instead.

'I assure you, they are not so quaint as those in other places,' I said with feeling, thinking of my adventures in Dartmoor.

'It has been very trying for father in recent months,' she said. She took my free hand. 'You see, so much of his fortune was bound up with the stolen vessel. Not only the cargo but the men, the ship herself. It was a terrible blow for him.'

'But to accuse a fellow merchant – that seems odd. After all, I hear Ralegh has lost his own ship.'

'I know,' she said, pulling my hand towards her slightly. I tried to keep away, but somehow she drew me nearer, her eyes shining with passion, her ringlets bouncing about her lovely face. 'Of course, I have tried to make Father see that the Raleghs would do nothing to offend him, and that they would defend his ships to the death, since all merchants must fear losing their living.'

'What do you think happened to his ship, then?'

'Pirates. The men of Lyme are always said to be very dangerous and will steal any ship.'

'Are there many pirates in these parts?'

'I don't know,' she said, with a charming smile.

'I had heard that some merchants instal spies in other men's businesses,' I said. Perhaps Lane had not been the only one. 'Has your father employed someone recently?'

'You must ask him,' she said.

We were quite close now, and if it were not for the bottler, I might well have succumbed to her charms, but just then the fellow poured more wine into my goblet, which I had not expected. The sudden increase in weight made me start, and a goodly portion sprang from it and up into the air, drenching my hand and then my foot as well.

'A cloth, fool!' my companion burst at a volume that could have shattered rocks. I confess that her sudden bellow made me start again, and I snatched my hand from her.

She made a pretty apology, expressing the utmost contrition. 'He is very new to his job. Our last bottler had to be let go, for he was ridiculously incompetent at many tasks. A very old man, I fear. You must know how difficult it is to find good servants – especially in a city like Exeter. I suppose it is easier in a great city like London?'

I considered my own servant – a scrawny young example of the worst dregs of London life – and could not help but grimace. 'If it is as hard as it is in London, it must be enormously burdensome,' I said.

She gave a rich little laugh and patted at her skirts as the bottler returned with a handful of linen and began to rub at my codpiece as though he was honing a block of granite for a cannonball.

'Hey! Stop that!' I shouted, and the fool dropped his cloths in sudden terror.

'Go, boy,' she snapped. 'You will need to lose your post for this!'

'But, Mistress . . .'

'Go!' I said, 'Go! Leave us, you fool.'

He scampered out, but thankfully we were not left unchaperoned. As soon as he passed through the door, Shapley himself returned, all effusive shock to have heard what had happened to me. 'My dear Master Blackjack, my most profound apologies! How that incompetent could have . . . pray, allow me to refill your—'

'No, no, I thank you,' I said quickly, taking my goblet out of his reach as he proffered the jug once more. 'I've already taken much more than I should.'

'Then food,' Shapley said, and this time he would brook no refusal.

The bottler was apparently forgiven. He returned a short while after, and I was forced to wait while he and two others made up a trestle table, smoothing a white sheet over it, and then set out a selection of pewter plates and all the paraphernalia of a good feast, while I was once more submitted to a detailed interrogation of my life, income, house and other details that a prospective son-in-law might be expected to divulge.

All the while, the maid Alice stood listening intently. She appeared perfectly content to have me examined, as though she had no interest in Richard Ralegh whatever. Before long, her mother joined us: a large, bustling, vacuous woman of some five-and-thirty years. She made up for the grim appearance of Margaret, the fierce maidservant who had dismissed me in the streets when I met her with Alice. I gave her a tight little nod of recognition, but she seemed entirely unconcerned by my attitude and put on a show of smiling, as though attempting to be convivial, but it was like trying to change a face cast from cold steel. It required a hammer to alter it – and I would have been glad to endeavour such a remodelling after she had left me to the mercies of Richard and William. She was not to know that they were moderately honourable fellows. I could have been killed, for all she knew. Bending, with an immense effort, the edges of her mouth into a faint approximation of happiness, I could see that her eyes remained bleakly suspicious of me.

There were some aspects of our conversation that did spark my interest, however. All the while, as you can imagine, my thoughts tended to run along the lines of *What if Ned, the Troll and Adam were to find me in the streets again?* I felt sure that the trio would forget any promises made to the dean about not harming me. After all, they had harmed poor Lane badly enough!

'Your dean at the cathedral, I met him last night,' I said at one point when the conversation was slowing. 'He struck me as a very forceful fellow.'

'He is quite the blade about town,' Shapley said. His mood became sombre at the mention of the dean. 'He's often muscling in on things. He *claims* it is because he is protecting his little flock here, but I believe he merely wishes to maximize the funds available to him – and the cathedral.'

'How does he do that?'

'By any and all means available to him. I have seen him employ the law, bullying or simple violence. He has a number of thugs I wouldn't let on one of my ships. They are supposed to be there to protect the cathedral's yard, but they swagger about the city like henchmen for a lord.'

'I have met some of them. Three, I am sure, were responsible for the death of the man Lane.'

Shapley lowered his head and glanced at me sideways. 'I should be cautious about telling that to too many people in the city,' he said. 'News of such talk soon gets back to the dean.'

'But what would a man of the cloth be doing worrying about things like that?' I asked.

It was, yes, a foolish question, and Shapley was perfectly within his rights to be sarcastic. Fortunately, he saved himself from inflicting that indignity on me. Instead, he pointed out that even canons in a cathedral have to eat, and although a dean would be well catered for in the hierarchy, still there was nothing to prevent him from enjoying profit from his own investments.

'He has a successful trade with several French vintners and brings over a lot of wine. Then again, he has a finger in many other pies as well, and, as I say, he protects his investments jealously. There have been times when he has brought in goods over my head and almost cornered the market in certain areas. Aye, and worse.'

'Worse?' Most cities tried to keep all transactions open and visible to any onlookers, so that the probity of each transaction was transparent, but some would still try it on.

'Some say he has tried to force the price up for some of his own goods by bullying other sellers to raise their prices.'

Suddenly, I had a vision of Ned. Perhaps that was his function for the dean: he was a bully who would go to stalls and force market traders to adhere to whatever price the dean wanted. 'Perhaps that is why he used his three bullies,' I mused aloud.

'The three you spoke of? Perhaps. They sound like his fellows, certainly. The poxed vipers,' he added with a scowl. He belched, put on a sour expression and drank again, moodily.

'When Lane's body was found, I saw Ralegh with the dean and another man, John Wolfe.'

Shapley nodded grimly. 'I count my fingers after taking his hand. I wouldn't wish him near me in a darkened alleyway. He's the sort of fellow who, when you greet him, it is worth a glance around in case he has brought men with him. I've heard of others who have been forced to suffer when they competed with him.'

'What would he and the other two have been doing at Lane's body?'

'Making sure he was really dead, I expect,' Shapley said sourly. He held out his goblet and continued while the bottler brought the level back up to the rim. 'Lane had a marvellous ability to annoy others – the dean by his constant complaining that he should be taken back by the Church, and we merchants because he accused us of many vile acts.'

'What sort of acts?'

'Hah! When Ralegh lost his ship, Lane had the damned impudence to suggest that another merchant in the city was responsible! As though we were little better than pirates!'

I said nothing at that point. If there was one thing I was quite convinced of, it was that a merchant would stop at nothing to prevent a competitor from growing richer. A man like Shapley would be sorely distressed to think that another might be happy and the proud owner of more profit.

'So there have been at least two ships lost recently?'

'More than that. At least three. Hardwick over at Exmouth lost one as well. It has been a hard few months. Odd, though.'

'What is?'

'Well, usually you would expect that other sailors would see wreckage of some sort, or perhaps find a body or two when a ship goes down. But these three sank without leaving a trace. As if the devil himself had a part in their disappearance.'

While we were eating, I had relaxed considerably under the influence of Shapley's wine and returned to the conversation about Lane's body.

'Tell me,' I said, 'I was chatting to the vicar of St Sidwell's yesterday, and he was most upset, I thought, to hear of Lane being killed.'

'That is little surprise,' Shapley said. 'Lane was the vicar's brother. He had been a priest himself, but he refused to consider giving up his wife and child with the return to the Latin faith. Besides, he was known to be incontinent. Few women were safe from his advances.' I noticed that his wife seemed unnaturally quiet at this, staring fixedly at a small hole in the wall. He continued, 'Of course, he was thrown from his church and livelihood. I understand he was a persuasive orator; when he gave a sermon, the congregation listened. There are few men who can hold a crowd like that. Hah! He put his skills to good use, persuading women into his bed.'

I smiled, but I could sense that Mistress Shapley was uncomfortable, and the conversation was swiftly changed. She cannot have enjoyed such talk over her meal.

After the meal, I was forced to remain while Shapley spoke to me at length about his mercantile interests, the goods he imported, the wool and timber he shipped abroad. He grew expansive, drinking more and more wine, his head gradually sinking to his chest, waving his wine with ever slower gestures, until the cup tilted alarmingly and emptied itself on the floor, while a low, rumbling earthquake could be heard. On further investigation, I found it was Shapley himself, snoring fit to make the cathedral tremble.

In the face of a concerted effort by Alice and her mother to prevent me, neither of whom was abetted by the grim-faced Margaret, I contrived to make my escape. It was not easy, and I was forced to declare a prior meeting, but in the end, I succeeded in leaving and made my way towards the Ralegh house. Not without many long sighs from Alice, who appeared to decline before my eyes at the thought that I might leave. It is difficult to have a magnetic personality like mine. So often it leads to women being disappointed. However, I was glad to evade her clutches. The thought of Richard Ralegh's anger, were I to make off with his inamorata, was not something I wished to dwell upon.

It was interesting that the vicar of St Sidwell's was related to Lane. The man was clearly upset to learn of his brother's death, and the speed with which he made off on hearing the news showed his affection. Or that he felt his brother might have left something in his estate which the vicar could take. No, on second thoughts, that was highly unlikely. The vicar had not struck me as the thieving type. I had known many thieves and fraudsters in my time, and I was sure he was not of their ilk.

I reached Carfax and glanced in, naturally, at the alley where Lane had been, and from whence he was stolen away. I stood there for some while, wondering. Someone had killed Lane. Ned and his merry confederates had definitely beaten him, although I could see no advantage to them in killing Lane. Had that someone then knocked down the watchman and taken Lane's body away? Perhaps with some idea of concealing it. More likely the murderer had just hurled Lane's corpse into the river. It flowed fast enough past Exeter to carry the body to the sea.

However, it was a long and weary march to the water's edge. A man might move Lane with the benefit of a wheelbarrow, but he would be an unwieldy encumbrance even then. And the fellow could hardly hope to wheel his burden as far as the water without someone passing comment. He would assuredly be stopped and questioned. The only way to avoid attention would be to conduct the passage at the dead of night – but that would hold its own difficulties. After all, the city's gates would be closed and barred. A lone wheelbarrow carrying a dead man would be held up by locked gates. I know many porters who would be happy enough to lift the bars on a gate for a small consideration of, say, two pennies, but there would be the obvious risk that the porter would deprecate a murderer passing with a decomposing and rigor-mortised figure in a wheelbarrow. It was the sort of thing that would excite interest.

The alley itself was closed at the farther end – a dead end – so the body could hardly be pushed that way. The wall led only to the cathedral precinct, and a member of the cathedral congregation would be likely to take offence at bodies being thrown over walls with the cheerful abandon of a man tossing away a chicken bone. Lane's body must have been concealed somewhere else if it could not be borne to the river for disposal.

And then I realized that I had not considered one important aspect of the affair: the vicar. The man was Lane's brother, Shapley had told me, and soon after I told the vicar about his brother's body lying in the alleyway, he had shot off into the city like a greyhound spotting a hare. But what would he want with his brother's corpse? Perhaps just to save it from the cost of an Exeter funeral. Shapley had mentioned that Lane had a wife and child. It was possible that Lane wished to save the bereaved woman from the cost of a funeral service in the cathedral. If Lane had managed to take the body away, he could have wheeled it to his own church, and surely the porter at the East Gate would have waved him through, since he was a priest, after all. And then he could install Lane in a small grave there at his church where he could give his brother the burial he craved and remember him in his prayers.

Yes, that made sense. Which priest would not want to do the best for his own brother? And if the brother was suddenly deceased, surely the vicar would want to provide him with a decent burial.

Of course, the problem with that was the potential risk. I imagined a vicar who stole a body from the cathedral could anticipate a severe mauling in the bishop's court, after all. The money he was taking from the cathedral coffers would be missed, and the bishop would not be pleased to have lost it.

It was none of my affair. I was glad to look to the future and start to plan my journey back to London, away from this madhouse of competing merchants and religious types. The courser had been expecting me these two days past, and assuredly his price would have risen, because there is little that would please a courser better than a customer who was desperate to leave the city but could find no beast to carry him. Kempton the courser would know full well that I could get no other mount, and his price would accordingly increase. It was the way of the business.

I considered going to visit the man again, but just now the evening was starting to draw in. The sky had begun to take on that silken sheen that indicated twilight was already almost gone, and the streets were emptying as people repaired to taverns and inns and prepared to relax at the end of a long day of work and struggle. It was too late to think of heading up to the north to see the courser. In preference, I was about to return to the Ralegh household when I saw Richard and William approaching. They hailed me with enthusiasm, and I was immediately bombarded with questions about Alice and how she fared? I shot a look at William, who merely rolled his eyes.

'Richard, Master Ralegh,' I said when he had stopped to draw breath, 'please compose yourself. Let us find a tavern and I will happily tell you all I can.'

We had no sooner settled in our seats than a happy, buxom woman entered. She took in the three of us at a glance, and it was plain that she recognized in me a man of no little position and importance. The fact that she turned to me first was proof enough, were proof needed, that she could tell which was a man of London. She smiled at me, and I gave her a happy Jack grin in return. So often these small, provincial inns are without the basic necessities, but looking at this woman now, I was fairly sure that she had a wayward eye that would be more than happy to see to accommodating any little desires I might have. As she passed, I gave her thigh an experimental squeeze, and apart from advising me to remove my hand, she made no comment. After my anxious experience with Alice Shapley, I felt sure that this woman would be an excellent bed-warmer and must ease my frustration. I would speak with her later, I decided.

However, first I had to speak to the infatuated Richard about the object of his desires.

'How was she? Did she look sad? She must have! We have not been able to speak for weeks now. Her mother is a vicious, cruel woman, Master Blackjack, is she not? I would fall on the ground before Alice if it would save her stepping into dogshit, or lay down my life for her if she was in danger. I would do anything for her. Dear Alice!'

William gave a grunt of frustration. 'You were happy enough to forget her charms when presented with the view of Moll Thatcher's house.'

'That was different, as you know. Besides, a man has a need for entertainment. If I marry her, I dare say I will be less in need of places like Moll's,' Richard said, but from his expression, his conviction was less than persuasive. He was one of those incontinent fellows who try to fool themselves into thinking they will change. For my part, I reckoned he would be as likely to give up the appeal of new female companionship as I was myself – and I had no intention of becoming thus entangled. Even though it was true to say that Alice Shapley would be an attractive bedmate. And with that, I was reminded of her apparent interest in me as a suitor, and a shiver ran down my spine.

Richard noticed my shudder and was instantly eager for news. 'Was she well enough, apart from her loneliness? Does she pine for news of her lover?'

I recalled her attention to me and managed to nod. 'She was plainly distressed, although she managed to conceal it from most of the party. But I have some experience of young women, and she could not fool me,' I said stoutly. I did not say that I had spent the entire interview full of concern that the bint might at any moment declare her love for me. I would not risk Richard's passion with such a comment.

The conversation flagged somewhat, since Richard's only topic of conversation was the welfare of his maid, and William appeared to have less interest in the woman than I, so it was with relief that I spied the vicar of St Sidwell's at another table.

He was drinking with a kind of unhurried determination, like a sailor who has just returned to port after a long voyage, and who is so glad that he wishes to attempt to drain at least one barrel of ale. I left the two, crossing the floor to sit with the vicar.

When he looked up, his face was not that of an accommodating priest. 'What?' he said and returned to his quart pot.

'My friend, how is Maud?'

'What is it to you?' He looked and sounded quite bellicose.

'I was only wondering what had happened to you after we saw her?'

He looked at me from brows that gave him little space for vision. His head was lowered, and his appearance made him appear to be glowering like a squirrel watching a boy walk off with his nuts. 'What is she to you? Eh?'

'Nothing, nothing,' I said hurriedly.

He peered closer. 'Do I know you?'

That was when he began to weep.

There are few things more disconcerting than a man suddenly bursting into tears. I mean, if Alice had turned on the fountains, I would have been mortified and would immediately have searched around for a story or anecdote that could have stayed her weeping and brought about a happier expression, and that would only be natural for a gentleman like me. But to be confronted with a man determined to water his ale with his own wellspring, that is confusing. Naturally, the usual response would be to make fun of such childish behaviour, or to give his head a buffet, but in this case, it would be distinctly ill-mannered. A fellow does not insult or make fun of a priest. Not in these days of Queen Mary's reforms and her determination to foist the old religion on a reluctant kingdom. To mock a priest at this time could cause a short visit to the Tower or a gaol of your personal choice, before being warmed by a serious bonfire before a large crowd of delighted onlookers.

'I . . . um . . .' I said.

'I'm sorry, my son. Sit, please. Take a seat. This will pass shortly.'

He sniffed and wiped his nose with his sleeve. Sitting next to him, I could see that his eyes were bleary and bloodshot, like a man who has been on a day-long drinking session.

'Poor Maud. She is sorely distressed. How can they survive without him? She was so distraught . . . she has no income and nothing put by. I would help if I could, but what can a poor priest do? Her daughter searches for food. I came here to remember poor Roger. How could I comfort his widow? Poor Roger. Poor Maud. He was my elder brother, you know?' he said and looked at me with the mournful eyes of a bloodhound who had lost his trail. 'He never hurt anyone, and someone struck him down in his prime. Someone knocked him on the pate so hard his skull was broken.'

'And now he is gone,' I said.

I don't know, sometimes, why I make such comments. It was obviously, now I look back on it, rather an insensitive comment. That fact was soon borne upon me by his fist. It shot out and grabbed the front of my jerkin. Pulling hard, the vicar managed to demonstrate to me that a man who works in his own church, lifting perhaps only the occasional chest, mostly spending his time with quill and parchment, can yet have the muscles of an Atlas. I yelped with alarm as I found myself hauled over the table until, to my startled consternation, I was mere inches from his face. His eyes were trying to focus on me, and I could see them moving until they almost crossed, before he closed one eye and peered at me with one glaring iris as black as night. Then he lifted his other hand, and I flinched, expecting a blow that would flatten my nose across my face like an old egg broken on a griddle. To my immense relief, he suddenly took on a pained expression, as if he realized that he had pulled the wrong fellow over the table.

'Sorry,' he mumbled. 'Wasn't thinking. Yes, he's gone. Dead. I'll never see him again, this side of Judgement!'

'No,' I explained. 'Someone has taken his body from the alley. The coroner hasn't seen him and held his inquest, but someone has already removed your brother.'

He let go of me and flopped back like a worm dropped on to stone. He goggled at me. 'Removed?'

'He isn't there.'

Suddenly, he lurched to his feet. It took a fair bit of wobbling back and forth before he was stable, but he showed spirit in attempting it. 'They promised me,' he declared to no one in particular. 'They swore! He was to be safe, no matter what!'

'Who did? Who promised?'

'The dean and his friends! The whoresons, they swore to me that they would not hurt him!'

It is possible that you are a little confused at this point. I can happily confess that I was.

So far, I had learned that the dead man had been a priest. He had been married, but his widow and daughter would soon be destitute. The dean had happily told me that the man was a pest and nuisance to all, and Shapley had confirmed that. The brute Ned, who worked for the dean, had admitted to beating him up on the dean's orders. So it was clear enough that Lane was disliked by the members of the cathedral. Perhaps Ned's attack, merely beating the man, had gone awry, and he and his two merry companions had in fact killed the poor devil? I know many people have been accidentally slain when knocked on the head, after all. Fellows in the street minding their own business, who were suddenly assaulted by robbers and coshed over the pate a little too enthusiastically, and who succumbed to the blow, never to waken. Yes, it has happened often enough. It was curious that Ned seemed to be quite angry when he denied that he had taken part in a murder. He was happy enough to confess to the beating, but the idea that he had committed a murder enraged him.

Yet now the vicar was telling me that he had been personally assured that his brother would not be taken away when he was dead? Or was he saying that his brother should not have been killed in the first place? I was about to ask when he swayed, stepped sideways to get past the table and then very slowly toppled to the side. A handy pillar was within reach, and he casually reached a hand out to it for support, looking mildly perplexed when he missed it by six inches. Still, he kept on leaning towards it, and I watched his eyes widen as he gradually succumbed; they focused momentarily on the pillar with a kind of accusatory horror, and then he disappeared behind a bench.

It took the assistance of both William and Richard to recover the priest from the floor. We pulled a table and two benches from our way first, because the vicar had managed to slide behind them and now lay comfortably squeezed between the wall and the bench. He had an alarmed expression on his face, like a child who has just realized that his theft from the biscuit tin has been noticed by both parents.

'Wha' 'appened?'

We eased him back upright and studied him. Nothing appeared broken or damaged, other than a slight swelling on his left brow and a small scratch that wouldn't even merit a scar. William and Richard hunkered down in front of him, speaking slowly and gently, while he carefully listened and made an effort to concentrate on them, although from the way he kept widening his eyes and lifting his brows, it was clear that their faces were little better than blurs to him.

'He can't make his way back to the church in this state,' William said.

The host stood wiping his hands on his apron. 'I won't have him stay here in the bar all night. If you will pay for a room, I have a bed upstairs he can use, but I wouldn't want to leave him alone like that. He'll sleep, but he might throw up and drown in his own vomit.'

It was hardly an attractive vision, but there was an appealing aspect to it. I had no wish to return to the Shapleys' home, and the Ralegh house was little better. This inn had the advantage to me that it was neither of those houses and, in addition, I might be able to make good my escape the following morning, hurry to the courser's paddock and rent a horse, and at last make my way from this horrible city and get home.

'Someone needs to stay with the poor fellow,' I said.

Richard looked at me with a curled lip. 'You want to stay here with him? He'll probably throw up over you in the middle of the night.'

'Better that,' I said virtuously, 'than he should be left to suffocate and die. I would not have that on my conscience.'

William was watching me with a cool expression. He nodded. I felt sure that he had already divined my intention. Now he gave a small smile and nodded. 'I will walk back to the Raleghs' house and fetch your belongings,' he said. 'That will save you one task.'

'Thank you,' I said. 'I would appreciate that.'

And thus it was that, within the hour, I was settled in the tavern's bar with a pot of ale before me and, at last, peace from the tumultuous folk I had met. In the morning, God willing, I would find a horse and make my way east, never to return to this festering land of Devon.

It was a cheery enough little hovel, this tavern where I was to pass the night. The fire was a glorious blaze, and because there was no market, the place was not overcrowded. I could be assured of a seat all evening, and my only penance was the conversation of a number of shepherds and cattlemen, from the odours they gave off. My chamber with the vicar was small, but it had space for two beds, and with the lack of market-goers, I would not have to share my bed with a snoring tradesman or farmer, who would fart and raise the bedclothes, or turn and throw an arm about me. Such things have happened to me at similar hostelries before now. Tonight, I intended a not-late night and an early rise.

The host was an accommodating fellow. He had a rather ingratiating manner and, like so many in his line of business, could talk for an age without seemingly drawing breath, but he was very attentive. Barely had I finished my first pot of ale than he appeared with a fresh jug.

'How many nights will you require, Master? Only the one? That is sad, indeed. But perhaps you will want to return before long, hey? And now, what about some drink? I have a small chamber behind here, where you will be alone in peace and comfort, if it pleases you, and I can bring a spiced wine, flavoured with a little apple and ginger, and some brandy to warm you, if you would like. And for food, we have a good stew, and bread, of course, but is that all you have in those bags? We will have them off you and . . .'

All the while he was leading me from his front room to a pleasant little parlour where the fire was already made up, and the smell of gravy and wine rose from the pots at the fireside. I sniffed the odours eagerly, and soon I was sitting on a high-backed settle with a large, hot cup warming my hand. While the place may have looked dilapidated from the outside, inside it was a snug, cosy place, and an ideal shelter from the chill of the evening.

I congratulated him on the quality of his drink.

'I am glad to hear it, Master,' he said, pouring from his jug to top up my cup and setting it back in its place. 'You are from London, I understand?'

'Yes. I travelled to Okehampton on business,' I said haughtily. 'But I am needed home. My master will be expecting me.'

'How is London? What is it like? Is it truly much bigger than Exeter?' he asked eagerly, and I sighed. This was one of those evenings when I was to be forced to give a full description of the city.

'Perhaps a little ale to ease my throat?' I said, draining my cup. I might as well gain a drink for my efforts.

Many are the times I have been forced to tell barbarians from distant towns and villages of the marvels of the great capital city of our kingdom, but although it is interesting at first to see how the listeners' eyes widen and their mouths fall open as I tell of palaces, the great carriages, the wonderful processions and celebrations on feast days, or the magnificent travelling players who entertain so marvellously, it is a pastime which soon palls.

I was glad of the food – he served a good stew with thick dumplings, then slabs of cheese and some bread, washed down with a good quantity of ale – but the incessant questions grew tedious. I longed for a little more robust entertainment. The host's wife appeared to have decided that my hand on her thigh was a gross insult, but it struck me that one or two of the serving maids were tolerably clean. Once I had given the innkeeper a surfeit of information, I decided to go and look at them. One of them might merit a small investment to keep my bedding warm. Meanwhile, there was an increasing amount of noise from the bar. When the host was content, I left my parlour and wandered through to the main hall again.

In my absence, the room had filled. A pair of overworked skivvies were doing their best to satisfy the thirst of a number of enthusiastic drinkers – most of them were youngsters, and from the look of them, I assumed they must be apprentices.

I sidled in at the door and tried to push my way to the bar, receiving a few elbows in the side as I went, as though only the young were entitled to an ale. I grew irritable enough to ignore their protests and continued until I had reached the first row behind the bar itself, and waited, attempting to catch the eye of a flame-haired beauty who stood looking alarmed at the rabble before her, as well she might. The host's wife was nowhere to be seen.

There was no shoving through to the bar itself. The apprentices were two deep, blocking all access. I tried to make myself known, but before I could, a tall, slim fellow before me bellowed at the congregation to be still, for their unholy row was terrifying the chit at the bar. Voices were raised rudely rejecting his words, but on hearing that, he growled a challenge. Even a group of youngsters were unwilling to take on the risk of being beaten senseless by him, and they subsided grumpily, while he turned, and suddenly I had a shock.

It was Wolfe.

He had a low brow, eyebrows that met over his nose, and piercing brown eyes. For all his bookish appearance, I was forced to modify my first impression of him as an ascetic. His frame was slim, but it had a wiry strength. He was lean and bronzed, and under his plain black cap he had steady, deep-set eyes with a scattering of crows' feet at the corners, but there was no humour in them just now. For a moment, I feared that he might have seen me with his wife earlier.

Glancing at me, he gave me a short nod, as of a gentleman greeting an equal, before bellowing, 'Keep the noise down, ye princocks! Have a thought for the poor maids trying to serve us! It's not their fault there are so many of us here.'

A few of the youngsters made jocular remarks about his appearance, and whether they should drag him outside and dunk him in a horse trough, but the hotter heads were quickly persuaded to be silent, and a space appeared before him, giving him access to the bar. I managed to barge in at his side and slipped the auburn-haired beauty a coin for an ale. She was a pretty little thing. Full, red lips, slightly slanted greenish eyes, cheeks like a pair of apples. Soon I had a foaming jug in my hand, and when my neighbour left, he beckoned me to follow him. I gave up my post at the bar and took my perch on a bench next to him.

He sipped at a cup of wine, but all the while his gaze was fixed on the group at the bar.

'Is there some cause for celebration?' I asked.

He looked at me for a moment without speaking. When his gaze returned to the brutes at the bar, he nodded slowly. 'Aye, these lubbers are all keen to enjoy their drinking. They had the day off to celebrate the anniversary of the release from the rebels, but they want to continue to drink themselves into oblivion today as well! Youth! All they think of is singing, swiving and sucking down ale.'

Luckily, after my last weeks in Devon, I could understand his speech. 'Ah. That was the procession, of course.'

'Aye, the celebration of the city's liberation from the siege. It was Jesus Day. The mayor and all the guildsmen have been up to the cathedral for a service, so now these wastrels stagger and brag in their drinks. Look at them! An unwholesome brood if ever there was one. I swear, the blood of the youngsters today is too thin. When I was a younger man, apprentices knew how to behave and show respect to their elders, but these young fools? I doubt half could tell you the hour of the day without asking. All they think of is women, ale and gambling, and not in that order.'

For all his surly remarks, there was a half-grin on his face, as if he wryly accepted that they were no better and no worse than any other apprentices over the years.

'I wonder whether they would have been guilty of a practical joke at another's expense,' I said, almost without thinking.

'What do you mean?'

'Oh, I was thinking of the fellow found murdered yesterday. You recall? You were there, with Master Ralegh and the cathedral's dean. The body was taken last night, and the man standing guard knocked down.'

'Why would anyone steal the body?'

'You may not recall, but I remember you,' I said, not to be distracted, and there was more than a drop of hauteur in my voice. 'I asked you and Ralegh about hiring a horse, but you were both in too much of a hurry to help me.'

'You were the stranger asking about a horse? Ah, my apologies. Seeing my clerk murdered had left me upset, and I was very short with you. Yes, I was there; you are right. Poor Roger. He was terribly beaten before he was killed. You knew him, I think?'

'Me? No, not at all. He was dead before I arrived in the city. I wonder who could have done that to him.'

'A thief, I have little doubt. He worked for me, and he was assiduous as a clerk. I always found him reliable and hard-working.'

There was something in his eyes then that I didn't like. A flare of anger, perhaps. He was watching me, and I could not be sure whether he was thinking of me or of the clerk. Lane was surely not the target of his ire – could he have noticed me when I was chatting to Mistress Wolfe? But he looked like a man who would have taken action if he suspected me of attempting the seduction of his wife. The thought that he could suspect that caused a small trail of sweat to run down my spine.

But the expression was already gone. In truth, I forgot about it as we continued to talk, because soon he would give me an idea that would save me the trouble of seeking a mount.

'Great heavens! A horse? You would be better served to take a ship. Go to the quay, ask for a passage to the coast and take a vessel to London. There are always shipmasters happy to take passengers who will pay their way. It would hardly be as expensive as taking horses every day, riding to a town and changing your steed, then seeking a fresh one to take you to the next town. Think of the effort! If you were so inclined, you could try to purchase a fresh mount, but think of the time involved and the difficulties! How much would a room at inns cost every night – and how clean would an inn in the wilds of some heaven-forsaken hole be? You would gather fleas like a hound! Whereas you could be sitting in your own cabin, with good food and wine brought to you. A comfortable cot in which to sleep, the gentle rocking of the waves – how could you think of a horse in comparison? You would be stuck in all weathers, burning one day and freezing the next, or drenched in a sudden downpour and forced to wait until the rivers subsided. Even if things went well, you would be stuck jolting along on the back of a spavined beast, constantly on the lookout for outlaws and footpads of all types, worried that you might be set upon and robbed or murdered. Well, it is your choice, of course, but for me, the sea makes for a better passage. That is my conviction.'

He passed me a fresh cup of ale and I was forced to admit the truth of his words. There was logic in them. I had seen enough of the rough peasantry of Devon to believe that the likelihood of robbery was all too great. And sitting in a warm cabin with a trencher of good food before me, a pot of wine to hand, was preferable to the idea of jerking about on the back of a feeble old brute that had been saved from the tannery and glue makers by the courser's attempts to steal my hard-earned money.

'Do you know of such a shipmaster? I would be able to pay a little for the journey to London,' I ventured hopefully.

'Aye, there are many,' he said thoughtfully. Then his face cleared and he slammed a heavy fist on to the table's top. 'By heaven, I have it! I have heard that the *Thomas* will sail in a couple of days. That would be perfect for you – a magnificent vessel, modern, strongly built, fast and sleek. She has a cargo to deliver to London, and I am sure her master could be prevailed upon to take you.'

'That is wonderful,' I said. It sounded like the perfect solution.

It did not occur to me then that he seemed very keen to see me aboard a ship.

After my discussion with my new friend, I was keen to return to my room and get a good night's sleep. Tomorrow I could recover my few belongings, and thence make my way to the quay to take a boat to the coast. It would not be long, Wolfe had assured me, before the vessel would set sail, and then I could hope to fly around the coast in comfort as far as London itself.

It was only a little later that Master Wolfe set off to his home. I remained in my seat, feeling that all was well with the world. A fresh ale in my hand, and I was keen to go to my chamber, but I was lonely. With the vicar in his state of utter inebriation, he would hardly be concerned were I to bring a bedmate with me, and I had my eyes on the auburn-haired temptress at the bar. She caught my eye more than once but made no effort to come and see what I wanted. She would hardly be able to ignore my advances. For her to gain the interest of a gentleman from London would naturally be enormously flattering. So I remained where I was, supping my wine and waiting for the crowds to die down a little, so that I might speak with her without having to bellow.

The apprentices were gradually disappearing. One or two sat still on their benches, mouths agape, sleeping off their gluttony; five still propped up the bar, discussing matters which they considered of great importance, and which would, truth be told, be hard for them to recall the following morning as they went to work. It was the sort of conversation to be heard in taverns up and down the country, wherever apprentices and other youngsters gathered. Each was astonished by the depth of their friendship for their neighbour, and all were determined to demonstrate their affection with back slaps, hugs and even a few kisses. Happily, though, the wench at the bar was soon free, and I made my way to her to offer her a cup of something strong. As I approached, she slipped out of the chamber into the room behind, and I was left standing at the bar.

Some little while later, the host returned and stood behind the bar as the last of the revellers collected their sleeping companions, and then he made it plain to me that I should go to my bedchamber. I thought of asking him about the auburn-haired beauty, but there was something about his manner that dissuaded me. I also took note of the fact that where his hair was not grizzled, it had a distinctly auburn tinge. Now, in

London, I am used to a cosmopolitan community, in which a father will be happy to sell a daughter for a consideration, but I did not get the impression that this host would appreciate such an offer. He appeared most unwelcoming just now. It was, I have to say, tempting to traipse out behind the bar in an attempt to see her and persuade her to keep my bed warm, especially since, were I to be embarked on a ship in the coming days, it was unlikely that I would see so appealing a young face for some days or even a week, but a second glance at the landlord's face was enough to persuade me that such an option was not likely to win me a bedmate. It was more likely to win me another knock on the head, and this time possibly a stronger one, like that which had felled Lane.

I returned to my bedchamber, grimacing at the sound of the vicar's snoring. There are some men who can snore moderately quietly and without irritating others who might need their own rest. Sadly, the vicar was not built from that mould. He had a curious, steady drone on the inhalation, and a whistling, whiffling out-draught. The problem was less the noise, but rather the delay. The snore would waken me, and then I would be forced to wait for what seemed like an age for the susurration of air over his tonsils.

It was intolerable. I threw a boot at him, which caused a near suffocating snort, but soon he settled back into his steady graunching and whistling like a windmill in a gale. In the end, I gave up and walked out to the corridor, where I sat down at the wall and dozed till morning.

FOUR
To the Sea

8 August

Anyone who has slept with his back to a wall in a corridor will know how comfortably I slept that night.

I woke with a strain in the back of my neck. My mouth tasted as though a small family of rats had used it for their privy, and I thought that one might have expired there, for my tongue was as furry as one of their pelts. I winced and smacked my lips; I was inordinately thirsty, for some reason. Rising, I realized that my backside was all but frozen, and my legs were as stiff as oaken staffs. This was my second night sleeping on a hard surface, and my body was advising me of this news.

When I managed to stand, I could not help but close my eyes. For some reason, the corridor immediately began to move. Not whirling, you understand, but just gradually slipping away from horizontal. It was rather like sitting on a ship and watching the prow gradually circle around the horizon.

No, it would not be a good morning.

In my bedchamber were two empty beds. I raised my eyebrows to see that the vicar was nowhere to be seen, but the way my head felt, I was not particularly bothered. I picked up my bags and bits and pieces, slung the straps of the bags over my head, and slowly, with several pauses while my hand touched the wall to reassure myself that it was not about to collapse, made my way to the stairs. These, very steep, had a rope for safety at one side, and I clung to this like a drowning man as I slowly made my way downstairs.

The bar that morning had a rather noisome effect on me. I entered, walked to a table and stood quite incapacitated for a few moments. Then the auburn-haired beauty appeared and walked past me carrying a jug of ale, and the odour of it unmanned me. I was forced to leave my bags on the table and hurry out to the privy at the back of the tavern to take some deep, wholesome breaths. The fumes promptly made me sick, and I was forced to return to the bar with a distinctly green feeling about me.

Walking in from that direction, I suddenly saw the vicar at his own table in another corner. I picked up my belongings again and walked to him, taking a seat and watching him with fascination.

He did not stop. At that moment, he was chewing a large, greasy piece of sausage, but he picked up an egg with his spoon and shovelled that in too, swiftly adding a bite of bacon and some bread, washing the lot down with a gulp of ale, from what I could see and smell.

I swallowed. It was close, but I managed to stop myself from running outside again.

The maid came to me and stood near, waiting, a jug of ale in her hand. On the basis that I was sure I could feel no worse, I accepted a pint and sipped slowly. The flavour was rank at first, but I assume it had to do its duty and push the rat's remains down my gullet first. Certainly, by the time I had moved on to my second pint, I felt considerably better. Not that it meant I would think of the sausage or bacon as a suitable filling for my empty stomach.

'Master Blackjack, come, join me!' the priest said, holding out a hand in welcome.

Reluctantly, I did so, watching anxiously as he speared another piece of sausage with his knife and chewed noisily, grease dripping from his chin. It took an effort of will to take my seat with him.

'I have to hurry. I need to see the dean this morning,' the vicar said. He scooped up the last of his egg and pushed that in on top of a slab of rough brown bread, gulped more ale and sat back with a look of repletion on his face. I once saw an adder with an expression like that, basking in the sun on a large rock. Not that the edge of distress had left his face. His brother was still dead.

'Vicar . . . I'm sorry, I've forgotten your name.'

'It's understandable, my son. I'm Father Walter.'

'Of course. Well, Walter, last night you were telling me about your brother, and that you had been promised he would not be hurt, or that they wouldn't remove his body . . . I don't understand. Now you say you must speak with the dean – do you think he was involved in your brother's death?'

He shook his head and glanced around the room. 'No, no, the good dean is a decent man. He would have nothing to do with murder, I am sure. No, but I am a vicar, and my brother was too, although not with Rome. When he chose his family over his post, it left him betrayed and desolate. Luckily, he was a very bright man and set himself up as a clerk. He had friends who were of his own religion,' the vicar added. He looked shifty for a moment, a man watching his words carefully. 'I expect he received some help from them at first.'

'It must have been a quick process,' I said. 'After all, he was still a vicar until recently.'

'Yes, but most of the city is . . . is torn between the old religion and the new.' Walter looked away. 'Look, Master Blackjack, you must know how difficult the last months have been. Here, with family turned against family during the rebellion, it has been even worse. We have seen priest pitted against priest, brother against brother, neighbour against neighbour. It has been terrible. And we have survived; our city has survived. That was the reason for the procession the day before yesterday, and the sermon for the mayor in the cathedral – because the city showed itself to be above such matters. This city tends to look after its children. Roger had friends here. I just hope that . . . that someone will aid his widow. She is a precious lady and doesn't deserve to starve.'

'I have heard,' I said slowly, 'that some families used to pit brother against brother on purpose. If one fought for the King, and another fought for the King's opponents, it meant that one brother could survive to inherit the family's lands without risking confiscation of all.'

'Perhaps so, my son. I don't think that works in matters of Our Lord,' Walter said.

'But you did remain friendly with him, even though he had left your faith?'

'He was my brother.'

'And he left the Church and became a clerk supported by others of his faith,' I mused.

'He did not deserve death!'

'Who promised he would be safe?'

He looked shifty at that, but he was no dissembler. 'The dean has grown dissatisfied with him recently.'

'In what way?'

'Roger would keep badgering the Church. He was committed, you see. Why should the congregation not see the words of God written in English? Why should they not hear prayers in English, speak the prayers in English? Why should peasants not understand the religion they profess? It is unreasonable! So, Roger wanted his church back. He never agreed that he should leave his wife and child. He worked tirelessly to bring the Word of God to the people. He had lost his post in his church, but that would not stop him from proclaiming the Word of God to all who would hear him. And that often meant deriding the cathedral, and then . . .' He looked away.

'He put himself in danger by upsetting the wrong men, you mean,' I said for him.

'They want to quash all debate. Obviously, there is no debating the Word of Our Lord, but my foolish brother sought to question the Catholic Church. I imagine he became a thorn in the side of men who sought to support the Church, and they decided to remove him. But I spoke to the dean and apologized, and the dean swore that he would protect Roger. The dean gave me his word that he would speak to his henchmen and ensure that Roger was protected. And now he is dead, and, worse, they have taken his body to hide it! How could someone dare to take his body and prevent it from having a Christian burial? It's one thing to kill a man, but to willingly threaten his immortal soul?'

He sat there shaking his head with confusion that at least leavened his anger.

I attempted to reason with him. 'Vicar, you should probably leave matters as they are for now.'

'How can I? I must find my brother's body so he can be properly interred.'

'But if you go to powerful men and say things you may have cause to regret very quickly . . .'

'I will regret nothing.'

'Vicar, if you are killed as well, what then will become of Roger's widow and child? What will become of them? They need you now.'

'I can do nothing, other than try to win them justice. I cannot – I must not – get close to them. That would be a short journey to ruin.'

After my own experience with the dean, I somehow doubted that I would see the priest again. Walter had a burning urge for justice, and I knew little about justice, other than that it was expensive, and very often deadly.

'My advice is, do not go to the dean today. It can only lead to danger for you, and for them.'

But of course, he wouldn't listen.

I left him a short while later, and after settling my bill with the host, regretfully taking my farewell of his daughter, I stood outside. It was a short walk to Carfax from there, and soon I was walking down the lane to the East Gate, where I hoped to find a craft to carry me to the sea.

The road was exceedingly steep and quite narrow. There was no need to build a roadway wide enough for carts, when no horse could drag a carriage up it, nor hold a carriage on the way down. At the bottom, it was so steep that steps had been used to tame the angle. These were themselves a trial to walk down with tired legs and a sore head, but I was determined. I was going to leave this hideous city at last, and without regrets.

There were many people here in the city, and a fair number were making their way down the same narrow way. I saw an elderly woman stumble and fall, and a pair of willing women ran to her side and helped her up again before she could roll too far down the steps. I could not help but think that either one of those women could have been a purse dipper, but if they were, they would have been desperate. After all, the old woman was little better than a beggar. If she possessed a clipped penny, I would be surprised.

I made it to the gate, and there I was told I had come to the wrong place. The best place to go if I sought a boat to take me to the coast was the South Gate, and then follow that down to the quay. Still, someone did direct me to leave the city and follow a track below the city walls, past the church of St Edward on the bridge and on to the quayside. That way, at least I should not need to go back up that hill again.

That was the path that I took, miserable and noisome though it was. It passed by the tanneries at Exe Island, a strange, muddy area with deep pits dug where the skins would sit with bark from oak trees and become leather. There were other substances there, too. For some reason, leather works best when it has been steeped in dogs' shit and piss. The scavengers would collect as much as they could every evening and bring the fruits of their searches to the tanners each morning, where they would be thrown into a pit and used to preserve the skins.

No wonder leather is brown.

I passed the tanneries with relief and was soon following a track down a slope towards a series of buildings at the water's side.

It was little more than an accumulation of hovels. Some fishermen had their sheds by the side of the river, and barrels of produce were being rolled and clattered about as I stood there.

I began to make sense of the muddle. Shipmen and their masters were bellowing at stevedores and labourers, trying to get their small craft loaded as quickly as possible. I was surprised to see that there were no larger vessels about, but then I recalled John Wolfe had mentioned that there was a weir, installed to stop Exeter from having a great harbour of her own. Instead, the great landowners of the area had maintained their control of the imports and exports of the city. All goods must be loaded here, shipped down to the coast, whence they could be loaded upon the ocean-going ships, which must in their turn be emptied at the coast and their cargoes laboriously brought up the river to Exeter.

I was worried. Any man would be, in such a barbaric area. I was careful to keep to the middle of such roads as I encountered, while avoiding the central kennel, which was little more than a sewer. I kept my purse in my hand, reminding myself that I had been robbed once already. I had no wish to lose my savings and the profits from the dean as well.

Where should I go? Wolfe had mentioned the *Thomas*, and I was keen to find my way to her. But there was no telling which little rowing boat or which of the small craft would be bound to her. In the end, I reasoned that it mattered little which boat I took. I could take any craft to the coast and there seek out the ship.

A small rowing boat was nudging against the quayside. I bent my feet towards it but had only continued a short way when I felt a familiar tug at my purse. Turning with a furious glare, snatching at the hand which had taken hold, I grasped a slender little wrist.

She grinned like a little imp. 'What, you thought I'd try that again? Not after you fed me, master.'

I released her hand. She had no knife or blade with which to damage my new laces, although I was fain to trust her. 'What are you called?'

Her face fell. 'Most call me—'

'No, what is your name?'

She brightened a little. 'I was christened Edith.'

'Well, Edith, I had thought you would be with your mother.'

'She's not there.'

'Even though you said she was very unwell.'

'Yes, well, she likely wanted to earn some money, so went out to work.'

I looked up. It was late in the afternoon now, and I could all too easily guess what sort of work would leave Maud feeling exhausted and unwell in the morning, and would require her to rise to go to work as dusk encroached. 'Oh,' I said.

'She won't be back for a while.'

'I see.' I looked at her speculatively. A strange feeling of sympathy welled up in me. After all, I had known loss at her age, too. My mother had run away from the beatings my father gave her when drunk, and I had been forced to fend for myself, much as she did. And now she was here at the quay – I wondered whether Maud was here too, plying the only trade a widow could be sure would guarantee a few coins for food.

It was an interesting thought. Many whores worked at docks, offering hard-working shipmen a quick knee-trembler to celebrate their return after a traumatic voyage or to relax before they set off again. Perhaps her mother was here? A brief encounter would hardly delay my journey, after all, and if I were to be aboard ship for days, there would be few enough opportunities for a good mattress walloping, unless I succumbed to the advances of a lewd shipman, and that was not likely.

I looked down at her eager, hungry face, and the thought died. Better that I give this chit a few pennies for some food. I put my hand to my purse, but just then the child took a couple of paces away from me. Soon after, a firm hand slapped me on the back. It was John Wolfe, and he prodded my belly with no subtlety when I faced him. 'Good morning, Master Blackjack. I hope I see you well?'

'I am well enough, I thank you,' I lied suavely.

He glanced up at the sky. 'You should hurry to the coast if you want to catch the *Thomas*. She'll be sailing soon, I daresay.'

I indicated that I was already hurrying, and he smiled. I thought it was like the smile of a leashed mastiff who knows he has chewed through his tether. While he spoke to me of Weston, the ship's master, my eyes were gazing behind him, wondering whether his wife was with him today. She would make an excellent partner in mattress wrestling, I thought, and her wayward eye while talking to me yesterday led me to believe that she would need little in the way of persuasion. Alas, I could see no sign of her.

Wolfe had soon exhausted his polite conversation and strode off, for all the world like a Spanish galleon under full sail, bucketing through the rough waves of people and leaving them scattered in his wake.

'You should be careful of John Wolfe. He's not a good man.'

'How do you know that?' I scoffed.

'He beats people with no money or home. Or others who cross his path. Any beggar will feel his stick. He's not . . .'

I held up my hand to stem the flow of anger, but it only served to make her gabble.

'He's a friend to the dean of the cathedral and his men, and they are cruel to everyone!'

'I'm sure he's horrible,' I said. I had heard enough. A beggar may well dislike an honest gentleman for a real or perceived insult, but another gentleman is a different matter, and obviously I was a better judge of character than this child. I was, I fear, a little peremptory. 'Well, no matter. I have a ship to catch, and that means I must hurry to the coast.'

'Don't you trust me?' she asked, and her eyes were filled with almost authentic tears.

I patted her on the head, dropped some coins in her hand and left her, musing that a fellow should ignore the ravings of children, especially when they had attempted to cut the man's purse.

It would be some hours before I learned how correct the child was about Master John Wolfe.

I ignored her warning. After all, what would a child know of men like John Wolfe? He was clearly a successful merchant, a man with contacts, who knew the ways of trade and business. I have known such as him, and they tend to be ruthless, yes, and not particularly considerate of the needs of young beggars, it is true, but as a man with contacts who knew about ships, he was invaluable. And a great deal safer than someone providing me with a horse and pointing me in the direction of London.

At the quay were scores of men. All were silent, while shipmen pointed to one or two and beckoned them, telling the rest to disappear. On hearing they were to be dismissed, the majority turned to leave, some making crude gestures, or shouting or whistling, as they went. These were, I later heard, the dockworkers looking for a few hours' employment.

Now there was the rumble of heavy barrels, some full, some empty. Men grabbed bales on their backs and traipsed heavily over the quay and up gangways to the small ships that would carry the goods to the coast. Others thronged the wharves and manhandled casks, bales and animals from one set of boats, while nearby similar goods were loaded to others. It was a scene of utter confusion to me, but the men appeared to go about their business in good humour and with an economy of effort that was astonishing. I could only look and marvel as huge cranes turned, their windlasses driven by sweating, bare-chested shipmen and harbour workers, and lifted massive tuns from holds and on to the quayside itself. A lone voice screamed as though the devil had just stuck talons in his back, but it was nothing more than a fishwife calling her trade – why such peasants find it impossible to speak in the Queen's English when calling their wares, I shall never know.

Suffice it to say that the quay was a place of raucous activity and reeked of fish and the sea.

A tavern stood at the roadside, and I repaired to it to enquire of a passage. At least, the dingy interior was less congested than the tavern in the city, and I was soon gripping a drinking horn and had been informed that Master Weston was on his ship supervising the loading of a new cargo. I supped the wine and was glad of the warmth that seeped through my body. As soon as I had finished it, I made my way outside to find the master.

He was a sly-looking fellow, as brown as a chestnut, clad in a leather jerkin and with a filthy, greasy cap on his head. His one good eye peered at me with suspicion. The other was curiously white, and it was plain to me that he could see nothing from it. He rasped a hand over his thin beard as he surveyed me. 'So John Wolfe sent you to board the *Thomas*? I was told he wanted me to take a passenger.'

I gave him my most open smile. 'That is good. I would be glad of a ride to London.'

'Aye. Perhaps.'

I would not claim that his was the most effusive welcome I had received in my six-and-twenty years. He told me that, to reach the weir and the *Thomas*, I must pay him. Grumpily, I did.

It was tiny. In size, it resembled a large wherry, but with a large canvas sail that had seen many happier days before the green and blue mottling had attacked it. There were, I swear, more colours on that sail than on the benches of the haberdashers in Exeter's streets. That, and the odour of rotten wood, was almost enough to drive me back to the quay, but I swallowed my pride and natural concern. Like a creature born to the sea, I strode to the side and stood there. A momentary surge forced me to grab at the nearest rope, but apart from that, I am sure that the master and his crew must have been impressed with my stern, martial appearance. They would have realized that I was a citizen of London, and that I would not suffer nonsense. I was not some mere peasant to be fleeced. I noticed that the shipmen all tended to avoid my eye. It was surely a sign of respect.

It was approaching twilight when the vessel finally cast off the ropes at fore and aft, and the great oars were thrust out into the water to take us to the middle of the passage, where the three shipmen suddenly started to scurry about, pulling on this rope, releasing that, and grabbing the rudder. Suddenly, there was a crackling of canvas, and the sail billowed and the craft heeled over, and I was forced to grasp the nearest rope again. The master bellowed something about sheets, but I just clung on as best I might. This was not a time to pretend to be experienced at sailing. It could lead to my being flung from the vessel. A glance at the grey-green waters over the side was enough to convince me that keeping my grip on the vessel's ropes was my best option.

The journey was, it has to be said, quite without excitement. The waters were calm and smooth, and after a little while, I could enjoy the soft murmuring of water at the planks of the hull, the sudden din of disturbed ducks and geese, the hiss of the wind, and the creak and groan of the timbers. As the light faded, I was anxious that the craft might drive into the banks on one side or the other, but it was plain that the master knew his vessel and the river, and we moved along at speed with nary a moment's concern. It was late when we arrived at the estuary, where there was a large weir, and beyond that – well, there was a multitude of masts. They appeared against the darkening sky like the pikes of an enormous army. It was a sight to strike fear into a man's heart, and I did indeed feel a great trepidation, but I forced it away. After all, I was a man of skill and ability, and no one has ever had cause to doubt my courage.

No, I stiffened my back and gazed ahead at the ships with a calm demeanour, as a gentleman should.

In truth, I was just glad to see the last of Devon. No more drunken vicars mourning their brothers; no more grim, unhelpful coursers or horse dealers refusing to help me just because of my accent; no more deans and their thugs, robbing me and trying to test their blades in my back or my throat. No, all was now peaceful and calm, and I was happy to be here, listening to the water rippling past the front bit of the boat. I even dipped my fingers in the water.

At last, things appeared to be going my way.

The ride was not long. It was still daylight when we finally reached the weir and docked. Now I had to discover where the *Thomas* lay, so that I might pay for my passage to London.

Gazing at the shore as we drifted with the river, I was reminded of a smaller version of London's docks. The port boasted cranes at the harbourside and a scattering of houses that ran up the hill from the water and along the road back towards Exeter. As we moved on, we passed greater or lesser ships at anchor, while more were lashed to the harbour, their sails furled neatly. We sailed to a handy spot, and the boat bumped against the wooden piles. I made my way to the gangplank, and before long I was springing down to the wooden planks of the quayside and could take a view of the scene.

It was typical of any port, I suppose. All about me was the sound of timbers creaking, the wind whining and howling past ropes, the clatter of blocks and tackle slamming against timbers, men shouting at others with incomprehensible commands, while, over them all, I could hear the cries of women offering services involving relaxation of a more or less strenuous form. There were some I saw who could have appealed after a quart or two of strong ale, but my natural instincts were to avoid them like the plague. A maid in a city like Exeter is one thing; a woman serviced by shipmen who had captured diseases from far-off lands was less than appealing, and I was sure that, were I to approach one of the women here with the benefit of a torch, I would not be keen to conduct any negotiations.

The ships themselves were models of efficiency, I suppose. Their ropes were carefully looped about protruding pegs, the decks cleared of all rubbish, their barrels lashed in place. Yes, the ships looked like perfect examples of cleanliness and tidiness. Off the ships, the place was far less salubrious. Men moved with a bustle and shout, like butchers at a market, urgently rolling barrels or hooking bales and hauling on ropes to heave them skywards, swinging them out to a deck and letting them thud down in the holds. It was a scene of vigorous activity, but also of filth, mess and disorganization. Men wandered aimlessly, and one I saw was almost crushed by a huge barrel. I saw a man in a dispute, poking another in the chest with a truculent finger, bellowing something that made his spittle spray.

It was not only the men. I saw a rat the size of a cat scuttle about some coils of rope and piles of garbage, and there was the ever-present odour of sewage from the sides of ships where shipmen had squatted to empty their bowels. When I glanced at the greasy waters, I could see things floating that were not sticks. I looked away. This place was less appealing even than Okehampton.

Under the direction of Master Weston, the little vessel had made good time. It only required one man to work the sail and help bring the vessel to Topsham, and now Weston pointed with a horny finger to a tall shape. 'There she is. That's the *Thomas*,' he said.

Weston gave more commands, and the sailors furled the sails and reached for long oars again.

'Are we to row all the way to London?' I said, half jestingly.

Weston looked at me. 'Are you mazed?'

'Eh?'

''Tis hundreds of miles to London. We're sailing in the *Thomas*.'

The men were not bothering to row, I saw. The great oars were used more as rudders to help steer the vessel towards the *Thomas*. It had enough speed already, I suppose, because of the river's flow. I turned to see the ship looming closer from the gathering gloom.

Over the years, I have met many shipmen, and all seem to have much in common. They are usually uncommon friendly towards other men – while sober. All of them have a streak of violence that is as wide as the ocean itself, and all are superstitious about almost anything.

Just now, seeing that great hulk bearing down on us, as it seemed, I was struck dumb with a sudden terror. I felt like a mouse as the shadow of the hawk appears overhead. There was something about that vessel that struck me with horror.

I can assure you that climbing up the rope to that ship was one of the bravest things I have ever done. My teeth were close to chattering the whole way, and I was convinced at the halfway point that I must release my grip and fall to my doom; instead, I made my way up the side of the ship and was soon standing on the deck with Weston. I was glad of his company, for about us there was an accumulation of some of the roughest-looking dullards I have ever seen outside of a brothel in London's docks. These twenty or so were, apparently, the crew. I was introduced to them, but their names washed over me like so much fog. All I knew was that I would not wish to get into a fight with any of them.

A little hatch gave access to a cabin under the rear castle, and I began to make my way towards it. I was keen to see the cabin that Wolfe had mentioned, and the idea of getting outside a jug of wine and some good food was appealing. However, I was soon corrected. My space was, apparently, a small area below decks with the sailors. I was presented with a tiny chamber formed by the oak of the ship's frame. Here, there was a collection of old sails and ropes, which I was given to understand was to be my resting place. Further, it seemed that this was also to be my place during the day if I didn't want to risk being thrown from the ship into the seas.

'But . . . my cabin?' I protested. 'Master Wolfe promised me a cabin, and said I would be served my meals in there and—'

'You would like my cabin?' Weston said with a bow. 'You want me to give you my cabin? It would be an honour, my Lord.'

I have always felt that sarcasm is the meanest form of humour. That was when I decided I should make a stand. 'I demand the use of a cabin!'

Weston leaned forward, and the bristles of his badly shaven chin came into hideous focus, as did his eye. 'You are a passenger, which is all well and good, and I will make your journey as easy as I may, but do not mistake me for a cuckold-horned churl who can be ordered around. This is *my* ship, and *I* am the law here.'

'Ah. Very well,' I said.

'Now, the seas can be violent,' said Weston. 'You may think you can swim, but in the miserable waters here, you'll drown. I hope quickly. A slow death is not to be considered. You don't want your body to be food for the fish and crabs and the monsters of the deep.'

His words made me shudder, and I was reminded of the sense of dread I had experienced on seeing this ship. I had no wish to become a snack for a monster. I have never been particularly religious, and yet just now the realization that I might not receive a grave for my corpse, that I might not have a body to be returned to life after the Day of Judgement, was like a lead cannonball in my belly. It was not an agreeable thought.

I was permitted back to the deck while the ship was in the safety of the estuary, and I enthusiastically clambered back up the ladder to the open air, where I stood at the rail and snuffed the air, and I confess that the scent was invigorating. I am not an enthusiast for the sea generally, but just now, after the excitement of the meeting in the tavern, I was glad to be here, safely away from the brutes.

Of course, I wondered what had given me such a foul sensation on seeing the ship for the first time. Perhaps it was the result of the violence shown me when I was knocked to the ground – or was it the mere sight of this great vessel looming from the dusky light? Whatever the reason, it had sent a chill into my bones. It was tempting to slip down the rope again and into the boat and make my way back to shore – but I wasn't sure I could. Sailing had looked like a lot of hard work when there were several men, and I was not convinced it was work for which I was suited.

Besides, when I glanced over the side, there was no boat. Someone must have taken it! I hurried to Weston and warned him of the theft, and he looked at me with his good eye like a man presented with an inmate from Bedlam. 'Of course it's gone. We have to fetch the rest of the crew, you hardhead!'

As he spoke, I glanced back towards the quay and saw the

boat again. There were lamps nearby, and I saw three men slipping down the rope to it, and soon it was making its way swiftly through the calm waters. I watched as it cut through the water as cleanly as a little knife, and as it came up closer, I was suddenly assailed with that sense of mingled superstition and horror that I had felt on first seeing this ship.

In the boat were four of the worst-looking sailors I'd ever seen. Two were Weston's last crew members.

My feelings of trepidation were not appeased.

If I could, I would have leaped over the rail, into the water, and swum for the shore – but I am no swimmer. I glanced about me. Weston was not far, and he watched me with a cynical smile tugging at his lips. I would get little sympathy from him, then. He had already marked me as a bullhead, a fool of no more use to him than a monkey – in fact, a monkey might be more useful than me. At least a monkey would be able to climb aloft without falling. I personally was less competent at heights, especially when the sole means of climbing was a rope that looked as safe and secure as a mere thread.

Oh, how I regretted ignoring little Edith!

The journey to London on horseback would have been arduous. Yes, I was glad not to be jolting along astride a beast. It would have been a wearisome ride, but I was sure that many of the shipmen on this horrible ship were little better than robbers and felons who would make my life hell. I spoke to Weston several times, first to ask, then to demand, that I be put ashore, but the ship, when the two had climbed aboard, was locked down. The boat returned to shore with its two sailors, but without me. I was left to think of all the ingenious ways open to a shipman who decided to remove a fellow traveller.

There were many. I could see weapons in every direction. I may not have known their names, but I was to learn a few. There were ropes on all sides, plenty enough to throttle a man, or to bind him and throw him overboard; the heavy wooden head-breakers were known as 'belaying pins'. They would save on rope. A quick bludgeon, then toss a body into the water – it would be easy.

But it was not only instruments of death or injury that had their own nautical term; everything was renamed just because it was on the ship. The ropes were not ropes but 'sheets' or 'stays'. I have no idea why. Every recognizable item on a ship had to have a new name, one entirely incomprehensible to an ordinary fellow like me. It is almost as though it is an intentional device to force land-based humans to accept that they are only secondary in importance, for, why, they cannot speak the language of the sea. Which is, of course, laughable, since the only reason they cannot converse with sailor men is the fact that the shipmen deliberately rename every aspect of their vessels.

However, I could not fault the seamanship of the men. Two – a short, swarthy villain called Hob and a scrawny, ill-fed fellow appropriately named Rat – looked the most unseamanlike pair, but put to work, they were impressive. They could rush up the ropes to the yards and loose the cords that held the sails aloft in a moment. They knew their craft, as much as the master knew his vessel. Weston need only mutter some incomprehensible words before the two were back aloft with others, and suddenly the ship moved less sluggishly and felt less like Hob's hippopotamus and more like Rat's greyhound. Indeed, they were both monkeys, scrambling up the ropes and seemingly dangling from them like creatures born to such a life. For me, it was all I could do to watch.

We spent that evening at anchor, and the next day we set sail.

FIVE

A Cruel Reverse

9 August

I woke, shivering in my pile of clothing and old canvas, to the sound of creaking, complaining hemp and timber. At first, I thought that the vessel was to sink, it sounded so appalling; but no: apparently, these whines, cracks and groans were all a part of a ship's music.

It was not the comfortable, easy journey that Wolfe had promised me, and many were the times, shaken awake in the middle watches of the night as a breeze caught in the rigging, that I cursed Wolfe. Surely, he must have realized that I was to be forced to suffer in this ignominious fashion. No doubt he laughed at the thought of my discomfort, although *why* I had no idea. Perhaps it was merely his sense of humour. Meanwhile, he had my passage to add to his profits for the journey. I soon learned from Weston that Wolfe was the owner of this vessel, and no doubt he would expect a sizeable reward for allowing me aboard. And when I had eventually been put ashore, there would be still more money for him to win from me, no doubt. I expected an atrocious bill for food and drink while I was aboard. Well, I would fight that! I saw no reason why I should accept any additional fees for my passage. Especially not on this mean little ship.

If it sounds as though I was full of self-pity, well, what would you expect? The only person who really cared about me was the child Edith. No doubt she was only kind to me from some guilt stirring in her breast after she had tried to deprive me of my purse, but for now she had shown herself moderately helpful and supportive. There were few others who had displayed such concern for my person.

I remained down in my makeshift cot for as long as possible, but the twin urges, one of hunger and one of vomit, caused me to hurry up the ladder to the deck, where I was immediately struck in the face by a bucket or two of water.

It was enough to root me to the spot, aware only of the cold that ate into my bones. I stood gasping, distressed at the sensation of water dribbling down my back and around my belly. It was appalling! Still worse was the sneering laughter of Hob as he caught sight of me. He was up on a spar, wrestling with a sail, trying to – I think this is the term – reef it in. I sincerely wished that a stray blast would blow him from the rigging and into the sea.

I moved towards the rear of the ship, away from the plunging front, which was rising and then smacking down into the water and throwing great gouts of water all over the deck. It was one such wave that had caught me as soon as I showed my face. The only relief to me was that it was not one of the sailors enjoying a practical pleasantry by hurling the water towards me intentionally.

When I managed to grip a rope to keep myself from being thrown headlong, I could take stock of the world before me. It was not a sight to inspire confidence. In fact, it was a sight to bring me to tears. Ahead of me was a grey horror. The seas were grey, the sky was grey, the ship itself was grey. Everything was as bleak as death, and I wanted to sob and beg the shipmaster to take me back to shore. If he wanted, I would pay for the journey so far. I just wanted to be off this rolling, creaking, horrible vessel, and find a tavern where I might dry myself before a roaring fire and recover. This was no means of travel for a gentleman like me; it was the sort of journey that only a fool could contemplate.

As I dangled myself over the rail, emptying my belly with each agonizing roll and plunge, I gazed long and hard at the horizon. Surely the coast should be visible? We should be heading eastwards, so the English coast should be to the left, I thought, but there was nothing but more greyness over in that direction. I was surprised that the visibility was so reduced, and looked over to the right to make sure, but there was nothing to be seen there either.

It was then that I turned and saw that the man at the tiller was Weston himself. I cautiously made my way to him, clutching at ropes all the way, and when I reached him, I demanded to be returned to shore.

He looked at me with a thoroughly unpleasant grimace. 'You want to go to shore? Swim. It's back there.' And he jerked a thumb over his shoulder.

I looked past him, and there, as a dark line on the horizon, I could see something. Perhaps it was the coast; I could not tell. 'But surely we are following the shore to get to London,' I said.

'Ah, usually, Master, yes, but not today. The wind, you see,' he said. 'It's too powerful; it could knock us on to rocks, so we're making our way nearer the middle of the channel to be safe from foundering.'

'Do we really need to come so far into the sea? Is it that dangerous at the coast?'

'You would not believe the dangers there. Reefs, rocks, sand-bars, all enough to rip the bottom out of the *Thomas* and cast us into a watery grave. And then there're the monsters.'

'Monsters?'

'Aye. They look like beautiful women, but then they snatch you from the deck and pull you under with them, and they eat you while you drown.'

I shivered and peered over the side.

He continued thoughtfully, 'Nay, we're best here in the open water.'

I nodded and hooked my arm through a dangling rope to steady myself. I was still hungry and still felt sick. I was as sure as I could be that I would soon bring up everything I had eaten the day before, but although I might be cold and hungry and weary, at least I was making my way home again. And that was something to be sincerely desired.

Within the week, I would be home again.

There are some matters about which an ordinary fellow like me is not very well informed. One of these is the movement of ships and another is the strange ways of sailors. I mean, the way that their vessels are forced to move is itself a mystery. If I were on a horse, I would point the brute's head in the direction I wished to travel and go straight to it. It is easy. But on a ship, the matelots insist on pointing first one way, then another. It is all to do with the wind, I suppose, and perfectly understandable to a man who lives on biscuits, strong drink and the companionship, of a more or less intimate form, of other men. There are no women on board to leaven the diet of blaspheming, beatings and buggery.

But by late afternoon there was something that I was beginning to realize was not right.

While the vessel was regularly swinging from one direction to another, in that strange 'Z'-shaped manoeuvre so familiar, I presume, to shipmen of all sorts, I noticed that the view behind us was remaining sort of midway between the two. I mean, as the ship swung to the left, the English shore appeared on the left side as I looked at it, and when the master turned his tiller, the front end moved to the right, and the shoreline appeared on the right side of the ship. Now, I may not be a sailor, but that to me meant our course was remaining perpendicular to the English coast. And that meant we were still heading away from England and towards France.

There are times to make a fuss and times when it is better to keep one's own counsel. Well, I kept mine for a good long time, but then I had to make a comment. It was clear that we did not need to travel as far as France to avoid rocks and shoals. There were none here in the middle of this vast ocean. I mean to say, I was not foolish.

'Master, surely it is time to turn and head east? If you continue on this course, we shall soon arrive in France!'

'Aye, what of it?' he said. He appeared to be speaking without thinking. He had his eye on the sun, then the sails, before peering ahead at a small smudge on the horizon. I saw it: it rose like a column of darker cloud against the grey sky.

'Well, I don't wish to go to France,' I said, somewhat at a loss for something else to say.

He turned and glared at me with what I can only describe as a rather startled expression, as though he hadn't realized who was speaking. 'You don't, eh?'

'No! You are taking me to London!' I declared with some heat.

'My apologies,' he said and bared his teeth. His one good eye seemed to be amused.

'What do you mean – "apologies"?'

'I would like to, but it's not possible,' he said and turned to stare at the horizon again. He appeared to have a slight frown when he looked at the smudge.

'You are being paid to take me to London!'

'No. I'm being paid to deliver you to France.'

'I . . .' I was nonplussed, as I am sure anyone would be. 'But I don't want to go there.'

'Others want you there. You've made yourself a nuisance, and I've been ordered to take you and leave you there.'

'Who paid you to take me there?'

'Master Wolfe. He wanted you away.'

'Why?' I asked, by now completely baffled.

'He said he saw you with his wife. He said you were trying to seduce her.'

'Me? I only met her once!' I protested, with all the vehemence at my disposal.

'Aye, he said you'd be convincing. Still, he's the owner of this vessel, and it goes where he directs. And if he says to put you down on France's shore, that's what's going to happen. Now be quiet!'

'No, look—'

'Be still!'

'I demand that you—'

His fist caught my head at the front of my forehead, a lucky blow, for if he had struck my nose with that force, he would assuredly have broken my nose and good looks forever. As it was, I fell back against the ship's sidewall, where I sat with a feeling of baffled confusion. Then the anger rose. Never let it be said that Jack Blackjack is a coward. I stood, and he glanced at me and then punched me on the cheek. I fell back once more and this time remained there.

'Why? Why does he want me in France?'

'I reckon he thinks they'll pay a little to have you as a slave,' the master sneered, and this time I rose with determination.

I pulled out my wheel-lock pistol and shoved it in his face. 'You will turn about, or I will loose this at you!'

He smiled then. It was more terrifying than his sneer. 'You think that will work after hours at sea? The powder will be sodden by now. But if you want, fire it. Kill me. But you only have the one bullet, even if it fires, and the crew will take you and throw you into the sea if you do. It'll be a long, slow death if you drown.'

I hesitated, and then he struck me again. My cheek was raw with pain, and I fell back once more. My head struck the side of the reeling, creaking vessel, and I felt sure I must throw up.

Which is where this story began. So now we have caught up. I was captured here on this horrible ship, and I was to be deposited in France for a future of hideous toil. I had heard what cruel folk the French were, after all. We all knew that.

That was when the gull appeared and took his ease on the rail above me, the bastard.

The rest of that day was spent sailing southwards. I passed the time trying to think of a means of escape from this living hell without using all my purse to save myself. However, my purse was soon in Weston's hands. That, for me, was the final straw. I had no hope left now. With my money gone, I had no chance of escape. My fate was assured. Much of my time was spent glumly at the rail, throwing up what remained in my stomach. According to Hob, I was still getting in everyone's way.

The master remained at the tiller, his eyes fixed on the growing smudge in the distance as if it mattered. Seamen are supposed to be able to tell the weather by glancing at the sky, but his absorption seemed bizarre to me.

A sailor called Elias seemed the only fellow who took any interest in me and my welfare. He seemed genuinely to care for my wellbeing, and when I was close to the sides of the ship, he would remonstrate with me, telling me I might be flung from the vessel if we caught a wave. At least, he warned me that first time. Personally, I didn't care. As far as I was concerned, the sea was welcome to me. The thought of being flung into the water and drowning seemed preferable to this extended torture, with only slavery under a French master to look forward to. When he saw me retching feebly, he left me hanging there, turning away with disapproval. Still, he did seem to care about me, and although I was the only fellow who was sick, other than a cabin boy who seemed to spend his entire time crying or throwing up, he appeared to want to help me. He even offered a heavy ale, which he reckoned would help my belly recover. It didn't.

On the other hand, Hob and his friend seemed to take pleasure in pushing me from their paths whenever they had a chance. Whether I was near the mast, at the sides or standing in the middle of the deck, I was equally at fault, and they would hurtle past me like gleeful children with a haul of scrumped apples or a sack full of stolen purses. Thrice the blockheads knocked me over, and after the third, I swore I would not succumb again, puking or not. The fourth time the pair of them ran at me, I stood my ground until the last minute and then stepped to one side. As the skinny one came past, I thrust out my leg, and the fool took a tumble to the deck, wailing and complaining loudly. Hob stood and glared at me, while his friend gripped his shin and wailed piteously. It was balm to my soul. Until the pair of them beat me to teach me to keep my legs from their path.

And so my day ended. After cold biscuit and some dried meat to chew on, I huddled below in my little corner, smarting from my punishment, wearily reminding myself of my lovely house in London, of the women in the stews, of the roaring fire in the Black Boar, and dreaming of all the various unpleasant tricks I could think up to make Weston's life miserable, were I ever to survive this hellish journey.

I did not sleep well.

SIX

Peril on the Sea

10 August

It was early the next morning when the ship suddenly hove to, as I believe they call it. Suddenly, all manner of things happened. There was a loud bellowing and the sound of bare feet stamping about on the deck, a short cry, and then creaking and rumbling, and a crashing of a chain rattling somewhere, before the ship started to heel over, and I sat up and cracked my head on a large baulk of timber. It hit right in the centre of my skull, and I cannot describe how painful it was. I was forced to sit there, clutching my pate and muttering every foul curse I could think of until the pain had somewhat subsided.

I had been dozing when the commotion started, and what with my head and the aching in every part of my torso from emptying my guts every few minutes, it took me a little while to climb to my feet. When I did so, I was struck by the stillness. The sails were furled and the anchor dropped, so the vessel was rolling uncomfortably as every wave hit her, but the last thing on my mind just at that moment was any thought of queasiness.

The smudge in the sky was explained at last.

There, ahead of us, was a hulk. It had recently been a ship, and probably one not too dissimilar to the *Thomas*, but now there was little to show above the water. There was a crackling as the mast tilted at a mad angle and then stopped as if waiting while the vessel smouldered.

Weston and Elias were up at the forecastle, staring ahead as best they could.

'No bodies in the water,' Elias said.

'Nay,' Weston said. 'But that means little. They might have jumped before they burned. Drowning is better than burning.'

'Aye. She could have caught fire some while ago,'

'I'd still expect a body or two in the water. Perhaps half would sink, but some would float, I reckon.'

'Poor souls,' Weston muttered.

'What's happened?' I asked.

Elias glanced round as if he had never seen me before. 'The ship caught fire,' he said curtly before returning to study the waters.

'How?'

It was the ship's master who answered, his one good eye fixed ahead. 'Mayhap a fire in the galley that spread out of control, or a candle that should have been snuffed, or a spark from stone against metal? Who can tell? There are many dangers aboard a ship like her. It only takes one careless man to let a fire take hold, and then the crew are all lost, as well as their master's vessel.'

There was an expression of grim sadness on his face. I was rather surprised to see that; I had thought that such a harsh, brutal group as sailors would have little truck with emotions such as fellow feeling for others. Perhaps it was less sympathy for the sailors on the ship, and more for the lost cargo.

'Sail!' a voice called. It was the greyhound, who was still up the mast in the little cradle at the top they called the crow's nest. I glanced up at him. For once, the gibbering fool was not giggling and moving about like a monkey on a leash but was staring fixedly.

'Where away?' the shipmaster bellowed.

'There,' the fellow shouted, pointing.

We all turned to peer, but there was nothing to be seen from the deck.

'Elias, you go and look. Your eyes are better than mine,' the master muttered, and Elias trotted to the nearest ratlines, climbing hand over hand with the speed and agility of a stoat chasing a chicken.

When he reached the crow's nest, he followed the greyhound's pointing finger, and at last called down, 'It's a sail, a vessel low in the water. I think it's a galley!'

The shipmaster stared up at the two men atop the mast, chewing at his cheek and swearing betimes. 'Any more?'

'They are coming this way,' Elias called. 'I think they might have seen us!'

Suddenly, all was bustle and haste. I was thrust from the master's path by a hand that felt like a large paddle, and if I were water I could not have been pushed aside with less concern. He was bellowing commands, and all around the men moved. Two went to the big capstan and began to turn it, so that soon there was a clatter and rattle as the anchor was hauled up. At the same time, other men were up the ratlines to the mainsail, Elias swiftly going to their aid. In short order, the sail was unfurled, and we were putting about, the ship heeling over alarmingly, to my way of thinking. I clung to a rope, somewhat bemused by all the clamour and urgency.

'What is it?' I said as one burly matelot pushed past me.

He gazed at me with fear etched into his face. If a man like that could be so alarmed, I thought, this must be serious. 'Pirates, mayhap. They're why that ship was fired.'

'But I thought the ship caught ablaze because of the cooking fire, or a candle, or . . .' I stammered to a halt. The master had mentioned possible causes of a fire. But that was before another ship had been seen. I opened my mouth to speak further, but the man was already gone. Pirates? I had heard of such felons, but never thought I would meet them. Pirates were dangerous men, I had heard. They were likely to attack a ship and kill all aboard, stealing the cargo as their plunder. They might capture sailors, but a mere passenger like me would be unimportant. I might be thrown overboard as soon as they caught me. Unless they cut my throat first for fun.

We could outrun them, of course. I looked over at the shipmaster. It was from him that I sought comfort in this troubling time. He would know that we were safe, of course. He must know that he could outrun the pirates. He was conferring with Elias now, and the two wore expressions which failed to convey any great hope that we were safe. Rather, they both looked seriously concerned, both of them staring up at the sail, then back to the burning hulk, whose smoke was concealing the approach of the pirates. When I caught Hob's eye, there was distinct fear.

That did not make me feel any more comfortable.

It was already late in the afternoon, and now we were plunging along in a roiling sea. The rain kept off, fortunately, but the ship rose and dipped like a boisterous lamb in its first run in the sun. It was exhausting, but at least terror kept the vomit at bay.

We were heading back directly to the coast, as far as I could see. There was little enough to indicate that the coast was there, but I was optimistic that the master knew his work. He was clutching at a rope, glancing up at the sail, then over at the sun, then back behind us. There was calculation in his features, I could see. 'What do you think, Master? Will we make it to the land before they catch us?'

'I don't know. They've a fast craft there.'

'What is it?'

'It's a galley. A ship low and quick, with slaves who row, so that they can catch anything else on the water.'

'What would they want with us?'

He gave me a long stare with his good eye. His bad one seemed to be studying me too, and I shivered, and not from the cold. 'They want our cargo, our money, and *us*! These ships work on slaves, and they need fresh slaves all the time. They don't feed and look after their slaves, after all. They wear them out, just like you'd wear out a donkey. And when a slave's no more use to them . . .' He made a big show of drawing an imaginary dagger over his own throat. 'They throw him over the side. That's if they're lucky. Most of them die at the oars.'

I gazed out at the darkening sea. Suddenly, there was a shout from the rigging. It was Hob, and he was pointing. 'Look! It's there!'

Behind us, there was a break in the thick smoke about the hulk. A fleeting glimpse showed me a slender vessel. There was a mast and reefed sail, but the ship wasn't using that. As it appeared, the smoke seemed to swirl about, a good few yards to either side of the craft.

'Aye, that's a galley,' the master grunted. He began bellowing orders again. 'Come on, you laggards! We have to outrun that bastard!' he shouted, and then he glanced at me. 'You have a pistol. You had best pull out the charge and reload it with fresh powder and shot.'

'One shot will not stop them,' I said.

'I meant it will save you from joining the slaves,' he said shortly.

If anything could have brought home to me how dangerous was our position, it was those words. He clearly believed that if we were captured, I should put a bullet in my brain. It was enough to make me half mad.

I ran down the steps to the lower deck where I had my belongings, and I was weeping and gibbering the whole way. It was a miracle I didn't lose my feet and break my neck in the narrow companionway, the way that I was behaving. I half fell at the side of my bag. My pistol was at my back, of course, because I needed all the protection I could find from these rough sailors, but I wanted to find my balls and powder. Weston was right: a man cannot leave a gun loaded at all hours at sea. The powder grows damp and useless after a short while. I had to pull out the bullet and tip away the old powder, then clean the barrel and firing hole before reloading with care.

Once I had succeeded in drawing out the old charge and cleaning it, I tipped a goodly portion from my powder horn into the barrel, and then took a waxed patch and ball and rammed them home securely. Just to be sure, I shoved a second piece of waxed cloth over the top, to ensure that the gun didn't allow any moisture into the barrel. I tipped a little powder into the pan and closed the cover, before winding up the clockwork mechanism and looking at it.

The gun was a heavy tool. Truth be told, I was not enamoured of it. The thing rarely hit any object I aimed at, and the few times I had needed it, it had been little or no use. Its main function, as far as I could see, was to terrify me personally. I was always convinced that when I pulled the trigger, the damn thing would explode and take my hand away. It was not a pleasant reflection.

I peered at the barrel, thinking about putting that to my head or my heart and pulling the trigger. Suicide was not something I had ever considered, and now, looking at it, I was not convinced I could do it. Pointing a gun at another man is challenge enough when you are a gentleman. Pointing it at oneself is an appalling idea. The barrel was like Ned Hall's mouth, a horrible black, gaping hole. I could thrust my finger into it with ease, it was so large. And then I had a few moments of hideous dancing about the decking, for my finger could slide into the barrel, but once there, it became stuck.

Eventually, I managed to withdraw it, and I stared at the gun with loathing. Holding my finger demonstrated how the thing was less a defensive weapon and more a trap for the unwary, as far as I was concerned. I shoved it back into my belt behind my hip and hoped I would not need to use it, because I was as certain as I could be that I could not destroy myself.

Pulling my sword's baldric over my head, I whimpered at the thought that the ship was gaining on us, and I must soon, very soon, face death or the hideous prospect of being forced to row a ship like a slave. Well, I would be a slave, I supposed. How could the galley's crew hold so many men against their will? There must be some sailors; perhaps they were used to enforce the cruel command of their captives. I shivered at the thought of whips and other forms of brutal suppression, and at that moment, I felt queasy again.

The idea of a chase is thrilling, I know – to those who have never been the pursued.

Watching a pack of dogs thrash over a field after a deer is no doubt exciting to all, except perhaps the deer himself. No one thinks of the target of the hunt, be it a rat, rabbit, hare or fox. Why would they?

Personally, I have always enjoyed watching dogs at work. They have an instinct for hunting, after all, and it is always worth seeing a pair running after their quarry. In the same way, it's enormous fun to see a hue and cry in full, bellowing search for a felon. There is little that is more fun than seeing them picking up their scabbards and staffs and making after some fool in a hurry to be somewhere else. Of course, it is not as enjoyable when you are personally the reason for their quest. I have often been on the receiving end of the interest of bailiffs, sergeants and watchmen, and it never brought me any pleasure.

However, one aspect of such chases tends to be the swiftness with which they are brought to a successful conclusion. A man hurtling through the busy throng in a London street will soon be taken down by an enterprising stall-holder, a dog or, once as I saw, by a child throwing a hoop at his legs. It is quick and sure, just like hounds catching a rabbit, or a terrier a rat. The conclusion is rarely long in coming.

This was different. Have you ever sat down and stared at a tree in the middle distance? Sometimes you can almost convince yourself that it is approaching you. There was one occasion when I was out at the East of London and had visited an alehouse for perhaps rather too long, and I took my ease on a riverbank, I became quite certain that a particular tree was creeping towards me. I stared and stared and was perfectly sure that it was indeed. It was a terrifying experience, and embarrassing when a local peasant discovered me hiding behind his privy.

I digress. The point is that standing and staring at that far-off galley, I could be persuaded happily that it was remaining at the same distance from us. It was as though there was an iron bar to which both vessels were attached, and which prevented them from gaining on us. I almost ruined my eyes by staring at the ship but could make out no discernible diminution of the distance between us.

'If they keep to this speed, we shall be in port before they can catch us,' I said.

The shipmaster grunted and cast a glance over his shoulder. 'You reckon, eh? I reckon she's catching up.'

'No, surely not,' I said. 'Your ship must be a great deal faster.'

'They haven't tried to use the oars yet. When they do that, they'll sprint along after us.'

I had not realized. When I looked again, it was clear enough that they were relying on their huge sail to drive forward, and not the strength of any oarsmen. But the ship was making good way, from the look of the white wings of water where her keel cut through the waves. Not that it made much difference to me. Our ship was splashing through, too, throwing up great gouts of white water with every plunge. It was exhilarating, now I was fairly happy that the galley would not catch us in a hurry.

And that was the thing. This was not a happy situation, obviously, but now that I was over the initial fear of being captured by these pirates, I found myself given over to a sense of slowly increasing terror. The appearance of the ship had been shocking, but now there was a kind of prolonged delay in the realization of my worst nightmares, and that was leading to this state of horror being postponed. And any boy waiting for a strapping for misbehaviour will be able to tell you that the punishment only grows in terror as the victim awaits the first lash. As we flew along, my trepidation increased to the stage where I could scarce speak without gibbering.

I glanced behind us. The galley was closer now. I could see that without straining my eyes. It made me panic to see it.

There is a curious state of calmness that comes with the anticipation of sudden death, especially when there is no possible escape. It is not the reduction of fear, but the slow, inexorable increase to the point where the mind cannot cope with it any longer. And short of leaping from the ship and willingly stopping the suspense, there was nothing to be done. Here, in the middle of the sea, miles from anyone who might help us, there was no escape. All we could do was attempt to squeeze every last ounce of speed from the old ship as we could. The master was constantly watching the sky, feeling the wind and issuing orders to reef this in, or let this out, or some such similar nautical instruction. It made no sense to me, and all I could do was stare in petrified stupefaction as the galley continued to close the gap.

It took so long! The wind was not strong, and our two craft were both moderately fleet, but our vessel was closer to shore, and suddenly I began to see a dark smudge on the horizon ahead. At first, I thought it must be clouds or smoke, but then I realized that this was the coast. We were in sight of England!

I called to the master, but he just growled something silly about me interrupting him with my squeaking or some such, and I was forced to watch the coast gradually becoming more distinct, while the ship behind gained on us. It was slowly approaching, so that now I could see dark-skinned, slender men at the front of the vessel. And now I saw a line of long oars suddenly thrust out on both sides, and I heard an enormous drum start to beat, and as if that ship was a great machine, the oars rose, dipped and rose and dipped again, in time to the beat of the drum. It was terrible, horrible, but also strangely inevitable. It felt to me that there was nothing we could do to stop that ship from capturing us all. We had no option but to surrender. The land was approaching, but already the ship behind us was reducing the distance between us with every sweep of those huge oars. Soon it would have caught us, and then we would learn what fate they had in store for us. Would I be sold as a slave? Or would they see me in all my finery and treat me as a valuable man to be ransomed?

Glancing down at my clothing, I was forced to admit that there was little about it to mark me out as an asset. After the journey from London, and my torments on the moors, there was not much of my London self left. Truth be told, I could have been mistaken for a mere journeyman in Exeter, compared with the figure I had cut in London. Any man seeing me must doubt my position in the world.

That was a truly miserable reflection.

A friend of mine once had a terrible toothache and had to visit a barber-surgeon. His mouth was swollen so he could hardly speak or eat, and his pain was something to behold, and yet he was reluctant to see the tooth butcher, because, as he knew, the treatment would make everything a lot worse before it improved. Having a tooth yanked out is painful at the best of times, and while the gum is bloated like a dead man's swollen gut, it is bound to be even worse. So he went and sat and waited unhappily. He watched while other men sat on the stool before him and the surgeon wielded his pliers and chisel enthusiastically, and his victims might groan and clutch at their seat with agony, while blood spurted from wide mouths, while teeth cracked and split, refusing to be pulled easily, and while friends gripped their head and shoulders to stop them trying to escape.

He said that those minutes spent watching other people, with his own tooth making him all but faint with pain, but dreading the short walk to that stool so that his tooth could be jerked free of his jaw, was the nearest to torture he had endured.

All I can say is this: he was never chased at sea.

'Why are they taking so long?' I whined.

'I'd guess they're all weary after chasing the burning hulk and then fighting the matelots on board her,' the shipmaster said. He spat over the side of the vessel. 'They'll catch us soon, you'll see. We can't outrun a damned galley!' He stomped off, casting fierce glances at the galley every so often from his good eye.

I was left to stare about me, hoping for a sign, any sign, of rescue. Anything would do for me: a ship that could help us, a small craft which I could jump into and try to get away – because surely the pirates would concentrate on the larger prize and ignore me – but there was nothing. Only the gradually defined land. Where once it had been a smudge on the horizon, now it was becoming a familiar landscape, with fields and trees, and even tiny dots that must have been sheep. There was a line of ochre at the foot of the fields, and I realized that this must be the beach. Following the line of the beach, I saw a haziness in the air and recognized the mouth of the Exe. The cottages' fires were causing the mistiness. And just now, with the sun gradually starting to sink in the west, the air was cooling.

Suddenly, I was pushed from my post. The shipmaster was at my side, glaring up at the rigging, then to shore, and from there back over his shoulder. 'Now!' he bellowed, turning the wheel.

I had no idea what he was planning, but the sudden turn made me skid across the slippery planks of the deck, and I had to grab a rope before I was hurled into the rail. I could well have been thrown into the sea.

'What are you . . .?' I managed, but no one was listening.

As far as I could see, the mad fool was planning to turn us back to the galley. If he did that, we would be certain to be boarded and murdered where we stood. I stared with my mouth open, until a stray wave struck the ship and burst over me. It tasted foul.

Looking behind us, I could see the galley was wondering

what his plan was. And then they must have guessed, just as I did, that the one-eyed lurdan was thinking to race to Exmouth. The lunatic can only have had the brains of a chicken, if that, because it was obvious to the most boobily knave that the galley would overhaul us. The ship had speed in those oars, and even if she had an exhausted crew of slaves and mercenaries, she would be able to cut us off by completing one long side of a triangle, whereas we must strike straight for the coast with the wind not ideal. I watched as the galley suddenly turned away from her pursuit of us, and instead began to point at the river's mouth. She seemed to lurch as the oars bit into the water, then sprang forward, faster and faster, until, at last, it was obvious that her bows were level with our stern.

I whimpered. This must not end well for us. Meanwhile, the shipmaster at my side was scowling at the galley with a keen concentration. I could not make out what he was planning, but it was plain enough to me that there was something afoot.

On and on we went. The galley's prow was ahead of our rear castle now, and I could see the same swarthy, black-haired villain on the foredeck waving a curved sword over his head and bellowing at his men. Over the water, there came the sound of a steady drumbeat, and I could hear weeping. I thought it was me at first, but then I realized it was the cabin boy. I cuffed him over the pate to teach him to keep quiet, and he shuffled away while I turned to the galley once more. It was not bothering to cut across us yet but was clearly intending to race ahead and block our escape. The man on the foredeck was joined by another equally disreputable-looking fellow who glowered at us as we rolled and plunged in the white, foamy seas.

'Any time now,' the shipmaster grated, and I shot him a look. Was he truly keen to see us all captured and thrown into slavery? It made my belly turn to lead. I was sure that I would be sick with the thought of sitting on a hard bench and forced to row for the rest of my life. I would never see my lovely house in London, never visit the Cardinal's Hat, never drink with my companions or . . .

'Hah!' said the shipmaster.

I peered at him with distaste. He could not hear me, I was

sure, and yet he appeared to take amusement in my reflections. And then I realized that he was not considering me; he was watching the galley.

Something had happened to it. Oars were thrust up in all kinds of directions. One of the men from the foredeck was in the water, making a great fuss with arms flailing, and the ship was halted. We sailed by with regal disdain, and the shipmaster bit his thumb in a fashion which indicated his contempt for the slavers, as members of the crew bellowed and roared and rushed about the deck.

'What . . . what's happened?' I asked weakly.

There was no answer for a long time. Instead, the crew of the *Thomas* took to the port rail and waved their hats and jeered, some making lewd comments, while the galley rocked as it was battered by waves at its side. The men on the decks were trying to throw a rope to collect in their companion in the water, and the oars were unmoving, some thrust upwards, others drooping into the water. It looked like a cockroach that had stepped into a fire and expired. An oar at the front, as I watched, slowly started to drop to the water.

'What happened to them?' I demanded. 'Is this some sort of magic? Are you a necromancer?'

The shipmaster gazed at me, and then his good eye narrowed, and his open palm slapped my cheek hard enough to make my brain rattle. 'Don't you call me that, you damned lubber! Of course it's not magic! It's seamanship. I guessed they didn't know this port too well, nor that there's a great sandbar out there. I just thought that they would see us hurrying to the port, and they'd think to head us off, and I hoped they wouldn't see how the sea moves just there. I was lucky. They didn't look where they were going, so grounded themselves.'

'What now?'

'Now? Now we tell the men of Exmouth that there's a slave ship out here that's just burned a ship to the waterline and is full of slaves and money.' He licked his lips. 'With luck, we'll make a good profit here today. You will have a share, too!'

I shook my head. All I wanted was solid ground under my feet, and the last thing I needed was a return to the sea to watch a bloody battle. I had seen enough of fighting during the rebellion, and enough of the sea already today.

He gave me a sneer and wandered off, scattering orders about like pebbles at his shipmen, and I remained at the rear of the ship, watching the galley as it remained fixed in its place. The man had been rescued and now stood, dripping, at the bow. Over the water, I could hear shouts and the sound of cracking. It took me a while to associate the cracking with the sudden yelps of pain. They were whipping their oarsmen.

That hideous sound was enough to make my stomach clench again. I had a vision of me sitting on a wooden board, shackled hand and foot, while a hairy-arsed brute wielded a whip and welted my back. I don't mind admitting that my eyes were filled at the mere thought.

While I was thus engaged, the oars started to drop and wait at the ready, and then there was a loud *boom* of a drum, and all dropped, and the water became white and frothed as the oars dragged through the water, but the galley did not move. I heard more whip cracks, more shouting, then a slow drumbeat, and the oars rose, moved forwards, dropped, and again there was a bright frothing at each blade, but the ship remained held fast. It was the most beautiful sight I had ever seen.

The long, slow progress to Exmouth was curtailed suddenly, as the shipmaster gave a bellow or two which caused men to scurry for the ratlines and scramble out over the yards, fiddling with the sails and reefing them, or whatever it is shipmen do at such moments. Another bellow, and the tiller was moved, and the ship began to heel over on a new tack. I was just wondering what the purpose of this was when I saw, emerging from Exmouth, three small craft. They were only large enough to hold some sixteen men, each grasping his own oars, so there were some forty men in total.

I gave a sigh of relief. Even if the galley were to free herself, these brave fellows were coming to help us. The galley couldn't fight all of us.

'Black-hearted devils!' the master snarled. 'Come on, back to the galley!'

'But you were going to get them anyway,' I pointed out. I didn't understand what his concern was.

'I was going to ask their aid and lead them to the ship, but now they see an opportunity. They'll have the nails from the planks of that galley in a trice, the thieving scrotes!'

I was at a loss here. Peering back at the galley, which remained firmly grounded, I enquired politely what we could do. Since the galley was already fixed in place on the sandbar, the *Thomas* plainly could not approach her. Our vessel was larger than the galley, with a deeper keel, surely, so if the one could be beached, so could we. I mentioned this to Weston, just in case he had not thought of this.

'Shut up, Master Whine-a-Lot! I'm a mariner. I know what I'm doing, and one thing I am not doing is leaving that vessel with her cargo of stolen goods to the men of Exmouth! They'd pull your teeth out if they could sell them! A right unsailor-like mob. You couldn't trust them not to break open your hold and take anything not nailed down, that lot! The times they've stolen goods from good, honest mariners, and admitted it, and made no recompense. I'd sooner trust the pirates on that galley than the men of Exmouth, the thieving turds!'

For now, I was at a loss as to whether the man had some knowledge that was concealed from me or he was a simple maniac. I shivered as the ship made a huge, slow, cumbrous turn, holding on to a rope as she did so, and ended up facing the galley again. The wind made our journey difficult, for as soon as we had moved forward some little way, there was a need to turn, making a 'Z'-shaped track in the water. And all the while, the little boats from Exmouth were nipping along like seagulls over the waves. They hardly seemed to touch the water, they moved so swiftly. It was good to think that they must surely get to the galley before us, and there take the risk of boarding and the hideous slaughter that was bound to take place.

I comforted myself that now I would be one of the last to climb up on to the galley's decking. I had no wish to die because I was one of the first. As I've mentioned, I have seen war and battle, and those who are keen to spill blood are welcome to the experience. I have never fought aboard a ship and saw no benefit in trying it now.

Master Weston gave a sharp order, and the ship tacked again. I was prepared, and was already clinging to a rope, and ran less risk of being thrown from the deck. When I glanced down and behind us, I saw that the nearest of the pursuing craft was only a few yards from our stern, and a very angry-looking man in the prow was shouting incomprehensibly, although I was more than convinced that his words did not include a polite request to overtake us. His meaning was put a little more forcefully, as I have noticed is common with sailors.

Weston may have had the intention of blocking all the three craft, but it was clear that the smaller vessels were a great deal more agile than our lumbering cog. The shipmaster managed to hold off the first two craft with his swift turning and unpredictable course, but the third began to sidle past on the port side, and when Weston began to tack to block it, the second little craft sprang forward like an arrow from a bow and shot ahead, her crew laughing and the two men who were not paddling with their oars making several unnecessary gestures towards us.

We gave up after that. The shipmaster turned the *Thomas* this way and that, but it was clear enough that he could not prevent the smaller craft from moving ahead, and soon I had a clear sight of the three as they reached the galley.

The first had a trio of grappling irons which they hurled up at the ship's prow. Three men went up the ropes like monkeys, and as soon as they reached the galley, one was cut down instantly. He fell back into the boat and lay still. A second was up and over the side, but even as he did, he received a buffet on his head from a curved sword. It looked as though the steel was snagged by the victim's skull, because the pirate was forced to try to lever it from the man's grip, placing a boot on the man's head to wrest it free, while the man's head jigged from one side to the other, the rest of his body entirely limp. The third man arrived on the deck as the pirate retrieved his sword, and the pair set to, while more pirates ran to support their chief and more Exmouth men threw themselves at the ropes and clambered up them.

As this was happening, the second boat arrived at the galley and more men threw grappling hooks and pulled themselves up.

'Bastard whelps!' Weston said. He looked about him at the ship. It seemed plain enough to me that the ship must soon hit the sandbanks which held the pirate ship. I moaned, waiting for the juddering halt that would herald the beaching of our vessel, but even as I clung more firmly to my rope, Weston bellowed to the man at the front of the ship. He whacked something with a maul, and there was a clattering and a splash. He had dropped the anchor. Instantly, the ship heeled over. Now the master shipman gave another order, and Elias led a group of sailors to the front of the cog, where there was a canvas-wrapped shape. They pulled the wrapping away, and there beneath was a small boat. I watched as the men attached blocks and tackles to it and hauled on the ropes to lift it. In only a few moments, the little boat was swung out into the water.

'Come on!' Weston said. He had grabbed a belaying pin in one hand and was tugging a sword's baldric over his head. 'With me!'

I felt as though my feet were rooted to the spot. I could only shake my head and mumble that I would remain to guard the ship, but Elias grabbed hold of my shoulder and jerked me forward, as though they all suspected that I would make off with their ship if they did not take the precaution of bringing me along. I strenuously declared that I would not go, but to no avail. I was grasped and hauled, and forced down the ladder to the jerking, bobbing craft. There, six mariners were already installed at oars. I was pushed to the rear, away from the oars, which was at least some relief, and two more sailors joined us. On the order, we slipped away from the *Thomas* and made our way across the turbulent waters to the galley.

I felt unwell, although whether it was well-founded alarm at the idea of a fight on the water or just the horrible motion of the vessel, I could not say. All I do know is that as the prow struck the galley, I looked up to see that the side was all red, and I wondered for a moment whether the ship had been painted. Then I realized the meaning of it and felt sickened once more.

The crew swiftly made their way up the side of the ship and

leaped on to the deck. I followed rather more cautiously, being unused to such strenuous exercise, and being more reluctant to climb aboard.

It was a scene of carnage. Men lay all about, some of them Englishmen from Exmouth, some darker-skinned men from the galley. I stepped carefully, trying to avoid the bodies and body parts. At one point, my foot landed on a finger and rolled away with it as the ship was prodded by waves as heavy as a whale. I almost fell into a pool of blood and was just congratulating myself on a narrow escape when a fresh wave struck the side of the ship, and my foot slipped on the blood, making my legs part in a most unpleasant manner. Suddenly, I was on my back and I knew the dampness I felt was not seawater.

I have been in battles before. I described my experiences in my first set of chronicles, when I was engaged to protect Queen Mary from the rampaging peasants from Kent under their leader Wyatt. I had been there when the peasants tried to cross London Bridge, and I had seen men with their limbs and heads blown off, and narrowly escaped the same myself. I had no desire to be hurled into another fight, and yet here I was once more, the unwilling combatant in a fight that was nothing to do with me. Still, the thought of money on the ship was tempting, and if I could gain a share by merely being present, that was worthwhile. So long as I was not in danger.

It gave me a thought. I clambered to my feet, looking about me. Everywhere there seemed to be men fighting, some clenched together almost like lovers, others slashing and stabbing, a few rolling over and over on the short deck. Meanwhile, two ranks of rowers sat silently below the deck, heads bowed, their backs bloody and scarred from whiplashes, each of them still gripping an oar in both hands. They looked like the dregs from a torture chamber. Turning, I was just in time to see a man from the slave ship aim a blow at me. He slashed with his horrible curving sword, and I darted back, fumbling for my own, desperate to keep away from the steel that danced before me, until I realized that there was no ground beneath my feet. This ridiculous vessel had no rail to guard against a fellow falling from the deck! With a wail, I fell from there to the lower level. I could have broken my back if I had landed on the central boards; fortunately, my landing was eased by two slaves, who moaned as I hit them, but who made the fall far less dangerous and painful for me.

I slid down their backs on to the legs of the men behind them. All bearded, all sweaty and thin, it was plain to me that they had been forced to endure great hardship with little food or water. Their lives must have been terrible. Gaunt and weary eyes peered at me with the uninterest of the dead. Their odour was enough to make me gag, and the sight of their terrible, haggard faces was enough to make me want to be sick. Uppermost in my mind was the thought that it could have been me replacing some of these poor souls if Weston had not been so thoroughly competent a seaman.

There was a sudden clattering and a scream from above, and then a fresh body fell from overhead, landing head first on the solid timbers of the walkway. This was a slightly higher section in the middle of the ship, and I thought that the slave masters must have wandered up and down here, inflicting their vicious wounds on the poor, defenceless devils.

I stood and, peering down, realized quickly that the slaves were not released to go and empty their bowels. With a grimace, I stood and glanced at the man who had fallen. The slaves expressed as little interest in him as they had in my appearance. They really were quite bovine. However, the dead man was another of the shipmen from the galley's crew. His neck was bent at an interesting angle, and his eyes were wide, as if in immense surprise. I did not get the impression that he would be rising any time soon.

There was more shouting overhead, and then a cheering, which to me sounded hopeful. There cannot have been many crew members. Only a few would be needed to control all these slaves, and as things stood, I thought that the men of Exmouth and the *Thomas* would have been more than enough to control them. I decided that I should return to Weston's side and see how matters had progressed. I made my way cautiously to the central walkway, over the body of the dead slaver, and thence to the ladder that gave access to the upper deck. There I found Weston glowering fiercely at a thickset man with the black hair and blue eyes of a Celt. I had met a few of these men in Okehampton and out on the moors. They were hardy, no-nonsense types, as quick to take offence as they were to smile.

'We took the ship.'

'You wouldn't have had the chance, if I had not brought the bastards to ground on the sandbank,' Weston said.

'That was very good of you, Master Weston. We are grateful,' the Celt said. He smiled disarmingly.

'And now I'll take my share of the salvage,' Weston growled.

There was a certain tenseness at that. There were still some fifteen men from Exmouth, most of them bleeding, but all fingering weapons. I had the impression of a pair of pirate hordes meeting. Suspicious wasn't the word for their attitude. This was the preamble before hostilities, I felt certain. I moved away from the altercation, casually moving to the rails and leaning on them nonchalantly as if clambering aboard a slave galley was an everyday experience.

While they bickered and their men started to face off against natural opponents, I happened to glance down. Among the poor devils chained to the oars, I saw one whose head was rocking slowly back and forth like an old man dozing. And then, without a word or even a grunt, the poor devil leaned back until his arms were outstretched, and as I watched, I saw his face turn skywards and his mouth sag open, and he was dead. It was that straightforward. He was alive – and then he wasn't.

I am used to death in many of its more interesting forms, thanks to my associate in London, but this sudden expiry was shocking. At first, it was the horror of a man losing his life in those hideous conditions, but then my feelings began to move into simple anger. While the sailors stood up to each other like stags over a doe, these poor fellows were losing their lives.

'While you shipmasters are arguing about your prizes, the poor fellows down there are dying of hunger and thirst,' I blurted, pointing. I stared at Weston, furious. 'If we had not been lucky and seen the hulk of their last victim, we might be dead or held down there ourselves! Hold your stupid discussion until we're on solid land and these fellows are liberated – at the very least, give them water!'

I confess that I spoke in a firm, blunt manner. Yes, because I was feeling sick, but that was not all. I had been beaten by Weston and the men of the *Thomas*, I had been unwell for the whole of my journey on the ship, and after falling from the deck and surviving the battle for the galley, I was out of sorts. Obviously, I would not usually have raised my voice in such a manner, making an enemy of two small armies of sea bandits, either of whom could easily hurl me from the deck and into the sea. But I was very angry. Who were they to count their profit when rows of men were dying below their feet?

Then I saw all the glowering men turn to me. I tried to step back, but the ship's wall was behind me, and I could go no further. I smeared a smile over my face and tried to look innocent. 'Where is the key to their chains, do you think?'

To my astonishment it was Weston who muttered, 'Yes, he's right. We ought to rescue the men down there.'

It was even more of a surprise to see the men from Exmouth gradually nodding their agreement. It would seem that there is a kind of brotherhood of the sea, and mariners tend to accept that they are all pitted against the waves, the weather and pirates. Finally, their weapons were lowered and sheathed, and the two groups of men began to take up less warlike postures, many moving down to the slave deck and offering support to the fellows below. A cask of water was broached and men from Exmouth carried a bucket with Elias ladling water to all the men.

Any man could weep to see them, these tattered remnants of men, and their pathetic gratitude. Some were barely aware of the water and had to have their mouths opened for it to be tipped in. Much was wasted, but as the men went down the lines of oarsmen, the difference was obvious in the way that they responded. Those who had not yet received a mouthful were wilting like a plant in the sun, but those who had taken a ladle were suddenly more lively and looked about them like men wakening from a dream.

For my part, I wanted to seek a means to release them from their fetters. I went below, to the rear of the ship, where there was a small chamber separated from the rest of the deck by a wooden wall with a door set in it. I tried to open the door, but it was locked. Rather than seek the corpse carrying the key, I held my pistol to it and released the wheel. Sparks flew and there was a sizzling and a flash from the pan, but the charge didn't go off. It took some time, blowing the pan clear of smouldering remnants of powder, then the judicious use of a splinter of wood to clear the priming hole before I could refresh the powder and try again. The charge went off this time; there was a great roar that made the oarsmen cower, and the door opened at my first kick.

Inside were various tools of the slaver's trade. Nasty-looking iron and steel devices, lots of hammers and other tools, and a series of whips. I took up a heavy hammer and chisel, and went to the nearest slave. He looked at me dully, but I had him lift his forearms to a beam, set the chisel against the manacles and hit it hard. It took three blows, but then the securing rivet popped from its rest and his arm was free. The second rivet took a little longer, but soon I was on to the next man. As I worked, I was aware that there was another man working on the oarsmen on the other side of the ship. It was Weston.

'Thank you, sir,' this man said when he was freed. He was little better than skin and bone.

'You are English?' I said as I moved to the next man.

'Aye, from Exeter. I'm called Harry Lydd. There were more of us, but they . . .' His eyes clouded.

'How long have you been here?' Weston said.

'Since our ship was caught, sir. I was working for Master Ralegh on *The Eagle*, and we were taken these few months since. We were forced to the oars, and if we refused, well, the sea holds many secrets.'

I had released a third man, but this one was dead to his environment. He looked at me briefly, with the blankest of expressions, and then set his hands back on the oars.

'Your master believed you were killed, his cargo stolen,' I said as I worked my way to the next fellow.

'All my companions, they're dead, and his cargo *is* stolen,' the man said. He spat. His voice was as ragged as the remains of his shirt. 'They worked us to death in this stinking filth. And made us row them away. Later, they caught Shapley's ship, too.

And it was all planned. They knew where the ships would be and simply lay in wait for them.'

'How could they know that?' Weston said sharply.

In truth, I was doubtful that the poor old man wasn't more than a little mad. A free Englishman, captured and forced into slavery – well, it was hardly surprising if Harry Lydd was driven more than a little lunatic. Even if he was only a seafaring peasant from Exeter. Still, Weston seemed to take him seriously. I smiled at him encouragingly.

The sailor looked at me very straight. 'How long does it take to vittle and load a ship, eh? Takes days. If someone else in a small, fast boat decides to tell someone else, it would take only a little time to sail over the channel here to meet someone and let them know where the vessel was bound, and how long before she might set sail. A ship like this one can cover the distance in no time and sit back to wait for its quarry to appear. And a ship like ours was full of choice goods. It was worth their while for the cargo, and then they also got us, the sailors, too.' He spat again. 'When I find out who was the messenger, and who told of our sailing, I'll feed him his own liver!'

For all the fact that he was as scrawny as a snake and had the face of a man dead three days, I believed him.

I managed to free nine men before I was forced to pause in my labours and pass the hammer to a man who looked like he could continue welting bits of metal for a week, and I went back up to the main deck.

Weston soon followed me. He grumpily gave the evil eye to the men from Exmouth, but he realized that a fresh battle would be foolish. It was more a matter of discussing what items in the hold would be taken by the men of Exmouth and which by him.

'Don't get any ideas,' he growled. 'You're still going to France.'

I felt the churning in my belly at that, but then I licked my lips. They tasted salty from the spray. 'Who told you to take me there?'

'You know that: Master Wolfe. I told you.' He was silent a moment, staring out over the sea with a fixed scowl on his face.

I pointed below. 'You heard Harry Lydd down there. He said he was on Ralegh's ship, that he heard a man come here and instruct the captain to capture other ships.'

'What of it?'

I could see he was labouring under great pressure. He was only a peasant of the seas when all was said and done. He was not a man of the world like me. 'If a man sent messengers to alert pirates, other seamen would have cause to remonstrate with him. That would be an act of betrayal and treachery.'

'Aye. Not even a Cornishman would act like that.'

I nodded, then frowned. 'How would he know where to go to alert the pirates? The sea is so vast.' I was trying to be reasonable. After all, I came from London. A fellow from London can usually see through to the nub of the matter.

He shot me a look from under beetling brows. It reminded me of a tiger's unfriendly gaze when confronted by a walking meal. 'If a man were to hear of a great cargo being sent from Exmouth, and set sail in a small craft while the ship was still having the cargo loaded, that little boat could be over the water before the ship had set sail, couldn't it? And if the craft were to go to rendezvous with a galley, for example, that would make the task of the galley very easy, if it sought to capture the ship, enslave the crew and steal the cargo.'

'And how,' I said, indicating the empty waters all about us, 'how would he know where the slave ship would be waiting?'

'Near the coast. It's easy enough to recognize landmarks there,' he said. 'Plenty of small rivers to hide in, too.'

I peered at him.

He continued, 'Well, I know enough about sailing and the sea, Master. It occurs to me that if someone wanted to make some money, he could send details of a ship crossing the sea and have his piratical friends pick up the vessel.'

'So?'

My obtuseness began to wear away at his patience. 'What if a man sent a message to the galley to stop the *Thomas*? And they lay in wait, knowing which harbour we would aim for?'

'Don't be so . . . They took the other ship first, remember?'

'They probably thought it was the *Thomas*! And when they realized their mistake, they killed the crew and fired the ship to prevent anyone from speaking of them. Then they saw us approach and realized that we held the cargo they wanted.'

'What do you carry?'

'Bales of wool, some copper and tin, and . . .' He stopped. 'Tin is worth a fortune, and the copper a pretty penny, too.'

'And for that, they were prepared to capture the ship and kill or enslave all of us?' I said. My stomach seemed to have caught some butterflies; I could feel them fluttering.

'It's a lot of money. Who would do such a thing?'

'Someone who knew you would be sailing. Someone who saw your ship being prepared and filled with cargo. Someone who hoped to benefit from your capture or death.'

He pulled a face at that and snarled, 'Who would think like that?'

I paused, mouth agape for a moment. 'Someone murdered Lane . . . did they kill him to keep him quiet? And then sent word of Ralegh's ship, and Shapley's, too! And this time it was your turn to die!'

Weston's face darkened, and he looked over the waves towards his ship, then to Exmouth and the rivermouth that led all the way up to Exeter. 'No man from Exeter would dare,' he said, and there was a degree of vitriol in his voice that made my hair stand to attention.

He stood staring out to sea for a long while. I tried to speak, but he waved a hand angrily while he thought. When he turned to face me, his mind was made up. He studied me. 'You can go,' he said. He reached into his jack and pulled out my purse. He weighed it in his hand for a moment, then passed it to me. 'You'll need that to get back to London.'

'What of you?'

'I have business in Exeter,' he said flatly.

The *Thomas* was to remain with the galley. More men had come from the town to help as the slaves were released and freed from their shackles, and now there was a great busyness all about the vessels, with strong ropes being fixed to the rear of the galley so that groups of rowers in small boats could haul it from the sandbank. I have no idea what the fellows were up to, but it looked like six larger-sized rowing boats were preparing to drag the galley backwards, and then they were going to pull it all the way to the town, where the cargo could be emptied and shared out. Weston seemed to hold little faith in the honesty of the men of Exmouth. Being a Devon man himself, I suppose, he knew how reliable they were likely to be.

For my part, I avoided him and joined forces with the men of Exmouth. They seemed happy enough to let me join them on the way back to the town, and I persuaded their leader that it would be good if I were to be able to fetch my bags and belongings from the *Thomas* on the way. A small handful of coins was adequate to persuade him, and before long, I was happily off the galley and on a boat with six men pulling hard for the shore, and five galley oarsmen, who squatted, blinking and huddled in the unaccustomed brightness of freedom. One was the helpful Englishman from Ralegh's ship.

We had almost reached the shore when there was a shout from the harbour, and a man stood pointing at us, or so I thought. On reflection, I realized he was indicating something behind us. Turning, I saw that the remaining boats had managed to tug the galley several yards backwards. It was plain that soon the vessel would be entirely free of the sandbank, and the men would be able to steer her to shore.

I should have remained there and demanded a share of the booty, but I had other thoughts in my mind. First was the fact that Weston may well have a change of heart and try to drag me back to his ship. He had seemed shocked by my revelation that he might have been betrayed to the pirates, but he was a man, so I thought, of honour. If he had given his word that he would take me to France, there was a good possibility that he would consider himself duty-bound to do so. I wanted no part of that.

Then again, when I reached the quay, there was a small craft about to set sail for the city. I dispensed some more of my money and took my seat on the small board at the rear. I had no idea how these boats worked, but there was, every now and again, a need to move. The sail had a rope connecting it to the rear of the boat, and when the master decided he must tack, the sail was forced to snap across the boat, the rope cracking taut and nearly taking my head off a couple of times. I gave the master a baleful glare on the first occasion, but he appeared blithely ignorant of the danger into which he placed me and my safety, whistling a merry little jig as he gazed ahead, oblivious of my presence. I could have been a ghost for all the attention he paid me.

At the quayside in Exeter, I happily left the man and shouldered my bags, making my way up the steep hill to the city walls and in by the South Gate.

I won't say it felt like home, because it did not. But it did feel like a city set firmly on solid ground, and for that alone, I was very grateful. I made my way up South Gate Street and to the inn where I had stayed my last night in Exeter. Soon I was ensconced in a chair before the fire, and the world, as I sipped a quart of ale, looked a much happier place.

The host provided me with a room, a thick stew with dumplings and a slab of cheese, and soon after eating it all, I was lying on a bed. It was full of bedbugs and fleas, I have no doubt, for I itched for a week, but just then it was the most luxurious bed I had ever lain in. I slept like a man would after my experiences, and nothing could have woken me until dawn slipped in by the shutters.

SEVEN

Return to Exeter

11 August

I woke to an itching that would not leave me. This is the problem with travelling – so often the hosts of inns will not clean their bedding properly. The lumpy mattress on which I had slept felt as if it were alive, and it was with great distaste that I hopped from it to dress.

In a small chamber, I ate a hearty breakfast of heavy bread and eggs, and negotiated with the landlord for him to keep hold of my bags until I sent for them, and set off to find a horse. I was determined to stay no longer than absolutely necessary in this horrible city.

However, I had made my way only as far as South Gate Street when I saw a familiar figure ahead of me. It was Richard Ralegh, and he hailed me, running to greet me with the infectious enthusiasm of a puppy. It was hard not to be flattered by his display of pleasure, but I have to confess that it was far from my mind to spend any time with him.

I explained that I was seeking a mount, and he assured me that, with the festivities completed, most of the stables should have beasts available for hire. The courser, in his mind, was not the best option for me now that so many others should be there for the taking. I was inclined to agree with him. I had not been impressed with the courser, and if there was a better man to deal with, I would be content. He gave me the names of two men down towards St Sidwell's, and the two of us began to make our way thence.

We had a useful time speaking to the two, and in short order, I was the proud possessor of a long-legged chestnut mare who looked as though she could cover forty miles in a day without sweating. She was ideal for me, and I closed the deal there and then. Returning to the city, I was happy to agree when Ralegh proposed a drink of farewell.

Soon we were ensconced in seats in the inn where my belongings were waiting. I sat and enjoyed a spiced ale before the fire, trying to tell him of my adventures at sea, with pirates, kidnapping and battles – but Richard just nodded as if it was a daily experience, and spent the time speaking of the merits of Alice Shapley, before waxing lyrical about a certain new recruit at Moll Thatcher's bordello. I began to see why William had been so grouchy on the night we were to go to the brothel. Richard was more a collector of women than a lover, it seemed to me.

All the while, I was aware of a certain tension. Don't mistake me: I was as keen as ever to return to London and escape the madness of this city of thieves and scoundrels, but I had an urge to see justice brought to Master John Wolfe. From the words of the man on the pirates' ship, Harry Lydd, someone had sent the *Thomas* into a trap, and only Weston's good seamanship and some luck had saved us all. And more than that, I wanted to see Wolfe suffer for what he had done to me. Persuading me to take a ship, and then arranging for me to be taken to France and left there – and why? Because he had seen me with his wife? It was enough to make me want to bed her in revenge. After all, I had not had the opportunity to cuckold him as yet. And she was a desperately tempting delicacy.

It left me thinking that I really ought to try to get my revenge on him. After all, if he had succeeded, I would even now be languishing on a French shore. Leaving the tavern, I reflected that I could leave, of course, as planned, first thing in the morning . . . but then I wouldn't have any satisfaction against the man who had almost caused me so much trouble.

I am no coward, as you will know. And the thought of bringing retribution to Wolfe for the harm he had sought to bring to me – well, that was very appealing.

It was thoughts of this nature that occupied me as I walked along the street, until I was aware of a man calling my name. It was poor Walter again.

He was in a terrible state. 'My friend, I hope you are well?'

I was grateful to find one man who was interested in my tale of woe on the high seas – but when I tried to tell him of my sufferings, he was quite short with me.

'I have no idea what to do for the best. It's Maud, you see. She is desperate. Would you come with me to see her?'

In only a short span of time, I found myself in that noisome little chamber again, with Maud sitting at a stool, wan and grey, staring at us both. I tried to avoid her look. It is hard to look at such misery, and I wasn't sure that Walter was aware of her ventures to earn some money. I suspected I was rather more worldly-wise.

'Maud, you must allow me to help you.'

'You can do nothing, Walter. You cannot support me. I don't deserve it,' she said.

'You have no other means at your disposal. Please, put such thoughts from your mind. Don't you agree, Master Blackjack?'

It was clear that he had enlisted me for moral support.

'You don't understand, Walter. I cannot accept anything from you. You have little enough – and think of the wild talk your help would occasion. You know how he was with other women. I won't have you being the target of such gossip. They'd say both brothers were the same, that you were after his widow before he was even buried.'

'But how will you survive?' he whined, wringing his hands.

'We shall get by, Walter. I have to go and find work.'

Walter was confused. 'What sort of work could you . . .' And then realization hit. 'No, Maud, you mustn't! We spoke of this before – what would Roger think? This is no way to—'

'What else would you have me do? Look on that shelf, Walter! That's all the food we have! Roger didn't care enough to save when he was alive. He was more than happy to go whoring, wasn't he? He'd be happy now – he's left us so little that I have to play the whore myself! He didn't think about what would happen to us if someone powerful took his life from him! He didn't think about us starving, did he?'

'I am sure he—'

'I'm glad for you. But I'm not. He's dead because . . .' She looked away. 'I don't know.'

'Surely, you must have some idea why? Or who might be responsible?' I asked.

'He didn't make friends in the Church or with married men in the city,' she said. 'He was a fool. He thought he was the most handsome. The times I caught him with other women, the times I saw him with them, flaunting them – would it be a surprise if a husband saw him too and took revenge? He was a fool!' She slumped against the table. 'Go away, both of you. I have to work. They've taken my husband, my future, and now my dignity. And they didn't even leave his body for me. I can't even have the relief of seeing him buried.'

'You say "they" – you must have an idea who,' I pressed her. I was sure she knew something.

She looked away pointedly, but suddenly, as though she couldn't hold it in any longer, she burst out, 'Ask his master! Ask Wolfe!'

I would have questioned her further, but she turned away from me. 'Walter, you're a good man. Your brother wasn't, and God knows, I'm not a good woman. But I have to scrape by however I can. Leave me to my shame.'

Walter continued to wring his hands, his face twisted into a perplexed grimace. 'That poor woman!'

I had to wonder what use the man would be to a parishioner in trouble, if he was so appalled by his brother's widow. She wasn't the first, and wouldn't be the last, to sell her remaining asset to get some food.

'This is *terrible*. If I only had a little money,' Walter was saying.

I wanted no part of a sudden demand to support the woman. 'This man Wolfe is clearly a dangerous sort of fellow,' I mused.

'He is considered one of the merchants most prone to . . . to taking risks.'

'In what way?'

'Oh, well, when the other merchants lost their ships, only Wolfe did not have the vessels and cargo insured. He said there was little point, when sailing only as far as France. The other men were keen to see their investments were protected, as most merchants will, but Wolfe said he saw no need. Why should he feel safe when the risks were the same for all?'

'And he did not lose his vessel,' I said. 'Although he was about to. It was only the skill of his captain that saved him.'

And then I had a thought. What if Wolfe had already decided to stop dealing with the pirates? He might have sent notice of the first ship, the one we saw smouldering, and then his own would see the galley and flee, as Weston did. His own ship was safe, and by seeing the pirates captured, further piracy would cease. That would be an incentive for a man to forego the costs of covering his vessel and cargo, surely?

'How much would such a policy cost?' I asked.

'According to Roger, anything from one-twentieth to even a tenth of the ship and all inside her.'

'A tenth?' I said, shocked. To think that a man could command such riches, in the full expectation that he would never have to pay out . . . that was astonishing. 'Who would they see to buy this kind of protection?'

'They arranged it between themselves and other merchants. Roger used to arrange the details. He was a most competent scrivener. I helped teach him myself. He would take the contracts, and those covering the risk would sign under the contract, so that there was no confusion.'

'So all the merchants here in the city could have been involved?'

'Yes. And not only the City's Guild members. Even the cathedral invests.'

'The dean himself, I suppose?'

'Well, he is the more senior member of the cathedral when the bishop is not here. And he is rarely here.'

My mind was whirling. 'So, if the merchants saw their vessels sink, they could claim back the money from the others?'

'Yes. It is all about the management of risk. They knew that they would get some return if their ships were sunk and they lost all. After all, if there was no cover for losses, they would lose all. And any man who had invested in their ship would also lose everything. A bottomry bond—'

'A *what*?'

'It is a loan. A man wants to buy a ship but hasn't the money, so he goes to another man with money, who lends it to him. The man has his ship, but only on the basis of a loan. And if the other man wants his money back, he can demand it. It is a loan, and the man making that loan can take it back when he wants. But if the ship sinks, both men lose all. That is why Ralegh and Shapley are ruined. They have lost their ships and cargoes. And Wolfe had invested in them, so his loan is also lost. That is why merchants and lenders prefer to control the risks to their incomes as far as is possible.'

'And Roger, your brother, was helping to arrange these loans and control the risks to ships?'

'Yes. But then he began to question the basis of the loans.'

'If he had learned of pirates who were capturing the ships and stealing their cargoes, I am not surprised.'

'I suppose so. It did not occur to me then.'

'Who did Roger work for the most?'

'Why, Wolfe. He was the man who wanted help most of all, I suppose. I never liked him. Roger used to say that he was a greedy, hard man. I cannot imagine him wasting any opportunity to beat another. He would grab it with both hands.'

'Why would he take your brother's body, I wonder?'

'Why would anyone?'

That was another question that made no sense to me. Why would anyone decide to remove a dead body? It was already discovered, after all. The coroner himself might not have viewed it, but he would at least know that it was a man who had been bludgeoned to death.

If he had any sense, he would immediately demand that Ned, and the other two, answer questions about Roger Lane's death. After all, they had already confessed to beating the poor fellow.

We parted soon after, Walter heading towards his church out by the East Gate, me wandering aimlessly, wondering how best to bring about my revenge on Wolfe for my incarceration on his ship.

I gradually made my way back to my inn and was glumly imbibing when Wolfe himself appeared in the doorway. He cast a glance about the room, not noticing me sitting in the corner, and motioned the large henchman whom I had seen on that first day to enter with him.

At the sight of him, I had a rush of genuine anger. I didn't care that he had a bodyguard with him; I was angry – very angry. He had pretended to befriend me, but he had deceived me. He had persuaded me to pay to take a ship to London, but he had ordered that I was to be deposited on the shores of France. I had been beaten about the head, run the risk of being run through on a pirates' ship – and emptied my belly more times than I could count.

The henchman followed behind Wolfe as his master led the way to a table in a corner, and I rose to follow them. I have to say, the expression of dumb shock on Wolfe's face when he caught sight of me approaching was an absolute joy.

'You're guilty, and I know it,' I said.

He jerked away from me, the shock at my accusation plain on his face. His guilt was plain as a dead rat in a sack of flour. Which was also the colour his face turned – pure white.

'I suppose you had not expected to see me again,' I said as I drew nearer.

Wolfe shot a look up at his henchman, and then back at me. 'My . . . my friend, I thought you would be halfway to London by now.'

'What, after an overnight in France? It would take me longer than that to get to London, wouldn't it?' I said, and I think it was cutting. I meant it to be.

'France? Why would you have gone there?' He smiled.

A servant appeared with a large jug of wine and a goblet. She set them before Wolfe, giving me a curious and slightly confused glance as if wondering whether she should fetch me a cup. I nodded to indicate yes; Wolfe shook his head and waved her away. It was rude, but I suppose he had not invited me.

'Why, because you had paid the master of the *Thomas* to take me to France and leave me there,' I said sharply. 'You were deliberately disposing of me. Why? What had I ever done to you? All I wanted was to get away from here, but you tried to set me on a distant shore where I would have been utterly without friends or support.'

'I don't know what you mean,' he said. He was recovering his poise, and a small smile of cynicism pulled at his mouth.

'Really? That is astonishing. You, a man who had a cargo of tin and copper to go to France, and yet you paid your shipmaster to take me with him. You knew Weston wasn't going to London.'

'I recommended a ship, that is all,' he said suavely.

'You paid Weston to take me and lie about his destination. I know. He told me.'

'Where is he?'

'He's still in Exmouth, I expect. He's helping unload a galley we caught yesterday: pirates.'

Wolfe was rattled, I saw. He had a way of jutting his chin forward as though in a truculent display, but from looking at him, I was sure he was more alarmed than angry. 'What are you saying? Pirates? A galley?'

'They have been raiding ships. It took Ralegh's ship, and Shapley's, and I daresay others besides. And someone was telling the galley which ships to take. It was trying to catch the *Thomas*.'

'What, it found you at sea?'

'Someone sent a messenger to the galley to let them know that the *Thomas* was preparing to leave the harbour. And that "someone" was prepared to see every soul aboard die, just as he was prepared to see the men on the other ships die or become enslaved on a galley.'

'That is far-fetched!'

'There was a man there, Harry Lydd, who was very convincing about it.'

'Did he recognize this messenger?'

His attitude left me flummoxed. He did not have the look of a man desperate to escape justice now that his crimes were found out; he was more like a man whose meal has been served too cold. He studied me with a quizzical expression on his face. 'So? Did he know this messenger? If so, we can have him captured and punished.'

I had to shake my head at that.

'They tell me that merchants in London are some of the sharpest and brightest in the country. Clearly, you are no merchant,' he said sarcastically.

'You tried to . . .'

'You should be most careful before making allegations you cannot support,' he said with sudden fury in his eyes. I leaned away. He really did look partly lunatic as he continued, 'In fact, you should be careful without exception! Perhaps you are not welcome in our city; perhaps you would be well advised to leave! Go back to your precious London and stay there! Exeter is a wild place for fools. They can be hurt. *Especially those who try to seduce other men's wives!*'

I blinked at that. After all, I had done nothing of the sort. I had not had the opportunity yet. 'I will go home as soon as I may.'

'Yes, I'm sure you will,' he said with a sneer. He flapped a hand, and suddenly I had a shoulder lifted by his henchman. 'Goodbye, little Master Jack. Do have a good journey home,' Wolfe added as I was pulled from the table and marched to the door.

I left him there, his henchman shoving me from the door and smirking at me as I walked from the inn. My anger knew few bounds, and if it were not for the size of the henchman, I would have run back in and attempted to remonstrate with Wolfe. But the man at the door was larger than the doorway. I wouldn't get past him. Besides, I needed to clear my head. There was something I did not understand.

If I had to wager, I would put my money on the news of the pirates being a surprise to him. He seemed genuine in his desire to find the messenger sent to the pirates and overheard by Harry Lydd. Yet he had reacted as a guilty man would when I accused him. Perhaps he merely realized that little I said had value in a court. It was my word against his, and I couldn't even produce the messenger.

Thinking hard, I walked without care. My path took me down towards the South Gate, and as I passed the entrance where I had been caught by the dean's bodyguards as I walked past with the watchman that first night, I felt a little safer. I could see the South Gate itself and, thinking I might wander outside the city walls and calm myself, I bent my way towards it and then felt a hand grab my belt.

I moved as quickly as an adder. My hand snapped around and grasped my pistol, and then I span and thrust it into the face of my assailant. It was a smiling Davy Appowell.

'You don't want to do that,' he said firmly, grasping my gun's barrel and taking it from my hand. Not that it would have made a huge difference had I pulled the trigger. It came to me then that I had not refilled the barrel with powder and shot since breaking into the cell on board the galley.

He smiled again. 'The dean would like another word with you,' he said.

It was the same room. I threw a glance over my shoulder as I was led in, but Ned was not there in the corner this time. My two captors pushed me ungently and stood still. I was propelled forward and stopped a scant four paces from him where he sat on a seat before the fire.

'I seem to recall suggesting that you should leave my affairs alone. You were to drop charges against Edward, and you were not to become enmeshed in my affairs. I had thought you would leave—'

'I tried to!'

'—but you appear still to be here,' he finished, as though I had not spoken. 'That is not pleasing. Further, you seem to be meddling in matters that do not concern you.'

'I'm trying to go home. I don't want to be here,' I protested. 'I tried to go, but my ship was attacked by pirates, and I've only just escaped from that, and now I want to just get back to London. I don't want to be here!'

'You are a determined protester, I see. What happened to your ship?'

'We were set upon. Someone told the pirates we were to pass that way, and they lay in wait for us. They destroyed the ship before us, slaughtered the crew, and then saw us.' Behind me, I heard a slight snigger. I turned to see Davy Appowell grinning. 'You think it's funny?'

The dean motioned to him to be silent. 'And they caught you? Because I don't think pirates tend to release captives without financial reward,' he said.

'No, they failed. And the captain of my vessel fooled them

into crossing a sandbank and grounded them. The pirates were all killed and the ship captured.'

'I see. How enterprising. And how were they told that your ship would pass by?'

'A messenger from Exmouth sailed and warned them. He was overheard by one of the galley's slaves.'

'Who was this messenger?'

'I don't know! I wasn't there!'

'I see. Why were you on this ship, when you were, as you say, trying to get home to London?'

'It was Wolfe! He told me his ship was going to London, when all the time he knew full well that it was going to France. He expected me to be dropped there, and never to see me again.'

'Why?'

'Eh?'

'Why do you think he would want to make you disappear?'

'I don't know! All I know is, he knew where the ship was heading, and someone warned the pirates.'

'I see. In that case, you should be wary of seeing him again. He must surely be a serious danger to you. If he was prepared to send you away, he might be equally willing to see you murdered.'

I gulped at that.

'Yet you are here again, and no doubt causing confusion and dismay wherever you go,' he said.

'I don't *want* to be here!'

'Perhaps,' he said pensively. He rubbed his hand against his chin, and the stubble rasped like a file on steel. 'If you speak the truth, he should be watched most carefully.'

'I feel sure he is,' I said. 'I think he was involved in Lane's murder, too.'

'Why?'

'I've heard that Lane was a thorn in the side of many, but he was also an honest man. He had made his oath to God as a priest in the Church of England and was not going to change his coat to suit anyone,' I said, gulping slightly. I didn't like to make such bold comments before a religious man. Such courage had led others to the funeral pyres. 'He would not lie, I am sure.'

'I told you once that he was a heretic: a devotee of the false religion imposed by King Henry and his son! I don't think a man committed to a heathen faith could be honourable. I would see all such fools brought back to the true faith, and if they are not, they should be destroyed!'

His anger was no display of play-acting. I could feel his rage.

'Yes, you are right.'

He frowned, calming himself. 'But what threat could Lane have been to Wolfe – or anyone else?'

'I have been told that he was a clerk for Wolfe.' I had an inspiration. 'Perhaps he suspected Wolfe's involvement with the loss of ships? If he realized that Wolfe was telling the pirates about Ralegh's and Shapley's ships so they could be captured, Wolfe might have had him murdered.'

'But Wolfe's own ship was threatened today.'

'Perhaps the pirates would have paid Wolfe the value of his cargo and ship. He could have shown he was in the same trough as the others, and suffering as much, and carried on without making a loss?'

'It is possible. I shall raise it with the coroner when he finally appears to view the body of Lane. Not that he will do much, I daresay, now the body has disappeared.'

'It has not been discovered?'

'No,' he said heavily. 'Nobody has admitted taking it, and it remains hidden. It is most perplexing.'

It was almost midday when I was deposited outside the cathedral close by the dean's bodyguards, as I was beginning to think of them, and I stood nervously eyeing every dark alley and doorway.

It seemed to me that each time I stepped out of doors, I was likely to have my purse stolen, be assaulted, or merely be grabbed and led in front of the dean. At least in some homes, I was more or less safe. At Ralegh's house, I could rely on a good meal, albeit at the cost of insults from the obnoxious Godfrey. It meant I was in a pensive frame of mind as I stood there watching the last of the crowds disappearing up the road or down through the South Gate.

On a whim, I began to wander morosely up towards the High Street, my mind whirling. I was more than happy to accept the dean's injunction that I should leave – persuading me to stay would have been a great deal more difficult. I needed to think; that much was clear. I wanted Wolfe to pay for his attempt to sell me into slavery, but it was vanishingly unlikely that I would succeed in bringing some form of justice to him. No, I would have to give up on ever getting my own back on him.

'Master Blackjack! Master Blackjack?'

It was the incompetent bottler from Shapley's hall. He pattered after me on light shoes as I walked across Carfax, and stopped a matter of yards away, panting like a dog in the sun, hands on his thighs and bent over. He looked at me as though he expected me to divine what the devil he wanted. Well, if he wanted a new job, or wanted me to put in a good word for him to get his old job back, I was able to correct his impression with a few choice words.

He looked offended. 'No, Master Blackjack, I am still employed by Master Shapley – he sent me to find you. He said you had returned to the city, and he wishes you to join him. I still work for him, Master, but I'm not allowed near the wine anymore.'

A good idea. Shapley clearly had the same view of the more foolish of the lower class of servant as I did. When I thought of all the wine that the hopeless woodcock and rogue Raphe, my own incompetent servant, had consumed without my permission . . . well, it was a lot.

However, this fool's appearance may well have been fortunate. I already knew I must speak with either Ralegh or Shapley about Wolfe. This was a perfect opportunity. Besides, I was aware of a gap where once I had possessed a stomach. I had not eaten since breaking my fast. At Shapley's house, I could be assured of a meal. With that in mind, I graciously indicated to the lad that he had my full attention and traipsed after him to his master's home.

Rarely has a reception been quite so warm, in my experience.

As I entered the front door, there was a commotion inside, and I had the distinct impression that the whole family had been waiting for me with bated breath. My hand was taken in a most accommodating fashion by the lady of the house, who expressed her delight to have me return and proceeded to kiss me enthusiastically on the lips. Then her husband appeared – if possible, with his eyes still more bulbous than before – making a great show of welcoming me to his hall, bellowing to his servants to bring wine, and ushering me into the chamber itself, where I was confronted by Alice and her maidservant. She stood most prettily and gave me a curtsey with the reverence due to a royal prince.

I was wafted past all the commonplace formalities of greeting and polite conversation and ensconced in a comfortable chair. When I blinked, miraculously a goblet of fine wine appeared. A second blink, and I was aware of a plate of sweetmeats. A third, and Shapley was at my side, grimacing in a horrible way that, I realized, was supposed to be a smile. He simpered. It was repellent.

'Master Blackjack, we heard that you were once more in our city. We are very glad to see you.'

'I was almost captured by pirates. It was a relief to return,' I said.

'That is terrible!' Shapley said. He cast a quick glance at his wife, who gave a shrill cry of horror and began praising my courage.

'It was a desperate battle,' I said. 'I had to board their ship and kill all the pirates. Still, I managed to rescue many of the slaves from their craft. Poor, starved creatures though they were.'

'Did the pirates speak of my ship?'

'No, we slaughtered them where they stood. I was not going to allow them to continue their depredations all up and down the coast,' I said with the cold, courageous tones of a man who was used to fighting.

I became aware that another chair was close to me. Somehow it had edged nearer as I was speaking. There was no need for me to look to tell that it was Alice. But I did anyway. She was a restful vision for the eyes, after all.

There were some urgent matters for Shapley and his wife to

deal with, apparently, and with much gracious bowing and scraping, they both made their way from the room. They even took Alice's maid with them.

I felt the tingle of danger. I am brave enough, as you will know, but there are times when a man recognizes peril. When an opposing army is running at him; when a cavalry charge is launched at him; when a volley of matchlocks are fired at him; and also when a very personable young woman, with whom a fellow's younger, fitter and more martial friend is besotted, tries to stick her claws in. Because that was clearly the intention of this household. That was why I had been sought all over the town, that was why I was so graciously handled here in the house, and that was why Alice had gradually moved her chair closer. She was a spider, and I was the unwary fly that had flown straight into her web. And now I was aware of my plight.

'Mistress, have you seen young Master Ralegh?' I asked. My voice came as a slight squeak, but she appeared not to notice.

'Who? Oh, no. Not since that day you boldly defended me from him,' she said. She leaned forward, slightly towards me as well, and rested her delicate little jaw on her left hand. 'Why ask about him?'

'He told me that you and he . . . that is . . .'

From beneath her coif, a few strands of her dark ringlets protruded. For all that I was in extreme danger, the temptation to take one and twine it about my finger was all but overwhelming.

'He and I are not engaged, no. He is a foolish boy, in so many ways. I believe he has decided where his own future lies, without thinking what others might desire.'

I looked at her face as a means of defending myself against such rashness and found myself entranced by her glorious eyes. Trying to distract myself, I set my eyes on her lips, which were smiling and slightly parted. Her tongue slipped out and slowly and lasciviously wetted her upper lip, from right to left, then left to right . . . It was intolerable. My codpiece was threatening to lift and demonstrate how she was affecting me. My last defiant attempt to divert the headlong charge that my mind was pursuing was to bring my eyes lower. That was a failure, too. It brought my attention to the swelling magnificence of her perfect bosom. The urge to press my face into that was almost more than I could bear.

'Mis . . . Mistress, I . . .'

'Yes?'

Her voice was low and husky. I dared not meet her eyes. I was trapped. I tried to cross my legs, but she put a hand on my thigh, and I was nearly unmanned.

'I . . .' I tried.

'Hush. I can see how warm you are . . . Would you like me to fan you? Perhaps we could loosen your clothing?'

I almost yelped. She leaned closer, and I was granted the feel of her hot breath as she whispered in my ear, 'I would like to get warm with you.'

And at that moment – had they been observing us? – Shapley and his wife made a loud entrance. He made his way to the opposite side of the table, and I was relieved to feel that the hot little hand had been removed from my leg, and Alice had taken up a more erect posture. As to my own condition, I leave that to my reader's imagination. Let me just say that I was feeling distinctly hot.

Shapley sat down with a look of gratification on his face. He looked now like a toad who has swallowed a particularly large and juicy dragonfly. 'I see you get on well together,' he said with overtones of smugness. 'I can see why, you both being such attractive fellows. Perhaps a union between our families would be of benefit to us all. Where does your father come from?'

I felt a cold sweat run down my spine. I had no desire to be amorously associated with this woman. When I thought of her, all I could see was Richard Ralegh's face and his well-worn sword. It was not a sight conducive to calmness or comfort.

'Master?' he said.

'My father?' I had a sudden vision of my father. A broken-down brute who had beaten me for complaining when I was hungry, who had made my life a misery after my mother left home. He told me she had died, but I never believed that. I think she grew weary of being used as his punchbag and suffering for his inadequacies. Just as I had. I left him when I was still a boy. I knew I would be better off among strangers than with him. 'He was a businessman, but he's dead now.' He was to me, anyhow.

'You have prospects, I think?'

'Um, yes,' I said, thinking of my master, John Blount, and my career as an inefficient assassin.

'You can see that my daughter has taken a clear interest in you,' he said.

I looked at her. She went through that lip-licking again, gazing very directly into my eyes. I shivered.

'I am sure, but my business is precarious,' I said.

'All the better. You can come here. I have a need for another man. You and I will be like father and son, Master Jack. We will build a business that will rival even a Genoese house! With us at the helm, we will achieve much!'

'But you have lost your ship,' I pointed out.

'Oh, yes, but there is still money to be made,' he said. 'With your funds and my acumen, we will build a new ship . . . a pair of ships, perhaps! We will take on all rivals. After all, with Ralegh as near to wiped out as he could be, and with Wolfe almost as bad, since he had put his money in our ships, few will want to invest in them, and if someone did, the insurance costs on their ships will be much greater now. Merchants like to manage their risks, and that doesn't mean throwing money at a man who is unlucky enough to have lost all when pirates took his vessel. That is no way to build confidence when your investors are shareholders in your cargoes.'

I did not like to point out that he himself was as unlucky as Ralegh.

Shapley smiled slowly. It was rather like seeing a ferret smile. It meant there would be pain shortly. He waved at his wife and daughter, sending them out, and then, when we were alone, he set his elbows on the table and leaned forward, shaking his head. 'You'll have to learn how business works, Master Blackjack. If you're going to join me, you'll best do so quickly.'

I tried to interrupt at this point, but he waved away my protestations. 'I have little doubt that Wolfe would have been broken if his ship had been taken. He lost much on my ship, and to lose his own as well would ruin him entirely. Now, with you backing me, we can take up the trade that Ralegh and Wolfe owned, as well as my own. People will be happier trading with you, a London merchant. You add credibility. Meanwhile, my expertise and contacts will make our business flourish. We will clear up all trade from Exeter. You and me together? We cannot fail! You will make more money than you could dream of, and in return for your investment, I give you my daughter, too. She is keen enough, I think. She looked it!'

I sat back and tried to get my head to accommodate this. To say I was startled would be an understatement.

'It was obvious to me, the moment I met you, that you were the ideal partner,' he said, his eyes narrowing as he smiled expansively. He waved a hand airily and let out a guffaw of laughter. 'I mean, a man from London! We all know how you conduct business up there!'

He began to regale me with tales of merchants, bankers and other thieving fraudsters he had known, and all the while my mind was reeling. I felt sickened, and the nightmare was unlikely to disappear anytime soon if this fool had his way. He had my future mapped out in detail, from the sound of things. He was providing me with a wife and a business, and he obviously thought that either would be enough to sway me – but with both, I was a certainty.

I could see my future stretching away into the distance – and it was not unpleasant. A life without the constant fear of Blount, my master, looking over my shoulder and deciding I was an unnecessary expense. Not having to maintain friendly relations with him was a genuine advantage. And this was the sort of work I was made for: a chance to settle down while someone else did the work, and all I need do was rake in the profits and spend them, meanwhile enjoying the thoroughly fruitful attentions of young Alice. Her smile and obvious attractions were the icing on the cake. I would have to leave London, which would be a hardship, but there were appealing aspects to this city, after all.

And then I remembered that I would be likely to die within moments of the banns being read. If I read the temperament of young Richard Ralegh correctly, and I was sure that I did, the first thing I would be likely to earn after announcing my betrothal to his inamorata was a swift blade in the belly. He was undoubtedly a doughty fellow, and a good friend in a brawl, but as a jilted lover, he would be quick to judge and bring punishment of a sort that would strike him as fair and reasonable. He might be an ardent patron of a certain brothel, but that wouldn't stop him from feeling jealously deprived, were I to take the woman he viewed as his own. He felt entitled in that way.

'Um,' I said.

Some little while later, I was outside the house and in a hurry to make my escape.

I managed it only barely, claiming that I must recover my bags from the care of the innkeeper, and Shapley, exuding glee to know that he was about to gain a son and my money, was content to receive my promise of returning soon.

Alice, who only a few days before had been such a temptation, was now an object of terror. She attempted to close with me when I took my farewell; I tried to remain stoic in the face of her charms, but when she slid in front of me and took a grip of my shoulders, pulling me closer, I confess that the odour of sandalwood and liquorice about her was enough to make me forget my concerns and pucker my lips hopefully. But her father appeared in the doorway just then and rescued me.

She whispered, 'Soon you will be able to have me without interruption,' and stood back, that teasing little smile playing at her lips once more. One hand knocked my codpiece, but I'm sure it was only an accident. Surely even she wouldn't be so brazen. Would she?

Shapley nodded and smiled, like some usurer certain of a solid profit. But like a usurer, there was a menacing side to his smile. He wanted me to give him all my money so that he could set himself up in business once more.

I had a suspicion that as soon as Shapley had approved of my coming nuptials, his servants would have been about the city telling everyone. And that would be certain to include the Ralegh household. I shivered at the thought of the worn grip on his sword.

With that happy thought, I set off for the inn once more.

There was an area on the left of Shapley's house, which was now an orchard. As I was trotting past, I was aware suddenly of a faint pattering, as of light footsteps. I turned, and there, on a path in the clearing, I thought I saw a figure disappear behind a tree. It was a fleeting glimpse, nothing more, but I was quite certain I had seen it. And it sent a shiver of pure terror down my spine. After all, it was gathering dusk, and the figure was a strange sight. Dark, with a small frame, just like one of those piskies the fools on Dartmoor spoke of, the malevolent little folk who would lead a man astray, take him from his path and to his doom. From the higher points of the city wall, the moors could be seen over in the distance: a grey-blue, brooding presence in the far distance, but not far enough to my taste.

So, yes, I shivered afresh at the sight of the small figure and hurried my steps still more. But as I went, I was sure I heard the little *slap, slap, slap* of bare feet behind me, like a ghost chasing me to rend my soul from my body and . . .

Yes, I was terrified. I am a cool fellow in an emergency – you can ask anyone who knows me – but this creature, clearly in pursuit, was enough to unman me. It made me want to cry out for mercy. I rushed on, gibbering slightly, which is perfectly understandable, given my immediate predicament. When I reached the roadway and was forced to slow because of the queue of people in the way, I summoned up the courage to turn and face my petrifying pursuer, but there was nothing to be seen. Whatever the thing was, it had concealed itself, somehow.

I breathed a sigh of relief, and you may be assured that I hesitated not at all in making my way swiftly to the inn. I had endured enough already for one day.

Once there, I took my ale to the back parlour, where I could sit with the fire to myself. I was in need of peace and quiet and no interruptions. At least in the back room, I was assured of solitude, or so I thought. I had only been in there for two quarts of ale, mostly to steady my nerves after hearing the pisky following me, when the door's latch was lifted, and I turned to see Ned in the doorway. He nodded to me seriously and then crossed over to the settle at the other side of the fire.

I was wary, as you can imagine, but to my surprise, he did not make an immediate move to attack me. Instead, he sat with his head hanging for a while, then stared at the flames for a little longer, and finally met my gaze.

'After Lane was found, we were the men everyone thought had killed him. No one had threatened us, but we knew people were looking at us like murderers. It's a short step from people thinking such to a dance at the hanging tree. Us, we'm grateful.'

'It was no trouble. But if you wish, you can buy me—'

'Now you've helped save men from the pirates. People trust you. So it seems right to tell you. We can't go to others without being asked many questions, but we can tell you.'

'Tell me what?'

'The body. If I tells you where un be, you can tell the coroner.'

I jerked in my seat, throwing a goodly quantity of ale over my hose. 'What? You know where it is?'

He nodded glumly. 'We di'n't realize. We thought the dean had seen Lane and bashed him on the haid, killed him accidental. He hated Lane. But we knew we'd get the blame. We'm the volks in the street. We'm the volks get blamed. If we say where to find him now, people will think it were us. And the dean won't save us.' His mournful expression lengthened.

'So you did murder Lane?'

His head shot up. 'No!' he declared hotly. 'We beat un, like us said, but left him sitting at the wall. Someone else killed him. Us di'n't break his haid!'

'Well, you have assaulted others in the lanes,' I pointed out, but he merely waved a hand airily.

'We knowed how it'd look. We'm had benefit of clergy, but that wouldn't stop others who wanted revenge. They'd come after us, and we'd be killed. So we took un.'

'You took Lane's corpse? Where? How?'

He gave a slow grin. That hideous maw opened before me again. 'Couldn't carry un all around town, could us? We tapped old Ham Barley the watchman on the haid and left un snoring, and took Lane to the end of the alley.'

'But that just led to the cathedral precinct wall.'

'Aye. Threw un over the wall. Hugh were on t'other side and caught him. Then us took un to the charnel chapel, hid un in there with the bones under the chapel. No one would look there.'

'And he's there now?'

'Aye. Best to get un out and give un to the coroner.'

'Why do you want me to help?'

'You'm a friend of the merchants, so if anything happens, you can explain. If it's us, us'll be hanged for murder.'

'I could be, too,' I burst out. I was very unhappy about helping with this plan. 'You should just tell the dean, explain why you hid him in the chapel. He'll be impressed you thought so carefully, and . . .'

'No. He'd push us out and we'd hang. Without the dean's support, we'd not last.'

There was a grim finality in his words. He had thought of this, it was clear.

'Why would he push you out? He still has a use for you, doesn't he?'

'Aye, but he's been difficult these last weeks. He doesn't want embarrassment to the cathedral. 'Tis all the men in the city who're still with old King Hal's religion. He reckons they'm difficult, and he don't want to give them any reason to rebel against the cathedral.'

'I see.' I could understand why the dean would be reluctant to have people think he was consorting with murderers, and if people were to find that Ned and his merry companions had hidden the body, it was more than likely that people would easily believe that men of a certain reputation had a hand in his death. No doubt many would wonder whether the dean himself had ordered them to kill Lane. It was easy to persuade a foolish population of any conspiracy, if they were minded to believe it. To protect himself, the dean would have to cast out his own servants.

'What do you want to do?' I asked.

I should have just continued to refuse to help. I *would* have refused to help – but Ned had the appearance of a desperate man. He wore the look that says, *I will be supportive to my friends, but my enemies will earn my everlasting enmity*. It was the sort of expression a mastiff guarding a house might wear, half welcoming, but mostly ferocious in case this newcomer was both a thief and edible. I knew Ned was fierce when roused, and I had no desire to feel his fist or his boot on my breast once more, so I nodded and said, 'Of course,' while thinking I should be able to escape him at some juncture and not go through his plan with him.

One thing was certain: he would never get me into that charnel chapel.

I was wrong.

He remained with me, and as evening drew on, he had me join him to walk to the alley where Lane had died.

There are some experiences that really do not bear recalling. This evening was one such.

I know of some men who, once imprisoned, were able to break free and find freedom. I've heard of others who would break into a storeroom to steal money. But never have I heard of a man willingly breaking into a cathedral's precinct and trying to steal away a body. Worse, breaking into a charnel chapel in among all the bones of the dead, to remove a healthy corpse. If you know what I mean.

'Here,' he said quietly at the wall blocking the end of the alley.

It was a good eight feel high, and I looked up at it with reluctance. The top might have broken pottery or anything to deter those who wished to enter without permission. Ned had thought of that. With us were Adam and Hugh, and Adam now passed over his jerkin. It had many cuts and tears in it, and now I was treated to a demonstration of how it had gained those injuries over time. Ned took it and threw it carefully over the top of the wall. It snagged on something and stayed there. Clearly, there were spikes or other deterrents up there. I swallowed at the thought of shards stabbing into my hands, but then Ned was already up and on the wall, peering about him carefully. He held his hand to me. I took it and was lifted up and on to the wall; I put a boot on it and then sprang down on the other side. I hissed an oath. A large stone was under my foot and twisted my ankle. It had thick black muck on it. A moment later, Hugh and Ned were at my side. Apparently, Adam was to remain in the alley to keep watch.

My heart was thudding painfully as I followed them over the soft grass. It was a fair length – clearly, the scythes hadn't been used here in a while – and I could feel the stems swiping at my shins as we went.

The cathedral's close was a large space, with graves dotted all over. Dead ahead of us was the cathedral, with the saints and angels of the image screen no doubt staring at us in distaste. I could almost feel their disdain as a barrier. They would certainly disapprove of our appearing here to steal a dead body.

The charnel chapel was like a small church over to our left. It stood like a reddish grey block in the midst of all the graves, illuminated by the poor light of a dim moon. In the dark, it looked menacing and a scene of horror. As, indeed, it was.

We made our way silently over the grass to the door. It was unlocked, and in a moment the two had slipped inside. I stood outside, and said, 'Wouldn't it be best for me to stay here to warn of anyone's appearance?' but a hand reached out, grabbed my jack and yanked me inside. My hand caught the latch and made it rattle, but not as much as my teeth, as the noise echoed, or seemed to, getting louder with every reverberation inside the chapel. I grabbed Ned to try to persuade him that perhaps we should leave, go back to the inn and leave this adventure for another evening, but he had already shoved me before him, and I went sprawling on the tiled floor.

It was as black as the inside of a barrel of pitch in there, but less pleasant. The upper storey here was where the chaplain would come to pray, and I could just make out an altar in the dim light. Hugh walked to it and fingered a cross with a quiet regret, but Ned hissed at him to steal nothing, and then we were on our way to the door over at the rear of the chapel. This gave on to a broad staircase that led to the bowels of the earth – or the undercroft where the bones were all stored.

Ned led the way, and Hugh pushed me after him. With a sense of dread, I did as told.

The chamber beneath was as cold as the devil's mercy, and it smelled – mostly of fungus and mould, but also partly of rotten meat. Ned had a small candle, and now he struck tinder and flint until he had a flame and could direct us to where the body was hidden.

It was a chamber of horror. The same size as the chapel above, the chamber had many arches on all sides, and all were filled.

I have to admit, I let out a short bleat of terror as Ned's light flooded the walls. They were all bones. Long leg bones, shorter arm bones, ribs and vertebrae, handfuls of tiny fragments, which I suppose were fingers, toes and other little bits, and a mass of well-stored skulls, their blank eye sockets seemingly watching our every move. I shivered as the flame illuminated more and more empty sockets.

'Shut up,' Ned hissed. It wasn't as though the priests were going to hear my cry, and when I looked to apologize, his face was unnaturally white as well, and he was glancing from side to side as though he too felt the presence of all the dead in the room.

He moved forward, past a pile of pelvic bones, from which I averted my gaze, and over to a wall of shin and thigh bones. They were stacked neatly, like so many fence posts. Ned went to them and crept around to reach behind. When he gave a muttered call, Hugh stepped forward. Ned had disappeared behind the pile of bones, and now he was hidden from view by the low arch, but we could hear his scrabbling and the sound of bones being moved, rattling and clattering like tiles in a game of dominoes. He had taken the light with him, so now as he worked, there were strange and deeply unpleasant shadows like long fingers of darkness reaching out to grab me and pull me in there with all the dismembered dead. It was all I could do to stifle my dread. Luckily, I am by nature brave.

'Shut up,' Ned said. He must have been talking to Hugh.

Hugh himself was bending round behind the pile of bones, and now he started to come out, backwards, pulling a large mass. 'He do smell!'

'He's been dead a few days. Wait till he's been lit by the sun an hour or two,' Ned said.

They brought the body out, and Ned jerked his head back towards the light. 'Bring the candle, Jack.'

I was sorely tempted to ignore him and pelt back up the stairs to the chapel itself, but a quick look at Ned's face told me it would not be a good idea. I nodded and went to the gap where they had brought out the body. It was a wide enough space, and behind was a muddle of bones of various ages. In their midst was the candle, which was standing in a puddle of molten wax on a skull. I reached for it and gave it a tug. The wax must have fixed the candle to the bone, because as I did so, the skull came away, only to suddenly drop loudly on to the other bones. The change in weight made my hand jerk, and hot wax flooded my fingers, scalding them. In my pain, I gave a cry and sprang into the air. The candle went out.

My boot landed on a thigh bone, which moved with a hollow, grating sound. I instinctively moved away, and my boot stepped on an ancient bone which crunched and made me shriek with alarm. I sprang back further.

'Ye daft—'

I heard Ned's agonized call, but it was too late. Trying to save myself by leaping from the leg bones, I encountered a tottering pile of ribs. I avoided them, but only by resting my hand on something like a stony marble. It moved. I gazed down and, with dismay, saw that I was resting my hand on a skull. It stared at me balefully for my presumption, and I snatched my hand away. For an instant, I knew peace. I was still, the world was still, the bones were all still.

And then there came that small sound of grinding as a skull began to wobble.

If I had retrieved the candle, I would have been interested to see the expression on the faces of my two accomplices, but as it was, we were in impenetrable darkness now, and only the constant low murmur of curses told me where the other two were. Fortunately, the door to the upper chamber was still open, and the doorway began to show itself as a slightly less dark area of the wall. Ned and Hugh picked up their burden once more, and we began to make our way up the steps.

Most reluctantly, I was left in the rear. I disliked this. It meant I had to go up the stairs with my back to the grim horror of the chamber, and I was sure I could hear dragging steps, or crawling, as unmentionable creatures followed me to try to catch me and hold me in that chamber of death. I tried to hasten up the stairs, away from them, but Ned and Hugh wouldn't hurry. I would have overtaken them, but there was not the room, and then suddenly we were in the chapel itself, and I could breathe again. I slammed the door shut on the hideous staircase and turned with a relieved smile to face the others.

I think the best term for their expressions is probably 'baleful'. Nothing was said, but it was clear that, in the opinion of my confederates, I was several dice short of a game. I tried to apologize, but all I got was a glare from Ned as he hefted the body once more. I opened the door for them, and we made our way into the dull moonlight.

It was so bright after the crypt that it felt as though we were walking into broad daylight. The moon was a sliver of silver, and the clouds seemed to chase across his face as if in a hurry to be somewhere else. Like me, perhaps they were desperate to leave this benighted city and go somewhere sane and civilized, like London.

We all three stood blinking a moment. It was not only the sudden brightness of the moon; it was also the fact that seven men were standing before us. One was Adam, but the others were all too familiar – especially the two nearest me. They were the cathedral guards who had dragged me before the dean twice already.

'Um.'

'Hello, Ned. The dean would like a word with you and your friends,' Davy Appowell said.

The interview was not a lengthy affair.

We were marched once more into that room, which was quickly becoming familiar to me, and found the dean sitting before his fire, clad in a thick cloak against the evening chill. He had a glass in his hand and sipped as he peered at us without expression.

'My Lord,' Ned began, but I could have told him he was wasting his breath. This dean was in no mood to be soothed.

'I have to attend matins shortly,' he said coldly. 'You have interrupted my sleep, and now I will enter the cathedral in the wrong frame of mind. And it is all your fault. What on earth do you mean by this?'

'Us di'n't think,' Ned said, head hanging.

'Do you ever?' the dean said in his most cutting, acerbic tone. 'Why was Lane's body in the crypt of the chapel?'

'Us thought the coroner might think you had a hand in his death,' Hugh explained.

'So, with your astonishing brilliance, you took it on yourselves to bring him here, to where I could have concealed him? That, to me, appears to show you attempting to put the blame for the murder on to my shoulders!'

'No, us were takin' him back to where he had been, so the coroner could find un,' Ned said.

'And how would that prevent his suspecting me?' the dean asked.

'There's nothing to say you had a part in his death,' Ned said.

'You are incompetent fools! And now you have laid yourselves open to accusations! I cannot protect you.'

'Let us go and take him, and you won't hear more of it,' Ned said.

'Let you go?' The dean stared. 'Half the cathedral knows you have been caught here with his body! How can I let you go? What sort of gossip would ensue? No, you will have to be arrested and held. The good Lord only knows what we should do with the corpse.'

'My Lord, you can't . . .'

'Take them away. Put them in the gaol.'

EIGHT

The Dean, the Merchant, and Conclusion

12 August

I will say this for the clergy: when they misbehave, they may be forced to suffer imprisonment in a cell, but at least it is a cell designed for them, by which I mean it was nothing like Newgate or the Middlesex Bridewell with their filthy, damp and dark conditions. Instead, we were installed in a spacious chamber that was in many ways better than most of the bedchambers I had used in Exeter. The blankets neatly folded on the floor were clean – and free from fleas, I was to discover. Yes, it was more comfortable than the inn.

'What now?' Ned said.

'I don't know,' I responded. Being a seasoned campaigner, I was not going to sit up and worry with Ned about whether he was going to have his neck stretched.

It was a curious position. These two, who had tried to protect their master, were now to be held for the coroner. He would no doubt make short shrift of them both. Meanwhile, I was also held, but at least I could state that I was not in the city when Lane was killed.

When the sun broke through the thick morning smoke from cooking fires, I was woken by the rattling of a spoon along the bars of the door. Looking over, I saw a servant carrying three pots steaming with hot porridge. I took one, and soon my belly was full enough. It was not the most exciting of meals, but it was adequate. I had scarcely finished my breakfast when we were called to the door.

We followed the gaoler out into the open air. He took

us to the dean's house. There, we were welcomed by the now overly familiar face of the dean's henchman, Appowell. He led us upstairs to the dean's room. I was glad of the roaring fire after my night in the cell and tried to sidle near to it.

He was sitting at his desk once more, writing, but he set aside his reed as we entered, and gazed at us with cold bemusement. 'You fools! I understand you were trying to protect me, but if I were guilty of murder, you should have alerted the authorities here in the cathedral, not tried to take matters into your own hands.'

Ned tried to speak, but the dean continued, ignoring his protestations and attempts at explanation.

'It will not do. I cannot continue to protect you. You will bring the chapter into disrepute. I fear I must take charge. I cannot help you further. From this moment, you are no longer servants of mine. You have no right to benefit of clergy.'

'But if they catch us, they'll hang us without the benefit,' Ned said despairingly.

'And if you remain in the cathedral, how could I defend you? You have brought this upon yourself. There are so many enemies in the city who would harm us, just because they despise the true religion, that your presence could bring about a fresh rebellion. I cannot risk that. You must go.'

He motioned to the henchman, who stepped forward and passed Ned a small purse of coin. 'Take that and welcome. But from now on, you are not my responsibility.'

A little later, we were at the gate to South Gate Street. Here the henchman motioned to us that we should leave. Ned and Hugh were off and through the gateway like two schoolboys sent to be caned.

The henchman looked at me. 'The dean says you're free to leave, but make sure you take advantage. Leave Exeter and never return.'

'With great pleasure,' I said, but then I hesitated. 'But what will happen to Ned and Hugh?'

'They'll run from the city, I daresay, and be caught and hanged.' He shrugged.

'But they didn't kill Lane,' I said. I was perversely sure of their innocence now.

'Perhaps. But if the murderer isn't found, they'll pay.'

It was a relief to walk out under that gateway and into the street again. When I glanced behind me, the henchman had followed me. 'Don't forget, Master Blackjack, you need to leave Exeter. You are bad luck – and you're bringing bad luck to the city. You aren't wanted here. Go!'

He chuckled nastily, turned on his heel and was gone. I disliked him more every time I saw him, and as I stood surveying the road ahead, I saw a familiar face. It was the gaunt features of Harry Lydd.

He looked at me with a face of tragedy. 'It's him,' he said.

I had not had an easy evening, and my weariness slowed my brain. 'What's who?'

'Him. The messenger! The one who brought news of the *Thomas* to the pirates! That was him!' he said, pointing.

I followed his finger. He was indicating the gatehouse to the cathedral. 'The porter?'

'No, you fool! The man that just called to you!'

With that, he broke into a shuffling run through the entrance to the cathedral, leaving me bemused. Appowell was in league with the pirates? It seemed unlikely to me. However, just then there was something else that snagged at my attention.

I had caught a glimpse of a pretty face above a slender figure. It was Mistress Wolfe. She stood staring at me with an eyebrow raised. She held my gaze for a moment, and then slipped into a doorway.

It was a clear invitation. I have been enticed by many women in my time, and this was the clearest summons I had ever received. I reflected that Wolfe had tried to send me abroad because he thought I had already tasted the favours of his wife; it seemed only reasonable for me to enjoy them now. I hurried to the same doorway and paused, glancing around me. As my gaze took in the street, I saw a small figure dart into a shop's doorway, only to be thrust back out by an enraged shopkeeper. It was Edith, I was sure, and she took one look at me and bolted away. Foolish chit was probably trying to steal something.

There was no one else there to give me concern, and I followed Mistress Wolfe inside full of hope. It had been weeks since I had been able to tempt a woman into my bed, and it would be a glorious means of revenge on Master Wolfe were I to partake of his wife's favours. Even without that incentive, the woman was one of those who could make a king think of surrendering half his kingdom.

Inside was a gloomy hallway. A passage led through the building to a door at the rear, but before me, I saw stairs rising to the next floor. I clambered up them, and soon I was at a door. Opening it led me to a landing with a series of doors on either side. One was a little ajar, and I walked to it and pushed it wide. Inside, there was a comfortable-looking bed, and beside it stood Mistress Wolfe.

What a sight she was! Her face was a little too long, her mouth a little too wide, her eyes a little too wide-set – but the overall impression was perfection. She smiled. I smiled. It was a matter of a moment for me to kick the door shut behind me and move to her side.

She smiled more broadly and sidestepped, coquettish as a woman not yet twenty. I took it as an invitation to continue pressing my suit and almost managed to ensnare her, but she stepped back.

'Wait, my precious,' she said. 'A moment; do not be in such a hurry.'

'Ah, to hold you in my arms,' I said. 'That is all I ask.' Which was a lie, of course, but I confess that I was feeling decidedly warm in such close proximity. I essayed a fresh attack, thinking to pin her to the wall, but she was too swift again.

Panting, I gave her my famous slow smile, showing my honour, integrity and lust. She didn't melt as I had expected, but stood staring, breathing a little heavily, just enough to make her embonpoint rise and fall deliciously. I stared at it, my smile broadening, while she tried to straighten her coif, which had been pushed a little askew where my hand knocked it trying to grab her.

'No! Wait!' she said, and this time there was steel in her tone. I hesitated.

She threw a glance out through the window before facing me. 'I am sorry, but I had to warn you. My husband is very jealous. He doesn't trust me and has had me followed, and he suspects you of trying to seduce me. Be careful, because he thought Roger Lane was . . .'

That was as far as she got before the door crashed wide, and I sprang a good yard into the air without effort.

There in the doorway was Wolfe's henchman, and behind him was Wolfe himself. I think it is fair to say that he did not look like a man who was entirely in favour of Master Jack Blackjack at that moment.

Our conversation was a little stilted. I made an effort, of course, as a gentleman should. 'Ah, Master Wolfe,' I said, but without the tone of enthusiasm that polite society would usually expect. Of course, this was not the usual meeting of two men. After all, I was in a chamber with Wolfe's wife, and any man finding his wife in the same room with another fellow would be reasonably suspicious about what might have been about to happen – or what had already happened.

He certainly was.

I could tell from the way he was breathing that he had a very unfortunate comprehension of what had been about to happen when he appeared. Which struck me as unfair. I had not enjoyed the opportunity to engage in anything more strenuous than chasing his wife about the room, and to be accused now without managing to bring the engagement to a satisfactory conclusion struck me as distinctly unreasonable. Not that I was in much of a position to argue my case.

'You!' he said, and it was rather like hearing an adder hiss.

It was decidedly off-putting.

'Um . . .' I said.

'You *London* men think you can come here and make free with good honest men's wives, do you?'

I took exception to that. 'That is hardly fair! I only—'

'Shut up!' Wolfe snarled, and I did. He strode to his wife and lifted his hand as though about to slap her, but although she averted her face, he never let his hand fall. 'Again, Margaret? You seek another man again? After Lane? He's gone, but you still whore about? Why? Just to humiliate me? Why would you want to hurt me? What have I done to give you cause? I've fed you, clothed you, protected you – and this is how you reward me?'

There was more hurt and regret than anger in his voice, I was relieved to note. It spoke of a degree of common sense and returning reason. I began to feel that perhaps I wasn't in quite such danger as I had thought. That fleeting sense of security soon fled.

'Take him out. You know what to do,' he snapped at his henchman.

Suddenly, my shoulder was gripped in a ham-like hand, and I found myself being directed to the staircase once more. This time, I was to understand, would be my last.

Behind me, I heard voices, and then a slap and a cry, and more hissed vituperation. It sounded as though she was getting her deserts for her treason – not that I felt any sympathy just now. My mind was fully occupied with thoughts of my own impending demise.

I had good reason.

As we descended the stairs, I tried to engage the henchman in conversation, mentioning that I was both moderately important and fabulously rich. I tried to reach down to my purse to demonstrate how beneficial releasing me might be, but the only response from the grim-faced bonehead was a painful twist to my upper arm that directed me around, away from the front door through which I had entered, and along a passageway that led to the rear of the building. Outside, there was a small area with fruit trees and some raised beds with some decidedly unhealthy-looking kale and some other plants which I would have liked to pause and study, but my companion was in a hurry. He pushed me onwards until we came to a gate in the garden's wall. Through this, and we were in an alleyway.

'I have lots of money. Perhaps if you were to release me—' I tried.

'Shut up.'

We continued along this alley and up another. There were

few people here, and those we did see appeared desperately keen not to see me. I was persuaded by the hand on my arm that I might prefer not to attempt to call to them or beg for help. The hand on my arm communicated very effectively that such a venture would be painful and potentially lethal. I was persuaded. But I was sad to see how these people would avert their eyes on seeing me, then turn and make off in the opposite direction. The cowardice of such folks was baffling to me. I was a stranger in this city; I did not deserve to be treated thus.

'Look, if you let me go, I—'

'Shut up.'

'If you kill me, you'll hang. If he killed me in hot blood, that would be one thing, but you?'

This time he didn't deign to respond beyond painfully tightening his grip on my arm.

We crossed an alleyway and came into a street, and then over that and into another alley, and now I began to recognize certain buildings. They looked familiar, and at first I couldn't tell why, until suddenly a very familiar voice called out.

'I think you want to pay the toll for entering here, Master.'

Rarely have I been so glad to hear a voice.

Ned was behind us, having just slipped from a doorway, I suppose. My escort was reluctant to stop and gave a rude retort to Ned's demand, but as he did so, two more figures appeared ahead of us.

'I think they want you to stop,' I said helpfully. In response, the brute twisted my arm high, and I was forced to whimper and bend almost double to save my shoulder from breaking.

'I'm not going to pay you, Ned Hall, so you can go swive a cat for all I care.'

'Ned, *help*!' I said.

'That b'ain't friendly, James. This un there, he's by way of bein' a friend to me. Don't think I want to see my friend injured.'

'Really? Then ye'd best leave us be.'

Instantly, I heard the rasp of a dagger being drawn, and it was set against my neck. I whimpered again.

'Hold, James Oldditch,' Ned called now. 'The dean would be very unhappy if'n you were to kill 'im.'

I quickly burst out, 'Ned, it was Wolfe who killed Lane. He murdered the clerk and left you to take the blame!'

I felt that knife on my throat very keenly now, and then it moved, and I felt it break the skin, and felt the blood leak from the red-hot wound and drench his blade. I knew then that I was to die. Oldditch let me go and I tumbled to the ground, weeping. I could hear the henchman's steps hurrying away as he fled. Ned was apparently uninterested in his involvement in killing me. He and his associates let Oldditch run away unmolested.

No man wants to die, and to die here, in this horrible alley, from the knife of a murderer's servant, was appalling. I mean, dying generally is unappealing, but to die at the hand of a mere servant so many miles from home . . . It would be less humiliating, were I still in London. At least there, I knew I had enemies. Here, it seemed so unreasonable to have had my throat cut and expire in the kennel in this grotty alleyway. Tears welled even as I felt the steady *drip, drip* of my life's blood falling into the alleyway's filth.

'Did you mean that?' Ned asked. Even in the midst of my death throes, he was asking questions in that blunt, unsympathetic manner of his. 'It were Wolfe?'

'Yes, of course. He as good as told me just now, and then told his man to kill me. And now I'm dying.'

'What, did he stab you?'

'My throat! He cut my throat!'

Ned chuckled. ''T'ain't more'n a scratch, that. You'll live.'

I stared at him, for an instant shocked into silence, and then I slowly lifted a hand to my throat. I shuddered at the slickness of the moisture, but when I looked at my hand, there was only a faint colouring of redness. The moisture was sweat. I stared at my palm and now I was aware of a wondrous elation. I was alive! For a moment, pure joy was the only sensation I was aware of. Alive! I rolled over to sit up, touching the sore wound with the sort of happiness that I could not remember since I was a child. Perhaps when I had been playing with friends, I had been this full of joyfulness, or when I had managed to bed a woman I had desired for a long while . . . but I could not honestly say that I had been so filled with euphoria even then.

'Why'd Wolfe do that?' Ned wondered.

'Hmm?' I was not concentrating. He had to ask again before I could apply my mind.

There was only one answer to it. 'From what he said just now, Wolfe discovered Lane had been playing hide the sausage with Wolfe's wife. When he saw that you had beaten him up, he must have come across the man in the alley and clobbered him with his staff, or a rock, or something. It was just convenience. He was lucky that you had beaten the fool first and knocked him largely senseless.'

'And he squealed, and he squealed,' Ned's brother said, capering.

'You're sure of this?' Ned demanded, glaring at me fiercely, while Miller shushed Adam.

'Yes, he just said so. Why?'

'Because we thought it were some'un else we saw.'

Now Miller joined in. 'You mean all that effort were for naught?'

'Aye.'

I ignored them. There was one thing uppermost in my mind now: Wolfe had to be captured and held for the next court. Otherwise, I would be in danger every time I went out into the street. When I suggested they should help, Ned refused. 'What, us arrest a merchant? Who would listen to us! We try to do that, we'll end up in gaol ourselves,' was his response. 'No, we're just packing some things and then leaving Exeter. We might go to London. Sounds like that's a good place for hard men like us.'

'You? Hard?'

I left them. I had two options to see Wolfe arrested: Shapley or Ralegh.

My reception was mixed. First to greet me was old Godfrey, whose face was that of a man who has just smelled urine in his wine. 'You're back, then?' he said. It was not the most enthusiastic welcome I've received.

Richard appeared a short while later, with William at his side. 'Jack! You miserable, good for . . .'

I perceived that he might have heard stories about Alice and me that might be detrimental to my health.

'Wait, Richard, you must be aware first that Alice's father has set his heart on forcing me to marry her. I will need your help to escape the city before he can entrap me.'

'Eh?' His never-too-fast brain was trying to catch up as I spoke. 'You don't want to marry her?'

'My friend, Alice would be a perfect wife for most men. I would be honoured, were she remotely interested in me,' I said, and I swear there were tears of sincerity in my eyes as I spoke. I was as earnest as a child demanding a sweetmeat. 'But she told me of her love for you, and, of course, hearing that, I could not even consider marrying her. It is you she wants, Richard.'

It was not an inconsiderable relief to see him swallow this hook, line and sinker. A smug grin overwhelmed his face, which was only thrown off when his father snorted. 'She'll never marry, then!'

This was my moment. 'You have heard of my vessel's attempted capture by pirates? It was nothing to do with Alice's father. Someone else had given instructions to the pirates to stop certain vessels.'

'Who?'

'I don't know yet.'

'Richard has told me about your journey across the sea,' Godfrey said. 'It sounds as though you endured a terrible time of it; I am glad to see you well.' His tone implied he was happier about the former rather than the latter.

It took a little time to have myself heard. At last, when they were quieter, I explained about Wolfe, his attempt to kill me and his confession to killing Lane. At that, even Godfrey was still for a while, staring at me with astonishment. 'You say . . . you mean . . . you imply . . .'

'John Wolfe thought Lane was making a cuckold of him, yes. So when he saw Lane in the alley, he took the opportunity to bash him over the head with a club or a stone and left him to die. No doubt he was singing a gay little tune as he walked home, thinking he had saved his marriage. Not that he has, of course.'

'Why?'

I put on a manly, experienced expression. 'I know of such

affairs, and they invariably mean that the wife is unhappy with her marriage. If she strays once, the second time is easier, the third more easy still.'

'She's a comely woman,' Godfrey said. 'And safe enough from him.'

'You think so? The man ordered my death,' I said, rather hotly.

'Yes, but he's a mere pawn in the hands of his wife,' Godfrey said. 'He would never raise a hand to her. The man's a eunuch when it comes to her.'

'Oh,' I said. It did explain why he had not struck her in that dingy little room, even though he had all the incentive a man could wish. I had heard someone being slapped as I was hauled away – but perhaps she slapped him? 'Still, we must arrest him. Whom should we call? The sheriff?'

'The coroner is returning soon. We should wait for him to conclude his own deliberations.'

'That might take days! He could flee the city in that time!'

Godfrey gave me what I can only call a calculating look. 'He might. And it might be better that he do, since else his arrest for murder would bring notoriety to the Freedom of the City. The damage could be great to people of importance.'

'What do you mean?'

He chewed his lip for a moment or two, warily watching me. Then, 'There is a deal of dispute between the city and the Church. The Church wields great power here, and it is using it extensively to hurt those of us who supported the new religion. Obviously, we have all embraced the return to Catholicism,' he added quickly, 'but the Church still suspects radical elements in the congregation which might one day attempt revolution. This city was always loyal to the old Church, but the Guild and other groups were tentatively drawn, I suppose, to the new Church of Henry. Anything that could be used to harm the merchants and our power here in the city would be detrimental to the city itself.'

'Is that why you were with Wolfe and the dean at Lane's body when he was found? Concealing something that would hurt the city?'

'That was different. Lane was a threat to many. He knew

much about our businesses. When his body was found, we had to confirm it was him and discuss what to do. And as now, we felt it was better to leave matters. The cathedral is full of men who would eagerly snatch any excuse to hurt merchants. Finding one merchant is a murderer would hardly help matters. Especially now our authority and wealth have been diminished.'

'That is no reason to allow Wolfe to get away with his crime,' I said, yet it was clear to me that Godfrey would not help. He peered at me, then at the fire. I added, 'It would be far worse, of course, were it to become known that merchants were protecting their own against accusations of murder. Better by far for the public to see that the Guild would not protect its own but would ensure a guilty man's arrest.'

His eyes flitted back to me, and he glowered. This time, when he gave a nod it was the gesture of a man choosing where to stick the blade.

We were kept waiting for some time when we reached Wolfe's house. Personally, I kept to the rear of the group. On our way to his house, we had collected a trio of bailiffs who were reluctantly persuaded that they should assist in the arrest of one of the most important men in the city. One of their number was the young fellow who had called me to help release Hugh Miller all those days ago. It seemed an age now. He was as anxious as a maid in a brothel to be told to arrest a merchant. His sergeant, a grizzled old warrior, seemed more enthusiastic about the idea, as if he had a grudge against those who wielded power.

The hall was large and could easily accommodate the two Raleghs, William and me, as well as the officers and three servants. On seeing us, Wolfe's bottler and the other servants seemed unsure what to do. Eventually, they herded us in, but then we were forced to wait long enough to make Godfrey Ralegh fret angrily, and he was berating the steward with some vim when Wolfe appeared.

He had dressed with all the ostentation that a successful merchant would in order to browbeat others less wealthy or important. His hat and jack were of a fine velvet that caught the light from the large windows, and I found myself thinking that I should consider buying a similar suit of clothing when I was back in London. There is no doubt that quality shows.

His face was perfectly calm, but I saw that his left cheek was marked. It looked as though someone had smacked him. I wished I could have seen it.

He spoke with a firm, authoritative voice. 'Master Godfrey, I am glad to see you. To what do I owe the pleasure of such company?' He glanced about the room at all the men there waiting; however, when his eyes lit upon me, there was a sudden venomous flaring. It made me slip a step backwards until I was a little behind Richard and William. I felt that if a look could kill, I would have been incinerated in that moment.

'It's about Lane's death,' Godfrey said. 'We have heard from Master Blackjack here that you admitted guilt for the murder.'

'I said what? I deny it utterly! The bastard-breeder deserved it, but it was not by *my* hand!'

'You deny the murder?' I blurted.

'It was not murder. It was homicide, but it was justice. He deserved to die. Few men more so. But I had no part in it. I would have liked to, but I am a civilized man.'

'You admitted killing him, Master, and tried to send me to my death! Do not bandy words,' I spat. I was quite incensed.

'Yes. With pleasure, I sent you to be punished. I told my man to beat you within an inch of your life and leave you outside the city walls. But I had nothing to do with the death of my clerk. You were attempting to seduce my wife, after all. You deserved your punishment,' he said with a curl of his lip.

'You accused your wife – you said to her "after Lane" and something about how could she flaunt herself again!'

He made a move towards me, and I slipped behind Godfrey. He glared at me. 'You talk nonsense!'

'I heard you!'

Suddenly, the dam controlling his choleric temper was breached. 'What of it? Eh? Perhaps the bastard son of a turd thought he could bed my wife. And if he did, he has surely paid for it, but it wasn't *my* doing. But when I found you in a room with her, I was determined to see you punished, you primping coxcomb!'

'You never suspected Lane?' I said. 'He was here in your house working on your business, and you didn't think he might have been guilty of misbehaving?'

'Damn you! Why should I suspect my own clerk? I had no clues until his wife came and told me!'

'That was how you learned of Lane's unfaithfulness?'

'Yes! She told me. It was that same evening, and she came here to tell me. She was at her wit's end and told me so that I could stop his fornicating with my wife.'

'What did you do?' I said.

'Do? I sent her packing! I would not listen to reports about my wife. It was only when I saw you with her in the street that I realized Maud might have been correct!'

We left him soon afterwards. Godfrey and his servants made their way home. For my part, after my late night and bed in a gaol, I was exhausted and was about to return to my inn when I heard a scream and saw a general rush to the cathedral's gate. 'What's happening?'

It was only as we reached the gate that I saw Davy Appowell standing over a slowly twitching Harry Lynn, who was clearly expiring, from the amount of blood that ran from his flank and neck. A number of men, women and children stood watching as his foot began to tap, and then there was the familiar but ominous rattle in his throat that announced his demise. Poor fellow: saved from a ship to be murdered here, by a man who . . .

And then I remembered Lydd's words: *Him. The messenger! The one who brought news of the Thomas to the pirates! That was him!* He had been looking towards the cathedral, but he had heard Davy Appowell's voice calling to me.

I felt like the horse who has had the blinkers removed. 'It was the dean!'

Richard looked at me blankly, but William was more astute. 'What do you say?'

'The pirates were alerted to certain ships. Harry Lydd heard a messenger telling them, but he didn't see the man's face or recognize the voice,' I said. 'But today, when I left here with that man behind me, Harry called to me and said it was him. I didn't understand what he meant at first. He came in here to kill the henchman, because he took the message to the pirates.'

'That man there?' William said, pointing to the henchman.

'Yes.'

'Why would he do that?' Richard said.

'Because his master told him to,' I said.

I spoke to the porter at the gate and led the way back to the dean's house.

It may sound strangely bold of me to accost the man in his room, but the death of Harry Lydd, whose only guilt was that he had been a victim of the dean's machinations, gave me courage. When we were in the dean's chamber, I stood before the fire and warmed my hands. He joined us a short while later.

'Well? I am told you wished to speak with me?'

'Yes, dean,' I said ungraciously. 'I would like to ask how you got in touch with your confederates the pirates, and how you persuaded them to take the ships which you suggested to them.'

'Me? Why should I do that?'

I licked my lips. This was, after all, conjecture. 'Because you dislike all the merchants and Guild members of the city. They are an elite that you despise, because you know that they are, in their hearts, no more Catholic than my dog. They are dedicated to the Church of England, as they showed during the rebellion over the new prayer book. And you want the city to be a beacon of Roman Catholicism. So you conspired to have their ships stolen, their goods taken, and the men bankrupted.'

'What nonsense!'

'And more – I expect you were handsomely rewarded by the pirates for the quality of the sailors, who could then be shackled as slaves. Which is hardly the work of a religious man. The pirates – where were they from?'

'I have no idea—'

'Oh, you know well enough. Just as I do. Harry Lydd identified your Davy Appowell as the messenger on the galley just now. It was Appowell whom you sent to warn them of the ships as they were prepared. And that way you were assured that your enemies in faith here in the city would be ruined and you could take over the cure of souls without interference.'

He shrugged. 'And?'

'You admit it?'

'It is a good idea. The Queen herself would approve. I am doing the best I can for the city – for the kingdom – for the Church.'

'Selling your countrymen into slavery or death?'

'If need be. At least they were treated by decent Christian men when they were captured.'

'They died as slaves. And what of those who were killed by the pirates?'

'They were Bretons, so Christian. If men died, God will treat those who believed with kindness.'

And that was all he had to say.

Of course, we could have taken the affair to the bishop – but he was out of the city just now in his family estates far to the north. We could have reported the matter to the chapter of the cathedral – but how many of them would have had any interest in the affair? They would consider the dean to have behaved understandably and well in the face of the recusants and heretics who clung to their short-lived faith. Such men did not deserve to be treated in the same way as – in their eyes – genuine Christians.

We left him as his bottler entered the room and refilled his cup with wine. He looked at me as we left, and when I glanced back at him, I saw that he was smirking. He felt secure.

He *was* secure.

'Another,' Richard said. 'And then we should pay a visit to Moll. Seal our day's efforts properly.'

'Nay!' I protested. 'I will rise early tomorrow and be off. I have a horse waiting for me.'

William sighed and puffed out his cheeks. 'You're off whoring when you have a wonderful, loyal, sweet maiden waiting for you? You are disgusting, Richard. You should save yourself for her.'

'She will wait for me,' Richard said smugly.

There really is very little as overconfident as a youth convinced that his woman adores him. I suppose Wolfe thought that himself once. Thoughts of him made my mind turn back to his wife and the unfinished business that I had barely been able to begin earlier in that room. She was a tempting baggage, but as dangerous as a loaded gun. Meanwhile, I was nervous about showing my face outside the inn for fear of meeting Wolfe's henchman or Davy Appowell. I was very sure that I would not be likely to survive such a reunion.

The two left, and I slumped in my seat, ordering more beer. I was sad. The deaths of Lane and so many sailors, and all for what? Just so a man could take revenge on his wife's infidelity, and so that a priest could punish those he disapproved of. It was a terrible state of affairs, and I felt quite shocked and exhausted by the whole matter. Now, with the sun beginning to fall, I was growing less weary, however, and my thoughts turned to Moll's bevy of beauties. Especially that little dark-haired woman who had so fascinated me. We had unfinished business.

I decided to brave the elements. It wasn't a long march to Moll's house, after all. What could happen to me over such a short distance, I thought?

There are times in everyone's lives when something happens that seems to have occurred before. You must know the sensation: you're walking down a road and see a horse and rider, and think you must have seen them only a moment or two before, or you walk into a strange room and feel that it's oddly familiar?

I had the same experience now. Walking the road, I was suddenly struck with the sense that I had been here before.

A hand had grabbed my belt, and now I was gripped as firmly as I had been on that night when the dean's man had stopped my progress. I turned. It was Appowell.

'The dean wants another word with you,' he said.

I groaned. Visions of Moll's wenches faded. Still, there was nothing to be done. Appowell had already proved himself perfectly capable of stopping me during our previous encounters. I submitted and turned back to head down towards the south and the entrance to the cathedral close, but he shook his head and directed me forward along the High Street towards a low-arched alley.

'In here,' he said.

I wasn't thinking too hard. 'What does he want?'

'Who?'

'The dean?'

'He'll tell you.'

I frowned. There was a tenseness in his voice that didn't sound like his usual confident bragging. When I looked at him, his eyes were all over the place, as though convinced someone was going to attack him.

'Where's your companion?' I said. Usually, he operated as one of a pair, after all.

The low arch gave on to a narrow alleyway between tall buildings, but as I entered and peered ahead, I could see that there was a wall at the farther end. 'We've come the wrong way,' I said.

'You have,' he said.

There was something in his tone I didn't like. 'What?'

'It was all your fault. No one would have cared if you had left Lane well alone, but you had to keep poking around. And then you brought Harry Lydd back, too. That made my life difficult, but the dean would protect me. But killing Lane – he won't forgive that.'

I admit that I was struggling to keep up with him.

'Don't look so dim,' he snapped. 'I knew it was dangerous when Ned saw me outside the alley that evening when they were leaving. I saw Lane in there and realized I could finish the job Ned had started.'

'But . . . why?'

'He saw me. Only a few days before Shapley's ship was taken, he saw me taking my little boat out. He put it all together and guessed what I was doing, and he threatened me. He said if I didn't get the dean to give him back a position, he would tell all that I had done.'

'Um . . .' I noticed he had pulled a knife from his sheath.

'I persuaded the dean to have him beaten up, and when Ned and the other fools had done all they could to him, I went in and finished him. There was a rock at the roadside, and I hit him. It took very little. And now you are the only man who can prove anything.'

I smiled thinly. You see, I knew something that he did not. As he began to step towards me, I watched as Ned reached around him and took hold of his knife hand and plucked the blade from him while the Troll gripped his throat.

I do not claim any special genius here. It was not my doing. Ned explained that after he and his confederates had beaten Lane, they had seen the dean's man but assumed he was there to witness that the dean's instructions had been fulfilled. It didn't occur to them that Appowell might have killed Lane himself. Later, when it did, they assumed that the dean was ultimately responsible, which was why they had concealed the body to protect him.

Later, when we had deposited Appowell in the gaol, sent a messenger to the dean and taken a few beers to celebrate, I managed to evict them from my parlour in the tavern. Exhausted, I sank back into my seat. It was too late now for me to travel to Moll's. My nerves wouldn't take another stroll.

Later, a shifty-eyed fellow visited me. He wanted to know that I was alone, he said, and slid out again, leaving only a faint and unpleasant odour behind him.

Shortly after, the door opened again, and this time there was a significantly improved scent. I looked up just as a dark-clad figure launched itself at me, and I gave a squeak, intending to fling myself from my chair, but before I could move, I was pinioned in a most satisfactory manner, with a pair of delicious, warm lips planted on my own. I was prepared to enjoy the moment, until a horrible memory came back. That scent was familiar: citrus and summery flowers . . .

I yelped and sprang to my feet, throwing her to the floor, where she sat on her rump looking more than a little bewildered. 'Master Jack?'

Her plaintive little tone would not ease my concerns. 'Maid, what are you doing here? If your father were to learn . . . if Richard Ralegh were to guess—'

'What if he does?' she said, pouting most prettily. 'Father wants you as a son-in-law, and Richard, well! He has a nice ankle and his legs are good, but he is so vain and foolish. And he thinks that going to swive all the whores in Moll's house is proof of his virility. Well, it's not. It's proof that he'll one day be presented with a little bastard! And I won't live in the same house as one of those! No, my darling, you and I shall be betrothed and happy, and you will raise father's business while I raise our children.'

It was a nightmare scene, and plentifully adequate to destroy any chance of my being able to rise manfully to the task at hand, if you take my meaning. I retreated until my back was against the wall, while she rose to her feet, with an agility that surprised me, and approached.

'Jack, you know you want me, and I'll be content with you, too. You and I will make a good, contented family with children to carry on the family name. Now, don't be so shy! Come and kiss me again.'

As if there was any possibility of shyness with this wanton! I slid my back along the wall until I reached a corner, and still she advanced, as unrelenting as the Mongol hordes.

'No!' I said pathetically, but it was no good. She was so close that she could grab my arms, and she planted a kiss on my lips once more. I confess, to my shame, that although in my mind there was still a small picture of Richard Ralegh's face, it was gradually being erased by other, much more appealing visions.

And then they too were erased in a second as a sharp knock came to the door. Suddenly, my mind was full of the well-worn hilts of Richard's sword as the door was thrust wide.

Fortunately, it was not Richard but Margaret Wolfe who stood in the doorway.

I was, just at that moment, still involved in a grapple with the young houri, and there was a moment or two of horror at the sight of Margaret before I could make an attempt to disentangle myself.

'Ah! I see you are otherwise engaged,' Margaret said with a voice that could have frozen the Thames.

'I—' I said.

'Were you expecting Madam Wolfe?' Alice said, in a voice that was, if possible, even more frigid. Notwithstanding the roaring fire, the room was rapidly dropping in temperature.

'Not at all,' I managed.

Margaret gave Alice a condescending smile. 'When you are a little more mature, you will know that in polite society young maids usually have a chaperone. It is to protect them from the unfortunate consequences of liaisons in taverns.'

'I suppose you must have had a lot of such experience, a lady of your age,' Alice riposted acidly.

I winced. I wanted to say something, but just at that moment, I had not the faintest idea what to say. Only a faint gibber escaped my lips. I smiled at Margaret.

'Don't look at me like that!' she snapped. 'You look like a whipped cur!'

She swept about, chin held high, and left the room with the elegance of a queen rejecting an offer of marriage. Which was splendid to behold, but rather fearsome at the same time.

It left me slumped against the wall, smiling slightly anxiously at Alice, whose expression had hardened to the rigidity of tempered steel. 'I, er—' I began.

'Why did she come here?'

'I, um—'

'Because she is married and has a reputation. Did you invite her so you could enjoy her charms? Clearly, you prefer those of a middle-aged woman.'

'I . . . no, Alice, I didn't—'

But I was talking to a closed door by then.

I sat heavily on the chair and recovered my cup. The beer had poured from it when Alice launched herself at me, and now I was forced to pour another from my jug by the fire to help me get over my shocks of the last few minutes, but as I sat once more, a small, tatty figure burst in, closely followed by a young servant boy. I waved him away and disconsolately offered Edith a sip of ale from my cup.

She pushed it aside and blurted, 'Master Blackjack, you must run!'

'Edith? Why, what are you doing in here?' I said, perhaps a little blearily.

'You must run! Master Richard, Godfrey's son, had a man follow Alice Shapley, and he's coming here, now!'

NINE
Conclusion

15 September

Some weeks later, I tried to review events in Exeter while sitting before my fire, bellowing at Raphe to fetch more wine and trying to kick his brute, Hector, from his position in front of the fire. The damned dog would sit up and stare at the flames, leaving me in the shade. He looked at me reproachfully but, on the third kick, moved over six inches to the side, leaving me access to a little of the heat.

My journey home had been long and tedious. Bumping along on a dreadful beast with little in his head other than raping every mare he came upon, he cost me a fortune, but I was able to buy him quickly and leave Exeter early in the morning after Richard came searching for me.

Edith's warning had given me time to leave the city before curfew, and I made my way to St Sidwell's, where Walter was able to give me a palliasse. Rising before dawn, I was early at a stables and rented a beast to the next town, where I was able to buy a mount. Edith had saved me from a lot of harm, and when I taxed her with her astonishing appearance, she confessed that she had been following me for some days. When I was attacked by Ned in the alleyways, it was her scream that alerted Richard and William to come to my defence; when I was walking about the streets, anxious that I might meet a pisky or robber, it was she whom I had seen. She knew where I was almost all the time I was in Exeter, seeking to repay me for one good meal.

The most important aspect of my journeys was the fact that I was home and need never see the city of Exeter again. I had no fond memories of it. However, at least I did know who was responsible for the affairs. Between them, Master Wolfe and the dean had caused all the trouble. Wolfe had been appalled by the unfaithfulness of his wife when Lane's jealous wife had informed him, but she had not expected to be made a widow by Appowell. Meanwhile, the dean was attempting to destroy the power of the elites in the city by bankrupting them, declaring to many that it was their own fault for their brazen heretical beliefs. He was as committed as only a true, faithful religious believer can be.

But I learned when I was back in London that his reign of terror was over.

I was in the Cardinal's Hat, a favourite watering hole, in the company of a pair of buxom hostesses, when a travelling merchant entered. He had come from Cornwall, he said, and was on business for his master and in London to see the sights. Well, I mentioned comfortably that if he was interested in sights, he would find the finest here in the Hat, and he concurred.

We chatted a little, and I boasted of my own travels almost to Cornwall and told some tall tales about Dartmoor and the City of Exeter, and at that, he told me of the dean's death.

'Aye, t'were sad. He were out an' walking about the cathedral close, just a little after matins, so they say, and someone set upon him in the dark – a group of three, so they say, and one quite touched,' he added, a finger to his temple. 'They beat and stabbed him, and made off somehow in the middle of the night.'

That was as much as he knew, but for me it was a strangely satisfying end to my tale. I recalled the expression on Shipmaster Weston's face when we discussed the man responsible for warning the pirates, and I felt sure I knew exactly who the culprits were.

And I would not betray them.